ADVENTURES OF MARY BROWN

BERNICE BLOOM

DEAR READERS

Hello,

A warm welcome to the world of Mary Brown. This is the second novel in the series about a charming, chaotic, wild and wonderful heroine.

In this tale, Mary goes on three huge adventures thanks to the arrival of her old school friend Dawn, who runs a travel blog for larger ladies.

The novel features handsome rangers, wild animals and ludicrously inappropriate clothing.

Also, look out for a delightful old man called Frank, who leads them off into Europe to find the place where he lost his friend in the war, and a less delightful man called Martin, whose testicles fall out of his shorts in yoga, making a loud slapping sound as they hit the wooden floor "like someone had slammed half a pound of Cumberland sausages on the ground." (Sorry if you were eating. That's a very disturbing image).

I hope you enjoy the mayhem.

Lots of love,

Bernie xx

"This is one memorable book with so many relatable and realistic characters."

"Mary Brown is just wonderful, and I challenge you to read this and not be amused by the book. I am so looking forward to reading anything else that Bernice Bloom writes."

"Bernice has a wonderful way with words and incorporates much into a few pages that make you think about maybe your own issues or of those you see around you. A wonderful pick-you up, feel-good read."

"I had to stifle giggles on more than one occasion."

"It is the first book in a long time that had me laugh out loud!"

STAY IN TOUCH!

Website: www.bernicebloom.com

SOCIAL MEDIA

Facebook: https://bit.ly/3iwKUOW Twitter: https://bit.ly/3iv7NlO Instagram:https://bit.ly/3nlBVUn

AMAZON

Books on Amazon (US): https://amzn.to/3cYuCwW Books on Amazon (UK): https://amzn.to/3lfPwui

AN OLD SCHOOL FRIEND AND A BIZARRE INVITATION

I should have known that it was the most ridiculous idea in the world. It had 'bonkers' written all over it from the start. Going off on a safari with a woman I didn't know. What was I thinking? It was weapons-grade madness. But somehow, it didn't seem like that at the time. Certainly, I had no idea as I sat there on that chilly September evening that things would get so out of hand.

I had no inkling that I'd be on a continent far away by the end of the month, stuck up a tree in my knickers with a couple of baboons screaming up at me while gun-toting rangers rushed to the scene. Nor did I realise that the video of my embarrassing episode would end up trending on Twitter. But - let's not get ahead of ourselves - we'll get onto all that. First, let me take you right back to the beginning...

It began on a cool autumn evening with a phone call completely out of the blue.

"It's Dawn Walters here," said a voice. "Remember me -

we bumped into each other in the garden centre last week. I know you from school."

"Of course," I said. I remembered her very clearly from Rydens High School - this huge, jovial, loud, larger-than-life girl who everyone liked but no one wanted on their netball team.

"How are you?" I asked. I had no idea why she was phoning. She'd been very friendly when we'd bumped into one another in the centre. I work there as a supervisor, and she'd come in looking through the outdoor plants for something to give to her mum on her birthday. I suspected her great friendliness towards me was motivated by her delight at seeing how much weight I'd put on since we last saw one another. I was always so slim and fit at school; she probably assumed I'd gone from a skinny-legged child to an elegant, size eight woman...then we locked eyes over the potted plants 12 years later, and she saw that the girl who once weighed eight stone was now around 14 and a half. She must have been overjoyed. I know I would have been in similar circumstances.

"You've changed," she said, almost delirious with happi- ness. "I mean - you've really changed."

"You're just the same," I retorted. She was about 18 stone at school and was now about 25 stone, so I was being generous.

We exchanged numbers and muttered something about keeping in touch, must go for coffee, lovely to see you, and that was that; I hadn't really expected her to call. To be honest, I'd thrown away the scrap of paper with her number on it. I thought we were being polite when we promised to keep in touch. But Dawn had followed through. Not only that, but she had a peculiar proposition for me.

"Look - this might sound odd, but do you want to come to Sanbona with me? It's a safari in South Africa?" she said.

I sat there in silence, realising I must have misheard her, but not quite sure what she actually said.

"Are you still there, Mary?"

"Yes," I replied. "I didn't quite catch what you said though."

"I know it's mad, but I just wondered whether you fancied a free trip to South Africa...with me...to, you know, see animals and stuff."

"Um. Gosh, yes," I replied, still not sure that I could have heard her correctly. I mean...who would do that? Who would invite someone on holiday when they hardly knew them? "When is the holiday?" I asked. "What will we do? How will we get there? Um - why are you inviting me?"

"I get free trips. I told you - I'm a blogger these days. I write a travel blog called 'Fat & Fearless' and I get invited to experience holidays and write about them."

"Yes, I remember," I said. "It all sounds amazing, but why would you want me to come? We don't know each other, except from Mrs Thunder's French class, and that was over a decade ago."

"I get invited to loads of places, and I try to invite different people to come with me every time. I just thought you might fancy it?"

"Yes. That would be amazing. Of course, I fancy it; I'd love to come. If you're sure?" I said.

"I'm positive."

"Great then," I said. "Great. I'll definitely come. Tell me a bit more about it."

"Well, it's a safari so it's full of animals."

"What sort of animals?"

"Hang on, let me just look it up," said Dawn, and I could hear her tapping away on the keys while I waited, wondering what my boyfriend Ted would say when I told him. To be honest, we hadn't been getting on very well recently, so he'd probably welcome the break. We didn't live together but we spent a lot of time at one another's flats. Both of us would benefit from spending time apart rather than continuing to see one another every night when we both knew that things weren't right.

"There are lions, giraffes, cheetahs, oooo, look - elephants," she said.

"Elephants? How cool! Can we ride them?" I asked. I don't know why I said that...I guess I didn't know how to conduct a conversation about elephants.

"No, Mary, we can't ride them. Have you seen me? I'm 25 stones. My car struggles to move with me in it, I wouldn't subject an animal to that sort of brutality."

"Fair point," I said, thinking of the terrible groan that my suspension offered up every time I got into the driver's seat. Dawn was about 10 and a half stone heavier than me, so I imagined her suspension must really have screamed every time she got in. Ten and a half stone! That was a whole person. Dawn was taller, wider and heavier than me. I felt petite next to her. I'd not felt petite next to anyone for about 15 years. I used to be a bit scared of her when we were at school...forever fearful that she might fall on me and crush me. Now I just thought it was nice that there was someone out there who was bigger than me.

"Look at their website," said Dawn. "The wildlife park is in the Karoo outside Cape Town, it's called Sanbona. That's S-a-n-b-o-n-a Wildlife Reserve. Take a look; it's bloody lovely."

I called up the pages as I chatted to Dawn.

"Bloody hell!" I said. It looked like an incredible place.

"There are lions, cheetahs, hippos and rhinos," it declared, showing them moving across the screen under the warm African sun. Birds swooped through the cloudless skies as panpipes played. If the reality of the place was anything like as captivating as the marketing films on the website, it would be sensational. "We also have leopards, giraffes, zebras and elephants," I read. It looked bloody great.

"This place looks amazing," I said, clicking onto the section called 'our people'.

"Really, Dawn, it's amaz..." I stopped short as a picture flickered across the screen. Not a wonderful animal, but an achingly beautiful man... dressed in khaki and clutching a rifle. It was one of the rangers who'd be looking after us on our trip. He smiled slowly at the camera, a vision of masculine beauty in a branded baseball cap.

"Dawn, get onto the 'our people' section now," I cried, my voice several pitches higher than usual. "I'm not joking. Go on there now. Take a look at the bloody wildlife they've got there. This one's called Pieter. He's based at Gondwana Lodge. Please tell me that's the lodge that we're going to. He's perfect."

"Oh Good God, Alive," said Dawn, reaching the short video on the website. "Oh hell, he's lovely. Wow. You know what, Mary Brown - we are going to have the best week of our lives."

ON THE WAY TO SOUTH AFRICA

Excitement about my impending trip carried me through the next few weeks. I booked the time off work and gleefully told everyone where I was going. Those I get on well with were chuffed to hear of my good luck, and those I don't care much for wrinkled their noses in distaste and pretended that they wouldn't give their right arm to be going on such a trip.

Ted was decidedly unimpressed by it all. Certainly, he didn't seem in the least bit bothered about me going to the other side of the world without him.

"I'm so stressed at work, babe," he'd said. "You know - there's loads going on, and I need to get my head down and really get a handle on it all if I'm going to make salesman of the year again. The financial year ends in a month...I'm up to my neck. You go, have loads of fun, and I'll see you when you're back. OK?"

"Yes," I said, both relieved that he seemed so fine about me going away without him and really unnerved that he seemed so fine about me going away without him.

Couldn't he just have pretended to have been bothered? Couldn't he have pulled a pretend sad face and said how much he'd miss me?

Mum was mainly just confused by the whole thing, and I admit that I completely understood her confusion. I was still none-the-wiser about why Dawn had asked me rather than anyone else in the whole world. Don't get me wrong - it was incredibly lovely to be asked on the trip of a lifetime by a virtual stranger, but it was also really fucking odd.

"Dawn?" queried mum. "I don't think I've met her, have I?"

"I was at school with her. Her mum was a dinner lady, and her dad had an affair with her aunty."

"Oh yes," said mum. It's coming back. Fat Dawn?"

"Yes," I replied, wishing mum hadn't called her that. I suppose it felt fine to call her Fat Dawn when I wasn't fat, but it felt far too close to home to call her that now.

"Blimey. Is she still as fat?" asked mum.

"She is," I confirmed.

"Well, you better make sure you don't ride any elephants then...you'll break them," she said

"I promise we won't ride any elephants," I told her. What was it with our family and riding bloody elephants?

"And behave yourselves – don't go getting drunk and silly like you do every time you go anywhere with that Charlie...I know what you two are like. Every time you two go anywhere, it turns into a scene from The Hangover."

"Indeed," I agreed, and it struck me, not for the first time, that I had no idea what it would be like to go away with Dawn. I knew nothing about her. Would she be any fun? Perhaps she was a lesbian? Oh My God. Had I done the right thing? This could all go so horribly wrong.

"Send me pictures of tigers, won't you," mum said while I was still panicking and running through scenarios in my mind where we were deep in the Karoo and Dawn made a move on me.

"Yes," I promised her. "I'll definitely send pictures of tigers."

"And I'll read the blog every day so I can keep up with what you're doing." I made a mental note to tell Dawn to keep the blog as clean as possible. I'd looked through it several times since she'd asked me to go on safari, and - I must say - it was very good. Quite witty and professional-looking, full of pictures, dry comments and clever observations. She'd obviously done a lot of travelling over the years, so the site was brimming with colourful tales from across the globe. It was also quite filthy. She didn't hold back on the swearing and wasn't averse to telling the world when she fancied someone...and what she might do to them if she got close enough.

Leaving day came around very quickly after the initial shock of the phone call. I'd had the immediate panic about Dawn being a predatory lesbian, then the panic that I had nothing in my wardrobe that was in any way suitable for safari life. The latter of these two issues was easily solved with some light shopping in Marks and Spencer's. Prior to my clothes-buying expedition, I'd read lots about safari life and watched films about colonial Africa. I had even printed off pictures detailing elegant safari wear. I'd bought the items I thought would be most suitable for the trip and packed them all carefully.

Now it was time to go, and I found myself standing by the front door of my flat, mentally running through everything I should be taking with me.

"Passport, ticket, safari clothing, toiletries," I said to myself. Was there anything else? I was paranoid that I'd forget something. I rummaged through my case one last time. Yes - all good. I must stop worrying.

All I needed to do now was to get to the airport, picking up Dawn from her flat in Esher en route. I'd promised to pay for the cab; it seemed like the least I could do when she'd organised a bloody holiday for me. To make the journey as hassle-free as possible, I downloaded the Uber app onto my phone.

We needed the cab for 4pm, so at around 3.45pm I put the destination details into the phone and waited for the car to show up. It told me that Ranjit Singh was nine minutes away in his Vauxhall Corsa. I was wearing my comfortable leisure wear, ideal for long-haul travelling. My outfit was in a muted, fudge colour. I hadn't gone for bright colours, having felt such a fool the last time I went on holiday. I had a very comfortable pink onesie, which I wore when I went to Amsterdam last year, but I spent the whole time feeling like an overgrown toddler or a Care Bear or something. This time, I wanted to ooze style and sophistication.

I checked in my bag for my passport one last time; then the phone bleeped to tell me that the car was outside, so I dragged my luggage out of the flat, bouncing it down the steps and making such a racket that Dave, my drop-dead gorgeous neighbour, came out of his flat downstairs to investigate.

"Going somewhere?" he asked.

"No Dave, I just like taking all my possessions with me wherever I go."

"Ha, ha," he said, unimpressed by my witty repartee. "Where are you off to?"

"South Africa," I said.

"What are you going there for?" he replied.

"To see herds of elephants!"

"Of course, I've heard of elephants," he replied. "What do you think I am? Some sort of dimwit?"

"No - a herd of elephants - like a flock of seagulls or a litter of puppies."

Honestly, it was like talking to a 90-year-old dementia patient sometimes. I can't believe I used to fancy this guy like mad; now I just feel half sorry for him and half maternal towards him.

"Oh. Herd of elephants! Yes," he said as I bumped my bag to the side of the steps and brought it to rest. Not once did he move to help me; he just seemed to be looking off into the distance. "The babies are lovely."

"Babies?"

"Baby elephants," he said. "Real cute."

"Yes," I agreed.

"Want a hand with that, by the way?" Dave raised his eyebrows and pointed in the direction of my case.

"I'm good, thanks," I said as I looked up and down the street for the Uber driver. I couldn't see a car with just a driver sitting in it anywhere. The only car I could see had loads of blokes in it.

I went back onto the app to check. It seemed like the right car, in terms of its colour, but I couldn't see its registration. It couldn't be right, though; it was full of people.

I stood on the curb as Dave watched me; for some reason, he seemed entranced and amused by the fact that I was going on holiday.

The car was close enough for me to see that it was definitely the right one; same registration number as the little car moving along the map on my phone. Presumably, the men in there were about to get out.

I put my hand out to indicate my presence to the driver, and he waved and pulled over.

"Hi," I said, and the three men in the car said 'hi,' back. None of them moved.

"Are you for me?" I asked. "I'm Mary Brown."

The driver nodded and jumped out of the car to help me put my bag into the boot. "Join the party," he said.

"Right," I replied, cautiously. There were three passengers on board - a large builder called Terry (who, it would turn out, knew everything in the world about sumo wrestling), a window cleaner called Ray who had his bucket and mops with him (his wife left him last week after 40 years of marriage but he never missed one window cleaning job), and a very large painter and decorator in his overalls, called Andy, who didn't talk much but snorted a great deal.

I squeezed into the back next to them. This was odd, but it was my first Uber. Perhaps this was how they worked? Little minibuses.

"We need to pick up my friend Dawn," I said, as the car trundled along, straining beneath the weight of us all. I waved at Dave, who stared back, confusion written all over his face.

"This friend of yours...," said the driver. "She is small, isn't she? There's not a lot of room for anyone else."

I didn't answer. And so, we sat there, me in my smart leisure wear with my handbag and travel documents perched on my lap while Terry demonstrated how he could talk in Japanese.

We were later than planned arriving at Dawn's house, so I phoned from my position cramped in the corner at the back of the car to apologise and say that I was on the way.

"Sure, heading out now," she said.

As long as I live, I will never forget the look on her face when she saw this tiny, overburdened car screech up outside, with me squashed into the back of it next to the large men. The painter climbed out along with the window cleaner, dropping his mops as he went, then the builder from the front, still snorting.

"In you get," I said. I tried not to look at the driver's face. Dawn was dressed in tight green trousers and a t-shirt and looked way fatter than I remembered.

"What the hell?" she said, easing herself into the front seat next to the driver, while the builder climbed into the back. "Why do we have a bunch of construction workers in the back of the cab? We're just a Red Indian short of a Village People tribute band. I can't arrive at the airport like this..."

"Konnichiwa." said Terry in his finest Japanese.

Ray scratched himself; Andy flicked through his phone, looking at pictures of his recently departed wife, sighing occasionally, and the car trundled along through the afternoon traffic, dropping off people along the way en route to Heathrow Airport.

"What was that all about?" asked Dawn as we took our bags from the boot and bid farewell to the driver.

"I don't know," I said. "I've never used Uber before. I wasn't expecting there to be people already in the car."

"Show me what you did," instructed Dawn, taking my phone out of my hand.

I showed her the app and how I'd just pressed the button for an Uber and put in the destination details. It was quite straightforward; even I couldn't have cocked this up.

"That's a bloody Uber pool car. You need to press this button," she said.

"Ohhhh..." I replied. "And what's an Uber pool car?"

"It's like a bloody minibus, for God's sake. Uber pool cars are for people who can't afford Ubers. They are for poor people. Don't ever tell anyone what happened, will you," she said. "I can't have people thinking I travel in uberpool cars with random builders. I won't put it in the blog, and let's not ever speak of it again."

"Sure," I said as Dawn wandered off towards the terminal, leaving me with all the bags. I wondered idly and with a certain degree of concern whether I was about to go on a long-haul flight and the holiday of a lifetime with the world's dullest person.

SCREAMING MONKEYS AND WILD RAINS

In the end, I didn't sit next to Dawn on the flight...would you like to know why? Because Dawn made the most astonishing fuss and got herself upgraded to business. At no stage during the incredible fuss did she suggest that I might be upgraded as well. So, I was stuck in economy, wedged between the window and a man and his wife who could not have looked less happy to be sitting next to me if I'd been carrying a bomb.

I do understand that it's a pain when someone is big and takes up more than their share of the room on a plane but - really - the snide looks and aggressive posturing weren't going to make me thinner, were they? They just made me feel desperately uncomfortable and ruined my whole journey. The rudeness also made me sad so I ate every morsel of food that was given to me to make myself feel better.

As I tucked into some terrible knitted chicken and plastic pasta, I could see the two of them whispering, and I just knew that they were talking about me and what terrible bad luck that they were next to a fatty and how appalling I was eating. Eating! How dare I?

I pulled my book out of my bag and read it aggressively. Can you read aggressively? Well, if you can - that's what I did. Although it wasn't so much reading as staring at the page and letting the words swim in front of my eyes while I tried valiantly to ignore the hostility brewing next to me. They would surely tire of feeling sorry for themselves sometime between now and South Africa hopefully before we left European airspace; then we could all just relax, watch films, eat the terrible food and arrive in Cape Town without me strangling either of them.

I didn't sleep much on the flight because of Mr. and Mrs. Angry next to me, and when we arrived at Cape Town airport, I was exhausted. My tiredness wasn't helped by hearing all about Dawn's magnificent business class experience.

"It was quite wonderful," she said, then began reading out loud what she'd written about it for her blog. The way she wrote about the champagne, the characters, the lovely beds and the nutritious food was really good. The whole thing made me feel jealous because I'd had such a horrible journey, but the writing was really classy. She might be an inconsiderate friend and a self-opinionated oaf at times, but I could see why people wanted to read her blog; she wrote with humour and warmth that was quite compelling. In the piece, she'd written about how she was looking forward to our gentle meander down through the spectacular African countryside to the game reserve. She'd made it sound fantastic, and I was cheered by the prospect of the picturesque journey despite my tiredness.

"Will it be a nice car for the trip to the safari?" I asked, charitably setting her up with the opportunity to tell me how special she was and how companies would always send the best.

"It'll be a lovely limousine," said Dawn. "I'm quite a big deal in the blogging world, so they always send the best."

"Excellent," I said. "This is really exciting, isn't it?"

"It is, actually," she agreed. "I've never been on safari before. I hope I've brought the right clothes with me."

"I watched some films about Africa for inspiration," I said. "Me too," said Dawn. "Out of Africa was beautiful."

"God, yes, amazing," I agreed.

Dawn called the limousine company while we were chatting to ask about the car. There was certainly no sign of a plush limousine or a driver in a peaked cap.

"A what?" Dawn said, turning away from me and pacing around. She wandered off towards the money exchange places and hire car booths, articulating wildly with her hands as she went. I could hear her raised voice but not the words she was saying.

All of a sudden, she spun around and walked towards me, grabbing the handle of her wheelie case and shouting, "Follow me!" I grabbed my bag and ran after her as we waddled across the concourse and onto the street.

"You need to know that this is not the way I normally travel, but there's been a cock up," she said, scanning the road for our transport to the Safari.

"Here it is," she said. "Oh my God, it's worse than I thought..."

Juddering to stop just next to us came an ancient

Nissan Micra. It was small and dilapidated looking and covered in dust. The driver looked about 14.

"Oh my goodness, two big ladies for my car," he said in a rather ungentlemanly fashion.

"How far is it to Sanbona," I asked Dawn.

"About three hours," she said. "This is a disaster."

I couldn't be sure the suspension on this damn thing would cope with the combined weight of Dawn and me for three hours.

"A complete disaster," repeated Dawn.

It wasn't a complete disaster, of course. Dawn had a habit of making everything that happened into a drama, but it wasn't the best of times - I'd had absolutely no sleep on the plane because I was cramped in economy next to anti-fattists, and now we'd emerged into the blazing heat to discover a dilapidated old car with no air conditioning was to take us down to Sanbona...which was three hours away. The plastic seats were already hot when we slid onto them. The temperature reading hovered around the 40*C mark. It was going to be the most sticky and unpleasant journey imaginable, and I was going to have to endure it all while sitting next to Dawn. There was no point in being miserable, though - I decided the mood needed lifting a little.

"It's not a complete disaster," I said. "I've got a couple of those little bottles of wine from the plane in my bag. We can stop for refreshments if it all gets too much. Come on we can do this."

I reached into my bag and handed her a warm bottle of Sauvignon Blanc. "Thanks," she said, giving me the first smile I'd seen that day.

“Cheers,” I said as we clinked the bottles together. I saw the driver shaking his head at us in the mirror. Had he never seen two enormous women drinking at 6 a.m. before?

The wine soon worked its magic, and we glanced at each other as the car flew over yet another bump on the ancient roads. "This is fucking ridiculous," said Dawn.

"Yep," I said in agreement as we sat there sweating and laughing as the sun beamed down on the little car driving through the Karoo.

The journey that was supposed to take three hours ended up taking closer to five in the dilapidated old excuse for a car.

By the time we arrived at our destination, the two of us looked like we'd been to war. The windows had been wide open because it was so scorching hot, and our sweaty faces had attracted the dust thrown into the air by the travelling car, so we looked as if we were filthy. I glanced over at Dawn; her dark hair was standing up on end, and her eye makeup that she had reapplied so carefully on the plane before disembarking was streaked across her face so she looked like Alice Cooper in one of his more aggressive videos. Sweat patches stood out on her tight-fitting khaki outfit. I hoped I looked better.

“How do I look?” I asked her.

She burst out laughing. "No one has ever looked worse."

The only thing that kept us sane on the journey was the captivating landscape and incredible scenery. It became easy to forget about the heat as we passed through the most glorious countryside... we watched baboons playing in the trees and birds dancing in sunny skies. When we arrived at Sanbona, the tensions of the flight and the heat of the journey melted into calmness and serenity. The beauty of the place was breathtaking.

The driver told us on the journey down that it hadn't rained for weeks, so the animal and plant life were struggling. The difference between rain and no rain in the UK may amount to little more than the difference between taking an umbrella and leaving it behind. Here it was a serious business, a matter of life and death. When there was no rain, the plants died so the herbivores couldn't eat, they grew weak and became easy prey, so the predators thrived. The very balance of nature shifted a little on its axis with a turn in the weather.

As we drove past the guards and into the game reserve, we could see baboons all over the rocks. As we drove past, some of them started screaming.

"Why are they doing that?" asked Dawn.

"They have seen the lions coming; they are warning the other animals," said our driver.

"How clever," I said. "All the animals looking out for one another."

"To a degree," said the driver. "Not always. Now, keep your eyes peeled. If we are really lucky, you will see the lions."

It didn't strike me as all that lucky to see lions, but I knew what he meant...seeing any of the magnificent big creatures that we only ever read about in books would be amazing. To see one on our first day would be great.

Sanbona was set in a beautiful 130,000-acre wildlife reserve at the foot of the Warmwaterberg Mountains in the Karoo region, an area rich with vast plains, rivers, lakes and a huge array of animals.

My heart was pounding a little in my chest at the thought of the days ahead and everything we might see. I looked over at Dawn, and she grabbed my hand and gave it a small squeeze. "I'm so excited," she said.

"Me too. Thank you for inviting me," I said.

"THAT'S okay I couldn't have invited anyone else," she said. I had no idea what that meant, but I was just thrilled to be there and delighted that I was the only person she thought she could invite. It was kind of sweet.

That night, we went to our rooms to unpack. I was relieved that we had separate rooms, but a shared bathroom was linking them, which wasn't such great news. I hoped that she was clean. I could tolerate mess, but not a dirty bathroom.

Dinner was to be in the outdoor restaurant, looking out into the magnificent countryside. We would be met by Henrique, the manager of the reserve, who would run through how things would work. Then we'd know exactly what the plans were for the trip, and hopefully, we'd get to ogle some of the rangers.

We walked down to the reception area to catch up with Henrique - a tall, slim, gangly man who looked like he'd never had a decent meal in his life. The polar opposite, in fact, of Dawn and me. He greeted us warmly and told us about the days ahead. There would be very early starts, so we would see lots of animals. Our ranger would meet us at breakfast at 4 am to tell us about the route we would be taking. I glanced at Dawn. We were both thinking about Pieter...wonderful, fantastic Pieter, who we were about to meet.

"There will be four other people in your group...a newly married couple called David and Alexa and two men, Patrick and Chris."

Dawn looked at me; I looked at Dawn. One handsome ranger and two unaccompanied men. Let the party start.

We sat there, enjoying pre-dinner drinks and looking out into the starry sky. It felt like we were the only people on earth. It was all so beautiful, so serene. Then, we saw flashes of lightning ahead of us, growing brighter and more intense as the evening wore on. By the time we had dinner, the wildest light show played out in the darkness, then thunder's heavy drumbeat joined the cacophony, and the rain came...a little at first, then tumbling down to the delight of everyone.

"It's rain!" screamed the head chef, running outside and praying up to heaven. "Thank God. It's rain."

OUT OF AFRICA

"Dawn, Dawn," I said. Silence. "Dawn?"

Still nothing.

Oh God. This holiday might have been the biggest mistake of my entire life.

"Dawn," I tried again, louder this time. Still nothing.

It turned out Dawn snored. When I say 'snored', I mean she made such a bloody racket that she could have woken the dead. It was a loud honking that left the room reverberating to its tune. I was surprised the whole place didn't wake up. I'd been standing in the bathroom shouting to her, but it was no good, so I walked through to her room and saw her lying sprawled across the bed - a hefty woman in a pair of men's pyjamas, wearing an eye mask that she'd clearly nicked from the plane.

"Dawn?"

It was no good...I couldn't rouse her at all. At least it didn't seem quite as loud now. When I'd been lying in bed, it had been unbearable. I walked back into my room, opened the doors, and strode onto the balcony. Once I opened the patio doors, though, the noise became even louder. Good God, alive - what on earth was going on with that woman...her snoring was so catastrophic that it somehow bounced through the walls and appeared to be coming from the lake outside. What sort of woman made that level of noise? I looked out over the water, shaking my head in disbelief, and that's when I spotted them: hippos...a whole load of them...honking wildly.

Ahhh...it wasn't Dawn at all. I smiled to myself. It might be judicious to keep to myself the fact that I'd confused her with a whole load of honking hippos. I scuttled back to bed, walking passed the gorgeous cream outfit I'd laid out for tomorrow. My size 20, elastic waist trousers in a soft cream colour, a white chiffon blouse, a long white, flowy jacket and a straw bonnet that I had tied a cream ribbon around. Next to them sat my enormous knickers and heavily constructed support bra. I was really excited about striding out in my finery tomorrow. I knew it was a bit over the top, but I was sure the others would be dressed up - it wasn't every day you went on a bloody safari, was it?

Morning arrived with all the subtlety of a nuclear explosion. It turned out that Dawn had the world's loudest and most annoying alarm clock. Really, it was absolutely terrible; it made the honking hippos from last night sound like choirboys. I took my eye shield off, sat up and looked into the darkness.

"We've got to get up," I shouted through to Dawn. "It's 3:45 am."

This was the sort of time I should be coming in from a wild night of dancing and drinking, not getting up. But this was the thing with safaris; it was all about early mornings if you wanted to catch the animals before the day got hot and they disappeared from view - into the undergrowth away from the hot African sun.

There was no sound from Dawn. "Hello, are you awake?" I asked.

As I prepared to get up and go and find her, the bathroom door swung open, and Dawn walked out.

“Oh,” I said. “You’re up already?” Then, “OH!” When she put on the light, I saw her in all her glory. She was dressed in cream...like Meryl Streep from Out of Africa. Exactly as I’d been planning to dress, she even had cream-crocheted gloves and a ribbon trailing from the hat perched on her newly styled hair.

“What the hell are you wearing?” I asked.

“You can see what I’m wearing,” she replied. She was wearing tonnes of makeup as well.

“I can see that you’re wearing the same thing that I was going to wear. Exactly the same clothes as I’d planned to.”

“Well, not exactly the same,” she said, indicating the cream shawl and the fact that she was wearing a long white skirt and not trousers.

“OK, not exactly, but - you know - you’ve copied my look.

“How can I have copied it if I was dressed first?”

“Oh God, forget it,” I said, clambering out of bed and heading for the bathroom. I did my make-up as carefully as possible, determined to look better than her. At least I was thinner, and there weren't too many people I could say that about.

We descended the stairs, and I knew how ridiculous we must look: two heavily overweight ladies with piles of makeup on, draped in ridiculous amounts of cream lace and white cotton. I was cross that we both had the same hat - bonnets bedecked with ribbons. Down below us, the others in our group looked askance. They were in fleeces, woolly hats and jeans.

Everyone was staring at us. I mean everyone...just staring open-mouthed in disbelief at these two heavily overweight women who looked like they'd stepped out of a coffee plantation from the 1920s.

"Hello, ladies," said the hotel manager, breaking the silence. Her name was Carmella...we'd seen her briefly when Henrique had introduced her last night.

"How lovely to meet you properly. You both look - well - amazing. Gosh. I am looking forward to seeing your blog. It's very exciting to have two famous British bloggers with us," she said.

"I'm the blogger; Mary is my friend," said Dawn, territorially. I had no desire to take any damn credit for her blog.

"But didn't we agree that the blog from the safari would be called 'Two Fat Ladies'?" said Carmella.

"Um, yes," said Dawn.

"Two Fat ladies?" I said.

"Yep," said Dawn.

"Really? Is that why you want me to come? Because I'm fat?"

"Well, kind of," she replied. "I needed someone fat to

come with me to get the gig. And also, you're fun too. I always liked you at school."

"Bloody hell, Dawn," I said. I don't know why I was offended. It's not like I could insist that I wasn't fat; it just seemed a bit - well - cruel - not to tell me why she'd invited me.

"Do join us for a cup of tea before we head out to meet your ranger," said Carmella, papering over the awkwardness. "Let me introduce you to the group."

There were two couples coming with us on the trip: David and Alexa, who were on their honeymoon and seemed to want to be alone, understandably. Alexa was a very beautiful and very young girl; David was much older...a good 20 years older, to be honest. And he seemed wildly possessive of his young bride. I tried to talk to her twice, and he all but shooed me away from her, wrapping his arms around her and claiming her as his own.

"He's bloody nuts," said Dawn. She was talking to me much more now, presumably spurred into social interaction by her embarrassment at getting caught out with the blog name.

"What possible danger does he think Alexa will come to just by talking to us?"

"God knows!" I replied. "It's not as if she's that interesting in any case. I'm quite happy not to talk to her; I was only being polite."

As well as David and Alexa there were the two men that we'd been told about: Patrick and Chris. They seemed really nice, and I had high hopes of friendships and maybe even something more if they played their cards right.

Chris was an artist of some sort - he said he did modern, progressive art, and his most recent works were shortlisted for the Turner Prize, which even I know is a big deal. He was great fun. Patrick was a food writer who did columns for men's magazines about restaurants and recipes.

Chris was quite gnome-like, with a full beard and sparkly, mischievous eyes, and there was nothing particularly handsome about him; Patrick, on the other hand, was gorgeous...classically beautiful with a square jaw and deep set, dark, brooding eyes.

The thing was, though, even though Patrick was 50 million times more handsome, I found myself much more drawn to Chris - he had such a fabulous personality that he seemed good-looking. Attractive personalities can make people seem so much more beautiful, can't they? In fact, there's nothing more attractive than a lovely personality. Kindness and funny always beat square jaws and muscular torsos. Well, usually. I suppose it depends on how muscular.

Patrick smiled at me and offered an Elvis Presley-type sneer as he shook my hand; Chris wrapped me in a big hug. That was the difference between them.

The other difference was that Chris was wildly politically incorrect and seemed to embarrass Patrick constantly.

"Does anyone want to ask anything before we go out?" Carmella asked.

"Any lesbian animals?" asked Chris, with a glint in his eye.

We watched as Carmella raised her eyebrows and

racked her brain trying to remember anything she might have learned about animal lesbianism at ranger school.

"I think it might be time to head out now," she said, her cheeks scorched red and the question lying unanswered in the air.

A FEMALE RANGER

"OK," said Carmella. "Your guide will be here soon, and we'll be going out. I'd just like to tell you a little bit about Sanbona. You'll find this a fascinating holiday...in many ways, all safari holidays are exactly the same in structure: you get up early and go out to spot as many animals as possible before returning to relax awhile. Then we go out to look for more in the late afternoon. After that, you enjoy sundowners and a magnificent sunset before a lavish dinner."

"Ooooo," said the assembled guests.

"But here's the rub," she continued. "The reality is that every safari you go on is completely different. Every time you go out, you see something new and hear something you haven't heard before – honking hippos, roaring lions or singing birds.

"You are moved in a different way with every trip. Safaris are living, breathing holidays that create their own drama as they unfold. They're an unwritten script, an unfinished symphony – a blank page on which your story unfolds daily. Every time you head out you have no idea what awaits you. That's why they're so magical and unique."

The lady had such a lovely, lyrical way of talking; it was a joy to listen to her, and I found myself lost in her words. Even Chris had shut up and stopped with the stupid questions.

"Now, the important job of the day: I need to find out what you want for sundowners. Mary - what do you fancy?"

Damn, why did I have to go first? I find it hard enough to think of what drink I want when I'm standing at the bar and about to drink it. The idea of deciding now what drink I might want at 6 pm tonight was very tough to come to terms with.

"A white wine," I said, and Carmella made a note in a pad adorned with giraffes.

"No, no. I'll have a Bailey's. Do you have Baileys?"

"We do," said Carmella, crossing out wine and turning to the others to take their orders.

"No, I will have wine. Red wine, though. That's what I fancy - a red wine."

"Right," she said, beginning to look as if she was losing patience with me. She crossed out Baileys with real vigour and wrote in my latest fancy.

"OK, next," she said, and I knew that what I really wanted was a gin and tonic. I hovered on the edge of the group until she had done everyone but Dawn then raised my hand like a schoolgirl.

"Sorry, but can I have gin and tonic instead? I promise I won't change my mind again."

"OK," she said, grimacing.

"I'll have a vodka and Red Bull," said Dawn.

"Ooooo..." I said, but Carmella was having none of it. The notebook had been put away, and she was gathering up her things.

"Now then, let's go outside and introduce you to the ranger who'll be looking after you during your stay."

This was the moment that Dawn and I had been looking forward to since first seeing Pieter's heavenly smile on the website. We both adjusted our outfits and straightened our bonnets. I hoped the fact that we looked like extras from a Jane Austen serialisation wasn't going to put him off.

"Do go outside, and we'll get going," she said, ushering us towards the door where an attractive, dark-haired woman was standing.

"This is Cristine; she will be your guide while you are staying with us at Sanbona."

"What?" Dawn and I looked at one another in amazement. A WOMAN. This was not right at all.

"It's lovely to meet you all," said Cristine. "I'll be looking after you during your stay. As long as you do what I say, I will be able to show you all the amazing animals we have here at Sanbona, and I'll be able to protect you and keep you safe. Please remember that this is not a zoo; these animals are wild. It's important to treat them respectfully and follow the basic rules I will outline to you as we go around. The first rule is always to stay on the Land Rover; don't get off for any reason. If you drop something, tell me - don't try to get out to retrieve it. Understood?"

There were muted sounds of agreement from us all, but I was too alarmed to join in.

"Any questions?" she asked, but my only question was WHERE THE HELL IS Pieter?

We left the luxury of the lodge and were immediately confronted by a muddy and filthy-looking vehicle. I realised in that second that I could not have been more inappropriately dressed. The Land Rover seemed terrifyingly open to the elements and rather too exposed, considering I was dressed like a bridesmaid, and we were going off to see animals that could tear us apart with their teeth.

I stood near the side, waiting for them to lower the steps for me to climb in.

"Just hop on board," said Cristine. Everyone clambered onto the vehicle except for Dawn and me. I knew there was no way on earth to get on there.

"Up you get," said Cristine.

"I'm not sure I can," I said.

I gave it a go, grabbing the handrail and trying to lumber myself on, but I just couldn't manage it.

"Hang on," said Cristine, running around to assist me. She stood behind me and pushed on my bottom, trying to heave me on board. Embarrassingly, it wasn't enough. Dawn joined in, and the two of them pushed with all their might as if trying to load an old sofa into a skip. Finally, I was in - headfirst, and with all my dignity gone, but I was in. Next, it was time to get Dawn on board. Carmella was called, then a guy sweeping the pathways came running, and the chef who'd been dancing in the rain the night before...together they huffed and puffed and loaded Dawn on board.

"OK, lovely, no problem," said Dawn, doing her best to hide the embarrassment we were both suffering. As we were about to set off, Henrique came running along with a step ladder. "Just to make things a bit easier," he said. Cristine stored it in the back, and we were finally ready to hit the road.

"Everyone comfortable?" she asked when she'd returned to her seat.

"Are there lots of rangers?" I asked, completely ignoring her question about our comfort. Of course I wasn't comfortable, I was squeezed into a ropey old four-by-four next to a huge woman with thighs the size of fridges. My elegant bonnet was precariously placed, and my clothes were dishevelled and certainly weren't comfortable. Even the elasticated trousers felt like they were digging into me, which is against all the rules of elasticated clothing; their very existence depends on them being comfortable.

"There are 12 rangers here at Sanbona," she replied.

"All men?" I ventured.

"Yes, I'm the only woman. Though around Africa, there are increasing numbers of female rangers. You'll find that..." "Do you know a ranger called Pieter?" I asked, cutting through her speech about female emancipation.

"Yes, he's the head ranger," said Cristine.

"Will we get to see him?"

"Sure you will," she said. "Is there any particular

reason? If there's anything you need or want, you can just ask me. I can help."

"No, that's fine. Just checking then. Um, so, when are we likely to meet Pieter? Do you know?"

"Will we see lots of animals?" asked Alexa.

"It's impossible to know," said Cristine. "The thing with safaris is..."

"Right," I interrupted. "Just so we're clear - is it impossible to know whether we'll see Pieter or not sure whether we'll see animals?"

"Animals!" said Cristine quite sharply. I could tell she was getting fed up with me. To be honest, I think she was fed up with me the minute she saw me. Cristine was thin and wiry and dressed in khaki shorts and a shirt. She was a no-nonsense, outdoorsy sort of woman, and I don't think she'd ever seen anyone as fat as me in her life. Or as oddly dressed. Or as utterly useless at getting into a Land Rover.

"OK," I replied, sitting back in my seat.

"Good try," said Dawn, expressing a sliver of solidarity.

I'd positioned myself so I was near to Chris and Patrick...they were on the seats just in front of us. It meant the lion would get to them first, which was reassuring. It also meant I could talk to him as we bumbled along the bumpy roads. I might have to turn my attention to one of them if Pieter wasn't going to appear. That's when I noticed they were holding hands.

Fuck! Two-thirds of the single men were gay, and the other third hadn't appeared. This wasn't going at all well.

A WHITE LION AND ELEPHANTS GALORE

"Now, the thing with a safari," said Cristine. "Is that you never know what you're going to see or not going to see."

"Too bloody right," I whispered to Dawn. "You head out expecting to see a gorgeous ranger with big thighs and a deep voice and end up with a woman."

"Don't make the mistake of thinking this is like going to the theatre or something," Cristine continued. "The animals don't come out and perform for you. To be honest - we might see nothing at all today."

"We saw nothing yesterday," said Chris. "No bloody animal in sight yesterday." His voice rose theatrically as he spoke, and he stroked his beard like some great Hollywood actor. Kind of how Brian Blessed might look if he lost about ten stone.

"We saw birds, but they don't count, do they?" said Patrick, shaking his head as if the lack of animals was entirely Cristine's fault.

"Well, hopefully, we'll see something today," she

replied. I had no idea how she kept her cool. She must have seen all manner of strange people gathering on the back of her Land Rover over the years, but we seemed like a particularly motley crew. I vowed to be as nice to her as possible for our trip.

"So, we'll head off now," she said, pulling away from the safety of the lodge and driving through the huge fences into animal land. "No one must get out of the vehicle under any circumstances. As long as you stay inside, I can protect you. I have a gun here and I've worked here for a long time. I know what to do, but whatever happens, you must not get out of the Land Rover. Do you all understand?"

We nodded mutely.

"What animals are you hoping to see?"

There were mumblings about cheetahs and lions, and Dawn rather alarmingly growled that she'd love to see a kill: "I'd like to see a lion tear down an animal twice its size and drag it off while it's still alive."

"Blimey - I'd just love to see some giraffes and elephants," I said plaintively. I've always thought that giraffes were sublimely elegant creatures - their gentle movements and that elegant long neck...kind of what I'd love to come back as if I had the choice. Elephants are great, too, with their long trunks and comical flappy ears, and baby elephants are adorable.

"OK, I'll do my best," said Cristine.

Within minutes, as if ushered onto the stage by an almighty director, giraffes moved ahead of us, gliding with such gracefulness through the trees that tears sprang into my eyes. They had lovely long necks and tiny heads...the supermodels of the animal world.

Without being able to help it, I squealed a little. This was amazing. I mean AMAZING. If you've never been on a safari - go on one. They are bloody fantastic. I mean fantastic. To be fair, I only came for a free holiday, and to ogle the handsome rangers, I didn't think about how properly captivating it would all be.

Next came the elephants.

"You're good!" I told Cristine as a herd of elephants trooped past us. The two animals I most wanted to see had appeared one after the other.

They lumbered close to the vehicle, and Cristine seemed quite comfortable. I was expecting her to drive away but she didn't move. I was so pleased. I wanted to stay here forever, close to these majestic, beautiful creatures. "No sudden movements and no sudden noises," she dictated. "But, besides that - don't worry - elephants are gentle creatures. They express all sorts of emotions. Elephants cry when other elephants die...you see tears in their eyes when they are sad. They are very lovely. So intelligent, kind, sensitive and emotional, as long as you don't do anything to frighten them, they will be quite comfortable in your company."

It turned out that Cristine was a world expert on elephants (how cool is that? Fancy being a global expert in elephants - that's the coolest thing in the world). She explained that she was studying their behaviour for a master's degree.

"Oh, hang on." With that, she jumped out of the driving seat and excitedly collected their droppings, displaying them for us to see. "Look," she said, as if showing us a diamond ring. "Aren't they lovely?" The droppings carry information about what the elephants have been eating that is useful for her research.

"I'm a very happy girl now," she said, dropping the contents of her gloved hand into a metal dish. "Lovely to have some fresh dung to play with tonight."

We saw so many animals that morning; it's hard to recount them all...a young tawny male lion trying to bring down an eland, failing miserably and having to wander away with his tail between his legs. Then, another lion had been spotted by a fellow ranger, so we were invited to go along and take a look. This was a white lion – a beautiful beast - white of fur and with the pale blue-green eyes of a film star. When we reached him, he was stretched out in the sun, his handsome face framed with a great mane of white fluff, his protruding belly testament to a good feed. A couple of feet away from him, under the trees, out of the sun, lay the remains of a baby giraffe he had killed that morning. "Can we get closer?" said Dawn, practically hanging out of the Land Rover to get a better look. "Can we go down there and take a look?"

"Really?" asked Cristine, losing her relaxed aura for a minute and giving Dawn a confused grin. "You want to go and stand between a male lion and his kill?"

"But he's lying down, he's full up, he's not going to be bothered by me. He'd have come up here and attacked the vehicle if he was.

"It doesn't work like that," said Cristine. "Lions completely ignore safari vehicles. They're just large, unthreatening, moving things that don't look very appetising and smell strange. If you get out you instantly look like a meal – with a head and legs and a tasty aroma of meat."

"OK," said Dawn, suitably chastised. "But if it's a slower animal that we could outrun, can we get out and see them?"

"No," said Cristine. "I want you to remember that for these animals - food runs. If something runs away, they'll assume they can eat it. And don't be fooled into thinking you can outrun anything. It may look big and fat, but even a hippo can run as fast as Usain Bolt and swim faster than Michael Phelps and a rhino can run over 30mph. You wanna take on one of those?? Not on my watch."

"What should we do if we're chased by a hippo then?" asked Dawn.

"Well, hopefully, you won't be, but if you are, I'd suggest climbing a tree."

We all nodded to ourselves, thinking this wise advice and words that we would be heeding should rhinos or hippos get in our paths.

We were only out for a few hours in the morning, and Cristine told us it was one of the best mornings of sightings she'd ever seen. I tried to persuade her that the animals had come to see Dawn and me in our finery...I even doffed my ribbon-bedecked straw hat in her direction, but she wasn't having any of it.

"It's because of the rain last night," she concluded. "It has brought them all out for the first time in ages.

In the late afternoon we went back out and saw rhinos and buffalos aplenty. I learned all about the safari world...how the buffalos die off first if there is a drought because they need so much water.

We saw birds and plants as well. My God, the birds were spectacular - from secretary birds which take off like aeroplanes, with a giant run-up, spreading their wings and swooping into the sky, to the huge fish eagles and the staggeringly pretty smaller birds in jewel-like colours, singing beautifully through the warmth and silence in this lovely part of the world. By the end, I was hopelessly in love with Cristine and wanted to stay here forever, learning from her and mixing with these fabulous animals.

A TERRIFYING SNAKE AND GUN-TOTING RANGERS

It was 6 pm, a very special time of day...sundowner time. This, in case you were unaccustomed to the ways and mores of the Safari set, was shorthand for drinking! It took place when the sun was just going down, so the ranger headed for the most picturesque spot imaginable, and we all consumed the drinks we'd selected that morning. Cristine had chosen the place with the best view of the sunset, and we were all set to enjoy assorted snacks and large drinks in front of the magnificent view.

We pulled up at the breathtakingly pretty spot, and Cristine began unloading the goodies she had packed into her cool bag. There was an alarming moment when it occurred to me that the pots containing crisps and nuts were astonishingly similar in appearance to those she had used earlier to capture elephant dung. I decided to share this with the group. It didn't go down well. We all steered clear of the chocolate peanuts after that.

Cristine handed me a gin and tonic and handed Dawn

her vodka and Red Bull. As soon as I saw her drink, I immediately wished I had also ordered one. My gin and tonic seemed far less exciting in both colour and flavour. I grimaced at Cristine like it was her fault, but she seemed oblivious to my facial expressions, so I took a huge gulp and felt the warming drink move down my throat like an anaesthetic and into my stomach, where it warmed me from within.

"Cheers," said Patrick, and we all raised our glasses. I realised that I was the only one to have taken a huge gulp before the 'cheersing' had been done.

"Cheers," I joined in, raising my glass with everyone else. We all sipped our drinks while zebras moved easily across the plane in front of us.

"See how the baby zebras stay close to their mums," said Cristine. "That's so that the mum's stripes camouflage the calf. Look...you can't see the baby next to mum...the stripes blend."

We looked over, and I could see what she meant. Nature was so clever.

"Wouldn't the lion attack the mum anyway?" asked Dawn.

"Could do...but mums are harder to attack than babies, and babies taste better. Younger meat."

"Down in one," said Chris, slightly ruining the rarefied atmosphere. "Come on - 1,2,3 and we all down our drinks."

"Excellent. Is there any other way?" I said, throwing my gin and tonic down my throat and smiling broadly. Chris downed his, too. The others just looked at us while they sipped theirs.

"We're not 14," said Alexa, which felt slightly ironic since she was the only one in the group who looked like she might actually be 14.

"It's a holiday," I said, exasperation dancing through my voice. "Chill out."

The only problem with downing your drink was that it was then all gone. Chris and I looked at one another, as the others continued to sip. Then there was a quite magical moment. A second of pure joy. Cristine unzipped her cool bag and revealed that she had more drinks in there.

"Another G&T?" she asked. "And a red wine for you, Chris?"

Honestly, I could have kissed her. We both nodded vigorously and laughed as we caught each other's eyes. Suddenly, it felt like Chris and I would become best friends after all this.

"Cheers!"

We both downed our drinks again. The others had wandered off to the other side of the small area we'd stopped in. It was a lovely little place...a little grassy area with a couple of trees, three benches facing out towards the most beautiful views and a big, wooden table. Buried deep in the undergrowth in front of the area was an old shack that we could just about make out; it was surrounded by trees and apparently contained an ancient toilet. I decided to hang on until we were back in the room before going to the loo. I didn't fancy wandering down there through the undergrowth.

Though the others wandered around to look at the views from all sides, and compare notes on the incredible day we'd just had, Chris and I stayed close to Cristine and her cool bag. Our devotion to her paid off when she unzipped the bag and took out more drinks. Jesus, how big was that bag? It seemed to have an endless amount of drink in it. I vowed to ask her where she got it and buy myself one.

"I only brought three of everyone's drinks," she said as she pulled out gin and wine. I didn't think people would want more than that since this is just a quick stop to see the sunset, not a massive piss-up or anything."

Alright, alright, I thought. Cut it with all the judgment.

"Perhaps we should drink these more slowly," said Chris.

Cristine looked out at the others, chatting happily in the distance.

"Unless the others don't want theirs, of course," she said. "Then you could have more."

"They definitely won't want theirs," Chris and I said at exactly the same time.

The thing was, I didn't imagine that the others did want their drinks...they were too busy chatting and admiring the views.

"I'll go for a vodka and red bull," I said.

"Yeah, I'll have Patrick's red wine," said Chris, and we downed them both while Cristine looked on, eyebrows raised and hand poised on the cool bag so she could replenish us when necessary, looking increasingly alarmed at the speed of our drinking, despite her professional demeanour.

"What's next?" asked Chris.

"What did the Americans order?" I asked.

I felt quite drunk. It felt lovely, to be honest. That

adorable light-headed feeling you get before the real feeling of hopeless drunkenness hits.

“Just these dwarf bottles of vodka and coke,” said Cristine, pulling them out of the cool bag,

“Dwarf!” said Chris, convulsing into laughter. “Dwarf. That's so funny.”

“Yes, funny word,” I said, though I didn’t think it was funny at all. Perhaps Chris was way drunker than me?

“No - not the word. It’s just the...ah, it’s hard to explain.” “Try,” I said.

“OK, well I need to tell you about our parties.”

“Good, then tell me,” I said, indicating to Cristine that we’d like the bottles of vodka and coke despite Chris’s hysterics.

"Well," he said, smiling to himself. "We really like to party... Or, should I say, I like to party, and Patrick just tolerates it."

"Go on..." I said, taking a big sip of my drink.

"We have these parties, and they're full of great people. You know, writers, artists, musicians... Just brilliant people who are so talented and artistic, and I want to make sure they have the best time possible, so the food I prepare is always magnificent – I will get someone in to make sure the food is restaurant quality, and I serve the best wines and champagne, and then – when everyone is drunk and having a great time and I think things just can't get better... that's when the dwarves come."

"Dwarves? Why?"

"Tons of dwarfs. Dwarves everywhere."

"I'm still really confused; you must tell me what the dwarves are there for."

"So people can snort cocaine off their heads. Why else would they be there?" he said.

I just looked at him, eyebrows raised, mouth open.

"Have you never done that?" he said, genuinely surprised.

"No, of course, I haven't. What's wrong with you?"

He laughed like a drain. "Gosh, you are funny. You have to try it. Snorting cocaine off the head of a dwarf is the best fun you can ever have. You are coming to the next party; just don't bring that bloody friend of yours; she is no fun."

"Okay, I will come," I said tentatively.

"Brilliant," he said. "You won't have to bring anything. I will supply the food and the booze. Oh, and the dwarves."

It wasn't long before the effects of the alcohol kicked in, and I found myself staggering, swaying, slurring and unbearably desperate for the loo. I knew that going for a wee here necessitated me striding through the undergrowth toward the small wooden shack. Before, I'd been quite worried about it, but with the false confidence granted by alcohol, it didn't seem to be half the problem.

"I'm going to have to go to the loo," I said to Cristine, shuffling a little as I lost my balance.

"Of course. It's all open - so just go inside but remember to shut the door afterwards so snakes don't go in there.

"Snakes?" I gasped.

"You're on safari," she said. "There are snakes everywhere."

Chris did a sort of little jumpy skip on the spot at the thought of them; it made me like him even more.

“I’m not a fan of snakes,” he said. I could see on his face that was a great understatement. He looked bloody terrified. To be honest, who is a fan of snakes? Only spotty teenagers with personality disorders who keep them in their bedrooms and feed them live rats.

“It’ll be fine,” said Cristine; she looked rather amused by it all.

“Will you come down with me?" I asked her, feeling like a lemon but now worried about what I might find down there.

"Okay," she said, leading the way towards the shack, a gun in her hand.

"What on earth do you need the gun for?" I asked.

"To shoot the snakes," she said.

"You are joking!" I squealed, terror, resonating through my voice.

"Yes, I am, hah!" she said. "I've just got my gun with me because we're not supposed to leave them lying around. I didn't fancy leaving it next to a drunk Chris. I'd come back and find he’d shot himself in the foot or something."

"Yes, very wise,” I replied. Cristine was quite funny really, once again I felt quite sorry for her having to deal with drunk English people when I'm sure she'd much rather have been studying elephants and talking to people who understood these things far better than we ever would.

She led the way through the undergrowth, knocking it aside as she went, purposefully striding with all the confidence of a woman who does this every day. I stayed close behind, jumping and screaming as every blade of grass touched me, now paranoid that there were snakes everywhere.

"Here we are then," said Cristine, opening the door to the wooden shack, leaning inside and putting on the antiquated light. It was a very basic, outdoorsy sort of toilet, but it was clean, there was a sink, and there was – crucially – toilet paper. To be honest, it was all you could ever reasonably expect from a toilet in the middle of the wilds of Africa.

I walked inside, dropped my cream trousers and crouched down gently. When anything is old-looking, I'm always extra cautious because I know I'm a huge weight and likely to break things. Breaking the toilet into would be too embarrassing for words, so I hovered slightly above it. That's when I saw it...in the corner of the room – a snake.

It's difficult to describe the huge scream that came from my mouth – driven by some inner terror and fear. I've never made a noise quite like it before. I heard rustling outside as someone came down the hill to my aid. I knew I should pull up my trousers and make myself decent, but I was so paralysed by fear, so utterly terrified, I couldn't move. The wooden door opened, and Chris's face peered through, seeing me sitting there with my lovely, frilly knickers around my ankles.

"I'm terrified," I said to Chris. "It's over there..."

I pointed to the corner of the room where the green snake lay.

I kept my voice low, eager not to disturb the vile creature in anyway.

"Oh my fucking God!" screamed Chris at the top of his

voice, piling back out through the door and running with all his might. At the top of the hill, Cristine had wandered back to the Land Rover and had started packing away the snacks.

I was alone

The only positive thing in this terrible scenario was that Chris's enormous scream didn't seem to have disturbed the snake in any way, and it sat there, not moving, coiled, poised, and ready to strike if my guard should be let down at any stage.

I knew I had to stand up from this uncompromising position and get myself out of the room, but I was terrified to move.

Slowly, I grabbed my trousers and knickers and tiptoed towards the door. I pulled the big wooden door towards me, and it made a horrible squeaking sound. Oh God, that was bound to alert the creature. I threw myself into the undergrowth, convinced the snake was following me but too scared to look behind. All I could think of was Cristine's advice to climb a tree. There was a big tree with low branches just to my left. I kicked off my trousers that were around my ankles and grabbed at my knickers, half pulling them up. From the corner of my eye, I could see that the party of fellow Safari goers was starting to move down the hill. Chris was in the middle, pointing towards me, presumably telling them the story about the snake in the corner of the toilet.

I launched myself into the arms of the tree, sure that if I was off the ground, my chances of being attacked by the horrible bright green slippery reptile were vastly reduced. I sat on the branch and looked down; Cristine was walking towards me; she would save me. She had a gun, and she was used to this sort of thing. I was bound to be safe.

"Are you okay?" she asked. I'd lost the power of speech, my fear had robbed me of any ability to articulate the sheer terror coursing through my veins.

I reached up to the branch just above, planning to climb onto it but unsure whether it was wise. I was drunk, trouserless and terrified; was tree climbing the best idea right now? I just felt as if I would be safer the higher I got off the ground.

"Stay there, Mary," said Cristine. "Don't move, okay, I don't want you to fall."

I clung on for dear life as Cristine reached for her radio and called for help, asking for another ranger to come and assist her.

I really wished I hadn't climbed up the tree. Every time I looked down, I felt sick; every time I looked out across the landscape, I became convinced that snakes were coming from everywhere to get me, and down below, I saw the fellow Safari-goers assembling. They shouted words of comfort and told me to hang on, and everything would be okay. Cristine was going to get rid of the snake; she was just waiting for assistance to arrive, and then she'd take care of everything.

"You okay?" she said. "I mean – you're not gonna fall, are you?"

"No," I said, with more surety than I felt. I was half-pissed; there was every chance of me falling from the tree.

Over at the top of the hill, Dawn was waiting; she hadn't come down to join the others and reassure me about my fate. Instead, she was taking videos of me for her blog. It struck me that I would either be eaten alive by snakes or featured on a blog wearing my knickers and with my stomach hanging out. I wasn't entirely sure which the worst of the two options was. Perhaps both would happen! I was fairly confident that even if snakes were eating me, Dawn would keep filming.

UP A TREE, KNICKERS ON SHOW, BROADCASTING TO THE WORLD

I heard the Land Rover bringing my rescuers before I saw it. It arrived at the top of the hill, pulling up by the picnic table where we'd been having such a lovely drink and chat just 15 minutes earlier. I could hear a handbrake being pulled on...then I saw him - like a superhero striding onto a movie set: Pieter. The magnificent, gorgeous, handsome Pieter, powering down the hill to save me. I just wished I looked better. This wasn't in any way how I'd hoped to appear when he first set eyes on me. I'd pictured myself like Meryl Streep, reclining decoratively in a wicker chair, sipping champagne, not half-pissed and clinging onto a tree trunk, terrified out of my mind, with my trousers on the ground in front of me.

"There's a green mamba in the toilets and a lady in the tree," said Cristine, her tone was quite matter-of-fact, as if this sort of thing happened every day. "Could you check on the snake first? I'll stay with tree lady."

Tree lady? Is this what I had been reduced to? Pieter smiled at Cristine and looked up at me.

"You OK up there?" he asked.

"Yes, fine," I lied.

He strode manfully towards the toilets as Dawn appeared under the tree below me, still filming.

"He's hot," she said.

I should have realised that it was the arrival of the handsome ranger that had forced Dawn to come down the hill to join us, and not any concern for my well-being.

"Yep," I replied noncommittally. Pieter certainly was drop-dead gorgeous, but it was strange how much that didn't matter when you were stranded in a tree and just wanted someone kindly and non-judgemental to get you down. I guess I was scared, and when you're scared, you want someone who cares by your side.

I looked to Cristine for help, but she watched Pieter's back as he went on a snake hunt. For the first time that holiday, I wished that Ted were there. Sensible, practical, reliable Ted would know exactly what to do...to be honest; he would probably have climbed up the tree by now and be helping me down, carefully and gently, telling me that none of this was my fault and that any one of us could have found ourselves stuck in a tree without trousers. It was to be understood. My tree climb was a sensible precaution, not the actions of a ridiculous, drunk woman.

"Was this the snake you were worried about?" said Pieter, walking towards the tree, holding the giant, luminous green snake in his hands.

"Oh my God, be careful," I said. "Those things are vicious."

I'd never seen anyone so brave in my life. How did he manage to carry it like that without looking utterly terrified? It was beyond me.

"I think I'll be okay," said Pieter with a slow smile. "This is a hosepipe."

"Oh!" I said. To say that I was embarrassed would be a dramatic understatement; I felt utterly ridiculous, crouching in the tree for no reason.

"Was this why you ran up the tree?"

"Yes," I said. "I thought it was a snake... I just ran away and remembered Cristine's advice that it was best to run up a tree."

"From hippos," said Cristine. "Not snakes."

"Pretty weird place to hide from snakes," said Pieter. "Because - let's be honest, you get loads of snakes in trees, possibly more than you get on land."

"I didn't think," I said, panicking a little. "I was scared."

"Do you want to get down now then?" he said.

"Yes, I want to come down, but I don't know how to," I said.

I was aware that my words were vaguely slurring as I spoke. I wasn't full-on drunk, but things were swaying, and I knew there was no chance of me leaving the tree unaided. Not without landing flat on my face and probably doing myself, and perhaps other people, serious injury.

Pieter was just looking at me. "I still feel very shaky," I said. "I'm scared to come down." "Okay then, I'll have to come up."

Pieter dropped the snake-like hose pipe onto the ground and easily climbed up to me. He reached the branch on which I was perching in about a 10th of the time it had taken me to get there. He crouched next to me. "How are we going to do this, then?" he asked, looking straight into my eyes.

He had these dreamy grey-green eyes that seemed to sparkle like a calm sea on a warm summer's day. He had been clean-shaven in the images on the website, but today, he had a rough-looking beard, which just seemed to add to his beauty. He stroked his chin as he spoke, the glint in his eyes growing as he thought through the options for getting a very large lady out of a tree.

"How about if I climb down to the next branch and help you down to it?" he said.

This didn't seem to be a very sophisticated plan, to be honest. But I knew I just had to do as I was told.

"Okay, I'll try," I said.

"OK, move your right leg down towards this branch."

He was issuing simple, straightforward instructions that should have been easy to follow. Perhaps they would've been easy for someone more agile and less drunk. The trouble was that I couldn't lift my leg as he needed me to because my stomach was in the way. Only people who have been fat understand how debilitating it can be.

Eventually, he realised the strategy was not going to work.

"Cristine, can you call for assistance, please? Tell them to bring the winch."

"Oh my God, what are you going to do?" I said.

"I'm going to get you out of the tree," he said.

And so it was that Mary Brown's mum casually

switched on the computer on that cool September morning in her suburban kitchen, hoping to catch a glimpse of her daughter enjoying the holiday of a lifetime.

She was with three of the ladies from bridge club when she opened Dawn's blog to see her only daughter being winched out of a tree with her knickers fully on show, her hair sticking up everywhere, and a team of rangers attempting to move her as if she was a bull elephant that had got stuck in the mud.

"Goodness," said Margaret, Mrs Brown's long-standing bridge partner. "What a time she's having."

MEETING THE CHEETAHS

Eventually, they got me down from the tree, but I'd be lying if I said it was a simple procedure. By the time I reached the ground, my fingernails and dignity were completely trashed. I'd screamed the whole time, which was very embarrassing - I just became convinced that I would fall and die. The only good thing to emerge from the horrible tree incident was that Pieter promised me that he would take me to see the cheetah close up the next morning.

"Close up," I said through unattractive sobs.

"Close up," he confirmed. "We'll walk up to them so you can see their beautiful coats. OK?"

"OK," I'd said. I realised he was talking to me as if I were a child, but I didn't mind. I didn't mind anything at the time. I just wanted to be back in the room with my trousers on. That wasn't too much to ask, surely?

Pieter was true to his word, and when we got back to the lodge, he said he'd be back the next morning to pick me up. I went to bed feeling a little bit ashamed of the way the day had progressed and a little chafed on my thighs where I'd been dragged out of the tree, but excited. I'd loved seeing all the animals, and the prospect of walking right up to the cheetah the next morning with Pieter was very appealing. It was also nice that I wouldn't have to get up at bloody 4 a.m. to do it. He assured me that if I let the others go off on their early morning drive, we'd leave later and go straight to where the cheetah always lay.

So, at 8 a.m., I sat in the reception area, waiting for Pieter. Cheetahs were his favourite animal; he knew all about them - I don't think he was an academic like Cristine, he certainly didn't seem like someone who did much studying, but he certainly had lots of experience of working with them; he'd been around them a long time. I had a feeling that this was going to be the most amazing morning ever.

I heard the Land Rover pull up outside, and - just for extra measure - Pieter beeped loudly and shouted my name. I jumped up, grabbed my bag and ran outside. I felt like a girl going on a first date.

"Hello there," he said, waiting in the vehicle for me to climb in, clearly unaware what a problem it was for me to get into the damn thing. We'd resorted to using the step ladder yesterday, which had worked well, but Pieter didn't appear to be aware of my difficulties.

"I may need a hand," I said to Pieter, trying not to look too pathetic. "I'm not great at climbing into these things."

Of course, of course," he said, jumping down and running around to help me. Rather than give me a hand up, he pushed my bottom so that I went into the Land Rover headfirst again. This time, I felt like a nervous foal being pushed onto the back of a horse truck against its wishes. Not the most unladylike or sophisticated move by any definition, but at least I was in.

"If we get going, we'll catch up with the others by the rock on the far side where the cheetah tends to spend her time," said Pieter. The words stung like an arrow to the heart. "What do you mean? Meet up with the others? I didn't realise they were coming."

"Yes, Cristine thought they might all enjoy it, so I said I would take them all. That's not a problem, is it?"

"No, no, not at all," I lied.

It was a rubbish idea in so many ways...firstly because if we were catching up with the group, it meant I could have gone with them in the first place and seen more wild animals. Also, it meant that Dawn would now be able to come and see the cheetah with us, and after the way she'd behaved yesterday... videoing me in my hour of great embarrassment, I didn't want her anywhere near me.

"Good – there they are now," he said, smiling and waving at Cristine. The two of them seemed to get on very well.

I'd had about 10 minutes alone with Pieter, and we hadn't even had the chance to discuss cheetahs. The plan to spend time with him and learn everything I could collapsed beneath me.

Cristine jumped out of her Land Rover and grabbed her gun; the others all climbed out after her, waving to me. "Hey stranger, there you are. I was worried about you when you didn't turn up this morning. Are you OK?" said Chris.

"Hi, yes, I'm fine. Ego a bit bruised, but OK," I said.

“Listen, I wanted to apologise...I came to your room last night, but the lights were off, and I didn’t want to wake you up if you’d gone for an early night, but I did want to say sorry.”

“What on earth for?” I asked.

“For being useless. For bursting into the loo and embarrassing you, then squealing and running out.”

“Honestly, don’t worry, I’d have done the same,” I said, though I knew I wouldn’t have. I knew I’d have tried to help.

I saw Dawn grinning wildly on the Land Rover's far side. She waved over and lifted her video camera to her face. Honestly, I was ready to shove that thing down her throat.

Pieter ran through the way things would work. He would lead the way, and we would all stay behind him and not run or move away from him, whatever happened.

"I cannot protect you if you all run off in different directions," he said. "Just stay behind me, and you will be safe. Understand?”

“Yes," we all chorused; it sounded amazing that he would lead us directly up to the cheetah. I shared my excitement with Dawn. But her face had turned a gentle shade of puce.

"He can't just walk up to a cheetah," she said. "That's insane."

“He knows what he’s doing, don’t worry,” I said.

"Okay, everyone quiet," said Pieter. “Stay behind me in a line; Cristine will be at the back. We are both armed, and you will be safe. But you must not run off, scream, or make sudden movements... just follow and stay in a line directly behind me. Okay?"

"Can I just confirm? Are we going to walk directly up to the cheetah?" said Dawn. "I don't think that sounds very safe."

"You'll be safe as long as you stay behind me and do as I say," said Pieter, a hint of impatience creeping into his voice. I could understand why - he must have told us a dozen times that we'd be safe if we did as he said.

"Right, off we go then." Pieter walked forward, striding up towards the rock.

It was fascinating to be walking up to a wild animal. I felt completely safe with Pieter leading the way. I stayed behind him, feeling the excitement grow as we walked, all of us in his footsteps as we headed towards the cat lounging in the sunshine, slightly tucked into the shade, by the huge rock.

"Can you see," said Pieter, whispering as loudly as he dared so as not to alert the cat to our presence.

I could see the cheetah clearly, its gorgeous coat shimmering in the morning sun. Wow, it was beautiful...I yearned to go closer still. As if sensing my thoughts, Pieter stepped towards the animal, and we all followed suit. We were all silent; all that could be heard was the gentle sound of twigs snapping beneath our feet. Then, suddenly, there was a cry.

"Oh God, I'm terrified," said Dawn. "It's gonna jump up and eat me; I just know it."

"Shhhhhh," said Pieter. "You have to keep quiet."

As he said this, the cheetah opened its mouth to give a giant yawn, and Dawn lost her mind.

"Aaaahhhh," she screamed, dropping her video camera and rushing back towards the Land Rover, screaming at the top of her voice.

"For God's sake," Pieter said, turning sharply and indicating to Cristine to quieten the hysterical woman at all costs. I picked up her video camera, which was still running, and slung it over my shoulder.

I could see Dawn and Cristine fighting down by the Land Rover as Dawn continued to scream and declare that she knew the cheetah would eat us all.

"Aren't you going to video her?" Pieter said, winking at me. "This is the moment to get your revenge."

"That would be cruel," I said.

"She videoed you when you were stuck in a tree yesterday and plastered it all over her blog," he said. "I was watching it last night - it was a nasty thing to do."

Oh no, Pieter had seen the video. I wondered who else had. I couldn't remember whether I'd given Ted the blog address...I really hoped not. Dawn was still shrieking.

"Go on, video her, you're missing it all," Pieter said.

I lifted the camera up and looked at it for a couple of seconds, and then I turned it off.

"I don't want to behave like that," I said. "What she did to me was humiliating. I'd rather go through life without humiliating anyone."

"You are one hell of a woman, Mary Brown," said Pieter, turning to lead us back down towards the Land Rover. "That was a very kind thing to do."

"Thanks," I said, feeling myself turn red.

"Sorry we couldn't spend much time with the cheetah," he added. "I know you were keen to see it, but it would have become terrified with all that screaming. It wasn't safe to stay."

"I understand," I said. "I just really wanted to know more about them. Is it true that you're an expert? Kind of like a professor of cheetahs."

"Ha," he said. "I guess you could say that. I have lots of videos of the cheetah, right from when she was a cub, and pictures of her when she was pregnant and when she had her cubs. There are tonnes of research notes that the conservationists made and left copies of because they knew how much I loved her. I should bring them round sometime for you to see?"

"Oh Pieter, I'd love that." I gently touched his arm.

"OK, why don't you come to mine tonight, and we'll have a cheetah evening. How does that sound?"

"Oh, thank you," that would be amazing," I said.

"No problem, I'll cook dinner or something."

So, that was a surprise. It turned out that Pieter was a nice guy despite being gorgeous enough to get away with being a shit. Who'd have thought?

A DATE WITH PIETER

The next day was really good fun out on safari, but we didn't see as many animals as the first day, and nothing special was planned, like walking up to the cheetah or tracking the lions. We did see some rock art; it was fascinating to think that people were turning to art so long ago to express themselves. It gave a real insight into their mindsets to see what they drew (men with spears, mainly! I guess they were pretty preoccupied with safety back then), but all I wanted to do was drive around looking for animals. I loved seeing them. I even felt sad on the late afternoon drive that day when Cristine talked about going for sundowners. I'd rather have had more time to look for rhinos or drive around searching for the elusive white lion.

Chris nudged me when I asked whether we could stay in the Land Rover instead of finding a place for drinks. "Don't spoil the fun...it's time for a drink," he chided. I smiled back, but the honest truth was that I'd much preferred to have looked for animals than drink gin and tonic...and that's something I never imagined myself saying.

Pieter was picking me up at 8 pm that evening to take me to his house for our cheetah night, so there wasn't too much time to prepare by the time we got back from animal watching and sundowners.

As soon as I got in, I tore off my clothes and lay back in a large spa bath, bubbles frothing all around me, sending soft scents into the air as I lay back and breathed deeply. It was such a huge bath; it covered me completely, which is a rarity. Most of the time in the bath, I'm reduced to splashing water over me to keep myself covered.

As I relaxed and melted into the soapy suds, my phone rang next to me.

"Hi gorgeous, how are you doing?" It was Ted.

"I'm OK; how are things with you?" I asked.

"OK, but missing you like mad," he replied. "It's lonely here without you. Are you missing me?"

"Of course I am," I replied. "I wish you were here instead of Dawn."

"Oh yes - so tell me - what's she like then? Is she good company?"

"She's OK," I replied. "I mean - she's let me come on a free holiday with her, so I can't complain too much, but she's quite - I don't know - she's not the friendliest person ever. I feel like she's trying to make me look an idiot."

"You mean in the Two Fat Ladies blog?" he asked.

"Yes - exactly. She said we'd always got on at school, and that's why she was inviting me on safari, but it turns out she only wanted me for the size of my arse...and there aren't many people saying that about me."

Ted laughed and told me not to worry.

"The blog's funny," he said. "You up that tree was hysterical."

"Really? Wasn't it mortifying? I haven't been able to bring myself to watch it...I imagined it was awful."

"Don't be silly," said Ted. "You looked scared but were still your usual funny self throughout."

"Thank you," I said, feeling a wave of warmth towards him.

"There's just one problem, and that's what I was phoning about - who's Pieter?"

" He's just one of the rangers here. Nothing special about him."

"He looks very handsome in the video."

"Ha!" I said. "Videos can be very deceptive indeed."

"Oh good," he said. "Because there's a whole montage of pictures on the site and it says you've got a hot date with him tonight."

"Whaaat? No - I haven't. It's not a date. For God's sake, Ted. Of course, it's not a date. He's just going to talk to me about cheetahs."

"How appropriate," said Ted.

"Why's that appropriate? What are you talking about?"

"Cheetahs. Seems appropriate when it feels like you're a cheater."

"No, I'm not. This is insane. Ted, please don't make this into something it isn't. He's going to talk to me about cheetahs - the animals - like lions and leopards. I wanted to go and see the cheetah yesterday, but Dawn got scared and screamed, so Pieter had to take us all away. He said he'd show me his collection of cheetah memorabilia tonight."

"His cheetah memorabilia? Really? He couldn't do better than that?"

"He's a ranger, Ted. He's just trying to ensure I have the best possible experience while I'm here, so we write nice things about him in the blog...that's all."

"OK," said Ted. "It's just hard, you know...reading all this stuff about you and seeing pictures of you having great fun with these gorgeous blokes, and I'm stuck at work."

"I would have stayed behind if you'd asked me to," I said. "You told me to go. You said you were busy at work."

"I know," said Ted. "I know. I wish I hadn't. I thought the break would do us good, but I miss you."

"It's only a couple more days," I responded. "And - you know - when you say 'having a great time with all these gorgeous men' - you're talking about me being stuck in a tree and having to be winched out. It wasn't the best time ever. It really wasn't. Whatever the guys may have looked like - it was bloody humiliating."

"No, I know. I'm sorry. Look, you have a great time, OK?"

"I will," I reassured him. "And I'll see you in a few days."

"Look forward to it, angel," he said.

The call from Ted left me feeling a little shaken as I clambered out of the bath and dried myself on the softest, fluffiest towels known to man. I knew tonight wasn't a date, but it was a shock how concerned Ted was. It was also a huge shock that he was reading the blog so closely.

And why was Dawn writing all sorts of nonsense about me and Pieter? Why the hell would she do that?

I had been quite relaxed with her and uncritical while she'd exposed my imperfections and errors to the world, but this seemed a deliberate attempt to embarrass me and upset Ted.

I could see that a video of a fat woman in her knickers stuck up a tree was funny and would attract viewers and followers, which was her job at the end of the day. I understood that. But putting a piece on there about me going on a date with Pieter...how was that supposed to do anything to drive traffic? She'd just got into the habit of putting everything on there and simply wasn't stopping to think whether what she was doing could be perceived as being just a little cruel.

I sent a text to her. "Dawn, can you not put stuff on the blog about me going on dates with Pieter? It's just a pleasant evening talking about cheetahs, not a date. My boyfriend saw the blog update and isn't very happy."

"Boyfriend?" replied Dawn. "I didn't know you had a boyfriend."

"You never asked," I replied.

"No, I suppose I didn't. I just assumed you didn't. I don't really think about people like us having boyfriends. Well, behave yourself tonight, then."

'People like us?' Thanks. By that, I guess she meant 'fat people'. Charming.

Since the entire contents of the wardrobe I'd brought with me to South Africa comprised cream linen, white cotton and lace, I had no choice but to look like Meryl Streep's younger, fatter, uglier British cousin for my cheetah night, so it was on with the lacy white top, and the long linen skirt. The straw hat was a bit much for evening wear, even I could see that, but I had a big cream jumper with me...kind of like a cricket jumper but without the cricket stripes on it...it would be perfect if the evening got cold. I draped it over my shoulders and pulled the lace top down. I needed the top to fall as low as possible to cover my horrible fat belly, but pulling it down meant that a whole load of cleavage was being shown. Given the choice between stomach and cleavage, I chose the latter.

So, just for the record - my cleavage wasn't showing because I fancied Pieter or anything...my cleavage was showing to ensure my stomach was covered. Hope that's clear.

I wandered down the staircase to the reception area where I'd arranged to meet Pieter. It was a lovely old sweeping staircase that you'd imagine appearing in a Hollywood film. It was beautiful, and I threw my hair back and strode confidently every time I walked down them.

"Oh, thank God," came a voice from down below. "Can someone help me?"

"Hello," I replied, walking towards the door from where the voice appeared to be coming. Cristine stood on the other side of it, looking confused and holding out two sets of car keys.

"Can you drive, Mary?" she asked, looking at me appealingly.

"Sort of," I said. "I mean - I've had lessons, but I never passed my test."

"That's OK. I don't need you to go on a public road just to move this car forward while I move the Land Rovers in to get the oil checked. Pieter has offered to help me by bringing the barrels in."

"Yes," I said. "Which car, though - I can't get into those Land Rovers, let alone drive them."

"This one," said Cristine, indicating a small car I felt much more comfortable trying to drive. It was around 100m away from where it needed to be. I could do that.

"Thank you, you're a star," said Cristine.

The road into the lodge was one way, so it wasn't a tough job; there would be no cars coming towards me and nothing I was likely to hit.

I pushed the seat back far enough to allow myself to get it and turned the key in the ignition. The car moved slowly forwards...excellent. I could remember what to do. This was all going to be fine. I drove forwards, heading towards the building that Cristine had asked me to park next to. But then, as I approached the building, I saw a car coming towards me...it was going the wrong way down the one-way street.

I flashed my lights at it, waiting for the driver to reverse so I could go past, but he flashed his lights back at me.

"Move over," I mouthed at him through the darkness. There was no way I would attempt to reverse back to where I started from, especially since he was in the wrong. I inched forward, but he inched forward, too; I flashed him, and he flashed back.

I had no idea what to do. I sat there for a while, then

flashed him again, but the guy just flashed me back. This was ridiculous.

Then, there was a knock on my window, causing me practically to leap out of my seat.

I looked up to see Pieter standing there, confusion on his face. "What on earth are you doing?" he asked.

"I'm trying to work out why that guy won't reverse out of my way," I said. “I have the right of way; it’s a one-way street, for God’s sake.”

"What guy?" asked Pieter, looking genuinely surprised. “You’re just sitting here, flashing your lights and beeping at no one.”

I looked up to point at the vehicle ahead, and at that point, I realised the car ahead of me was exactly the same as mine...and there was a good reason for this - the car ahead was mine. What I'd been looking at was the reflection of my own vehicle in the mirrored exterior of the building ahead of me.

"It doesn't matter; the car is gone now," I said, moving to drive the car forwards a little way and park it where Cristine had asked me to.”

"You were looking at your car in the reflection on the building, weren’t you?” said Pieter with a loud guffaw.

“Of course, I wasn’t,” I said, winding the window up and parking where Cristine had asked me. It was a huge bloody relief that Dawn wasn’t there to witness it.

I wandered back into the reception, where Dawn was talking to Pieter. He turned to me as I walked in. "That is the funniest thing I've ever seen," he said, laughing uproariously; you just sitting there, flashing wildly at no one in particular and beeping your horn like a loony. So funny."

"Yeah, hysterical," I said. "Really funny."

I was excited to see where Pieter lived, not just because of a natural interest in anyone who's that good-looking and an eagerness to learn more about him, but also because I was genuinely interested in the lives the rangers led. On the surface, they seemed to have such an attractive way of living - out in the wild all day with amazing animals, carrying a gun around and getting to feel like Crocodile Dundee, but I guessed there was a downside to the job, and it seemed most likely to me that the downside was that they didn't get paid very much and they didn't have great places to live.

"Here we are," said Pieter, as we pulled down a dirt track and came to a standstill outside what looked like an old shack. It was a miserable-looking building - so different from the beauty of the lodge where Dawn and I were staying. The fact that it was pitch black everywhere made it all the more sinister looking, so dark and isolated.

"Come on then." Pieter jumped down from the driving seat and moved towards the door. I scrabbled out, stepped down onto the muddy ground and followed Pieter to his front door. He kicked off his boots and put on the light, sending brightness over the sketchy furniture in a rather dim and dirty-looking room. It was the sort of furniture thrown out by students, the sort of stuff a charity shop in England would refuse to take.

"Have a seat," he said, and I perched on the desperately uncomfortable brown tweed sofa, reluctant to sit back for fear of never getting up again. The springs were gone, and it looked like the seat covers hadn't been washed since the 1960s.

"What do you fancy to eat?" said Pieter, walking into the kitchen.

"I don't mind."

The truth was that I'd already eaten at the lodge, but if he were prepared to cook, I'd happily eat a second dinner so that we could sit romantically across from one another and break bread.

"It's not looking good, to be honest," he said, rummaging around inside a fridge containing little except beer. "I've got nothing in here, food-wise, but a little bit of stale bread and some fruit the farmer gave me last week. It's looking a bit mouldy. I haven't even got any milk. I've got one beer; do you want half?"

"Oh," I said. "OK,"

I just assumed he would have gone shopping in advance of me coming over and have some food prepared.

"I'm not much of a one for sorting out fancy dinners," he said, predicting my thoughts. "I tend just to live one day at a time."

It wasn't so much that he couldn't provide a fancy dinner; what was odd was that he couldn't even provide beans on toast...or beans on their own...or toast...or bread, or anything. The man couldn't even provide me with my own beer bottle.

"Okay, well – should we go out somewhere?" he said.

"Is there a pub or anything like that nearby where we could grab a bite?" I suggested.

"There is a cafe in the village. We could have a beer and a sandwich there," he said.

"Okay, let's do that. Then we can come back here and have a look at the cheetah stuff afterwards."

"Good plan," he said, grabbing the car keys and heading for the front door. I struggled my way out of the huge sofa, my knees buckling as I tried to stand up, and pulled my top down to make sure it was covering my stomach before waddling after him and closing the door behind me. He seemed to leave the door open and not be concerned about who (or what!!) might enter in his absence. I'd have been terrified about what wildlife would call in while I was out.

He hitched me up into the Land Rover, and we drove for about 10 minutes into the local village; then he pulled over outside a small but cosy-looking place. He had called it a cafe, but it was so lively that it was more like a Gastro pub or a small family-run restaurant. I could see through the small windows that there were tablecloths and candles out everywhere, and really pretty flowers in the window boxes outside. My spirits lifted straight away.

"I love it when restaurants have white tablecloths," I said. "And candles. I always look for restaurants with tablecloths and candles."

Pieter looked at me as if I'd gone stark, staring mad. "I'd never noticed that. I've been coming here for 17 years and never noticed they had candles. Women are mad."

"This is perfect," I said, clambering out of the Land Rover again in my effective but undignified way. I'd taken to rolling myself out, clinging onto the doorframe as I did so. Honestly, Land Rovers weren't designed for anyone over about ten stone.

Pieter led the way into the café, and I followed close

behind. As soon as he swung the door open, the warmth of the atmosphere inside enveloped us. I heard a band playing cover tunes, and the waitresses smiled and said hello to Pieter, each of them drooling a little as he walked past him. He sat at a table which was clearly his regular, and ordered two beers before I could say that I preferred wine. I looked up, and the waitress had gone. It didn't matter – I'd drink beer and have wine next time.

"They do a great steak sandwich," he said. "It comes with chips.

"Great, that will do for me," I said, although I had imagined something a little more romantic... Perhaps some beautifully cooked seafood and a glass of chilled wine.

Pieter ordered our food, and I leaned forward on my elbows and looked deep into his eyes.

“So, go on then, tell me everything you know about cheetahs.”

But before Pieter could answer, we were interrupted by a small commotion as three very large drunk men came bundling over to our table.

"Hello matey, what we got here?" they said to Pieter.

When I looked at them more closely, I realised it was three of the rangers.

"Pieter, my old man, so this is where you are. We been looking for you."

"This is Mary," said Pieter. "Do you know Marco, Liam and Steve?"

"No, I don't. Nice to meet you," I said.

“Five beers,” said Marco, waving his hand at the waitress. “Hang on, no - make it 10, no point messing around.”

"Oh blimey. I think I'd prefer wine," I said, but my words were lost in the sound of chatter and cheering as the men downed their beers. This wasn't turning out to be quite the night I was hoping for.

"Come on, Mary, down in one."

I confess that I downed my beer, despite not enjoying it, and knocked the next two back with equal gusto, just to keep up appearances. My food arrived, and it was like a free-for-all, with everyone reaching in and grabbing chips.

All that remained on the plate was a little garnish of lettuce and tomato...I nibbled at the edge of the tomato as the men chatted. They'd moved into talking Afrikaans, which meant I was completely excluded. I don't think Pieter was doing it deliberately...it was just habit - beer and steak and a chat with the boys in their native tongue.

As the men chatted on, I looked around the pretty restaurant which had filled up considerably since we'd first arrived. To the right of us was a young, attractive couple and something about their body language drew me to them. I tuned into their conversation and soon realised they were debating whether or not to have an affair.

'I'm really attracted to you...' said the man.

"I'm attracted to you too," said the woman, more shyly.

It was captivating to listen. The man leaned over and took her hands, and they sat there staring at one another. Another beer arrived on the table in front of me, distracting me momentarily. When I turned back to them a large man had entered the restaurant and was storming towards their table prompting them to jump apart quickly. "Holy fuck," I said out loud. Pieter and his mates stopped their conversation and looked at me for the first time in about 20 minutes.

"What's the matter?" asked Pieter.

"It's about to kick off big time over there," I said. "Just watch."

By the time they all looked it was, indeed, all kicking off, with the husband having grabbed the affair guy round the neck. The woman started screaming for them to stop. Pieter raced over to the fighting men, with his three musketeers in hot pursuit. I loved how much of an action man he was, how confident in his own abilities, and how fearless. It was very alluring.

He arrived and easily separated the warring parties, much to the delight of the manager, who told the duo to leave and sort out their issues elsewhere. By the time Pieter returned to the table, I was shaking a little...whether it was adrenalin, excitement or fear, I didn't know. Pieter wrapped my jacket around me.

"Come on, let's get you back," he said, leading me to the Land Rover and heaving me into it. "You can tell me what all that was about on the drive home."

UP A TREE: AGAIN. THIS TIME WITH ADDED BABOONS

Dawn and I were up early and ready for our penultimate day on safari. There was a sort of sadness as we got ready, knowing that so much of the holiday had already gone.

"I can't believe we fly home tomorrow night," said Dawn.

I couldn't either. I'd got so used to life here. "I hope we see some amazing animals today," I said. "And I'd love to see the elephants close up again."

"And another kill," said Dawn. "I'd like to see a load of lions kill something big right in front of us."

"OK," I said with a fake smile. "Yes, that would be lovely."

I was really into this holiday now. It's odd how the rhythm of a safari starts to come naturally after just a couple of days. I don't feel traumatised by the early mornings like I did when we first arrived. I enjoyed waking up early, knowing that the day ahead was an unwritten page and that we might see things that we never imagined witnessing.

"Oh wow. I've got 600 new followers," said Dawn, lifting her head up from where it had been engrossed in her phone. "I was hoping to get 500 newbies in total, so that's good with a couple of days to go. Although, when I went to New York and bumped into Tom Cruise, I gained about 10,000 followers as soon as I put the video online."

"I guess me in a tree in my pants isn't quite as exciting as Tom Cruise," I said.

We went to breakfast at 4 am, me sweeping down the stairs, Hollywood style, as I'd taken to doing every time. I found it impossible to descend without pretending to be Marilyn Monroe in Gentlemen Prefer Blondes. I wished I'd brought a long red dress instead of just white and cream; then I could have done the staircase routine justice.

Breakfast was a quiet affair...Alexa and David had left the night before while I was out on my 'date' so there were only the four of us left. I regaled Patrick and Chris with tales of the couple from the restaurant the night before and how manly and confident Pieter had been, then we set out on our morning adventure, heading down by the lake to watch the hippos.

Cristine explained that when the hippos open their jaw right up and look like they are yawning, they are not yawning at all but showing signs of being scared. She said we would be backing away as soon as we saw anything like that. I hoped the hippos would play ball and not do the mouth-opening thing because I wanted to stay and watch them for as long as possible; they were such peculiar-looking creatures.

"It's been lovely driving you lot around," Cristine said suddenly, out of the blue.

“Has it?” I asked, the surprise evident in my voice. I imagined she was fed up with us because we were a bit useless, but she said our enthusiasm was real joy.

"And you are keen to learn; that's been lovely," she said. "You seem genuinely interested in knowing about the animals, not like other people I've had to show around."

"Oh, do tell..." I said, dying to hear stories of really stupid people on Safari.

"Well, there was one time when a couple arrived at the wildlife reserve and the guy told one of the rangers that he wanted to propose to his girlfriend. He asked whether a giraffe could bring the ring to them while he was on one knee. It was baffling to all of us that he thought these wild animals could be made to perform circus tricks.”

"Tell us more," I said.

Cristine laughed. "There was a couple from Germany who asked whether the animals got bored, and whether we couldn't bring out a TV for them so they could watch it during the day. They also asked whether the animals had access to a fridge."

We all laughed and smiled at one another, united in the warm glow of hearing that other people were much more stupid than we were.

Back in the lodge, I decided to have a shower before lunch. It was so warm that morning that I felt hot and sticky. Also, the shower in the lodge was the stuff of fantasies, so I tended to go in there quite a lot; all these settings allowed you to have it raining on you, pouring on you, dripping on you or coming down at you with such ferocity that it almost bruised your scalp. I once tried the scalp bruising setting and decided it wasn't for me. The other settings, though, were lovely. Rainwater was the best - a fine spray that tingled as it touched your skin - light, airy, and refreshing. I stepped out and wrapped a towel around my hair and around my body, padding into the bedroom to get dressed. Dawn was out on the balcony trying to look for hippos. She'd become utterly fascinated by them since Cristine told her they could run faster than Usain Bolt.

I slipped into my knickers and left the towel wrapped around me while I applied the lovely scented lotion that had been left in a straw basket in the bedroom. It was gorgeous - it smelled of everything lovely - like clouds and rainbows would smell if you could get close enough to sniff them.

I was aware of quite a commotion on the steps outside the room as I rubbed the lightly scented lotion into my thighs. It sounded as if there were loads of guys all jumping up and down. It was very odd. Then, it all went quiet for a moment.

I popped my head out of the door but couldn't see anything. It was a beautiful sunny day, and a lovely feeling drifted through me when the sun's warm rays touched my skin, still slightly damp from the shower and lotion. I stood there awhile, enjoying the sensations.

But as I was enjoying the tingling of sunshine on my skin, I noticed some movement in the bushes just in front of the steps to the apartment. It looked like a couple of people were there.

"Hello," I said. I had the sudden feeling it was Pieter. Perhaps he'd brought the cheetah stuff to show me after last night's disaster. But why was he hiding in the bushes?

"Pieter," I tried. The figures stood still but didn't respond; it was the oddest thing. I walked slowly down the steps. “Pieter?”

I pushed my way into the bushes, and that’s when I saw them. It was two bloody baboons standing there. One squealed, and the other just stared. I stood there, rooted to the spot, unsure what to do.

One of the baboons crouched, turning his head slightly to one side and staring intently at me. The other baboon moved around so he was standing to the side of me. I had no idea what would make them go away. Perhaps if I threw something, they would turn to look at it, and it would grant me a few minutes’ grace in which I could escape back up the steps to the room. I moved to bend down but was terrified of taking my eyes off them. In any case, there was nothing to throw, nothing big enough to distract them. Then it occurred to me...there was only one thing for it...I removed the towel and hurled it with all my might. The baboons looked round as if flew through the air. I panicked and climbed up into the tree, screaming as loudly as I could as I went. Don’t ask me why. Don’t ask me why I didn’t leg it back to the room. I guess my throwing of the towel was pretty feeble so the baboons weren’t distracted for long; I didn’t think I’d make it back there in time. So, there I was - once again up a tree to escape from an animal that was perfectly able to get into the tree should it want to.

The baboons were screeching up at me, and I was screaming for help. We were making a tremendous amount of noise; surely, someone had to hear us soon.

In the distance, I saw the sight of khaki green shirts running towards me. Thank God. It was Marco, Liam and Steve, the guys I'd met in the pub with Pieter.

"Here," I shouted, waving hysterically.

The baboons shrieked louder and one, then the other, jumped up into the tree next to me.

By the time the rangers arrived all three of us were in the tree, sitting on the lowest branch, me covering my breasts with my hands, them looking at me quizzically. We'd only been there only a couple of minutes, but they had shuffled over so close that we were all sitting next to one another like we were waiting for a bus or something.

Unbeknownst to me, Dawn, the intrepid blogger, had witnessed the whole episode. She had seen the drama unfold, heard the screams, and had done what a reliable blogger would always do in such circumstances - she'd filmed it all. With scant regard for my feelings and no regard for my privacy, Dawn had shown the world the picture of me half-naked in a tree with two baboons. Then, when gun-toting rangers had arrived, she had filmed that too, finishing her recording with the sight of Mary's larger-than-average bottom descending. She marked it 'Fat Girl stuck in tree: Part Two. This time, with added baboons' and loaded it onto the blog.

A NIGHT WITH PIETER

After everything that had happened during the day, the last thing I wanted to do in the evening was to go out drinking. I felt drained. It had taken four rangers to rescue me, and Dawn had again captured it on video. When I spoke to her about it, she hugged me, said she loved me, and was sorry if I offended. Offended? Try humiliated. The damn thing had been trending on Twitter all afternoon, and she now had 10,000 more followers. I'd matched Tom Cruise...or, more likely, the screaming baboons had matched Tom Cruise. It was all bloody exhausting. I just wanted to curl up on the bed, watch some terrible South African television, and get lots of sleep. Tomorrow was the last day, and we were doing something called 'walk on the wild side' in the morning, where we'd go out on foot to get closer to the animals and see more of the insects and plant life. I knew I'd enjoy it much more if I did it without a hangover.

I slipped on my pyjamas, tied my hair back from my face, and prepared to relax for the evening.

I pulled back the sheets and climbed in. I curled up into a little ball and found myself thinking about Ted. The holiday had taught me many things, and one of them was that Ted was a really good guy, and I should be making more of an effort to make our relationship work. He was worth sticking with, even when things weren't perfect. He was one of life's good guys.

As I was lying there, lost in my thoughts, I suddenly felt water on my legs. I put my hand down and could feel that my pyjama bottoms were soaked.

Oh my God - I'd wet myself; this was a nightmare.

I leapt out of bed, my pyjama trousers wet through, and went to head for the bathroom, but before I could get there, there was a knock on the door. It must be Dawn; probably come back to check I was OK. We had been leaving the door ajar so that neither of us needed to take out keys with us, but tonight, I'd closed it firmly against the world, fearful of baboons and the looks of pity from everyone who'd seen the video.

But, when I swung the door open, Pieter was standing there, clutching a carrier bag in one hand and two bottles of wine in the other.

"I thought you might be feeling low. I wanted to cheer you up," he said.

I stood before him, my large body encased in unflattering, too-tight pyjamas; having wet myself minutes earlier, my hair was scraped back off my face. It's possible that no one in the world had ever looked worse. I smiled at him.

"I wasn't expecting guests," I said.

"Clearly," he said, smiling back.

Then we both burst out laughing, and I swung open the door.

"Come in," I said.

"Look, I saw what happened today, and the blog and everything, and I wanted to check you were OK. He wandered over and sat on the edge of the bed. The bed in which the sheets were soaking wet from me having peed myself. To say it was mortifying was a gross understatement.

"Why don't we sit on the balcony," I said, opening the French windows and trying to tempt him away from the wet bed.

"Oh no," he said, spotting the damp sheets. "Did it break?" "Did what break?"

"I asked housekeeping to put a heated water bottle in the bed to warm it up for you. Looks like it's leaked everywhere."

"Oh thank God," I said, abandoning all efforts at decorum.

"I thought I'd wet myself."

"You thought what?"

"Really - I thought I'd wet myself. That's why I was trying to get you to come outside...to get you away from the sheets." "You're mad," said Pieter, pulling out a broken hot water bottle from the bed before following me towards the French windows. "I'm happy to sit outside, but won't you get cold out here in just your pyjamas?"

We compromised by bringing the duvets out and wrapping them around us while we sat, drank wine, and dunked crisps into hummus.

"This is great," I told him. "I'm so glad you came over."

"I'm glad too," he said, squeezing my hand, leading me to drop a chunk of pitta bread into the dip.

"You know - if I'd realised that Dawn had been filming everything, I'd have said something to try to stop her," said Pieter. "None of us knew she was doing it. She's very sneaky. I think she's behaved appallingly. I told her just now."

"Did you? I didn't feel like I could make a massive fuss because she's the one who got me this holiday, and it was always stated that the point of the trip was to write the blog."

"Yes, but not like this," said Pieter. "I think she's been incredibly cruel."

"Thanks," I said. It felt good to know that he was on my side.

"Anyway - I told her she owes you big time, and she's promised to look after you in future and not stitch you up."

"Thanks," I said again, giving him a small hug. As Pieter spoke, I could hear my phone ringing in the room...it was coming from somewhere deep in the tangled, wet sheets. I decided to leave it. It was probably Dawn, ringing to apologise after her chat with Pieter.

"More wine," he said.

"Thank you," I replied. "This is so lovely."

Ted pushed his phone into his pocket and sat back in the seat at Johannesburg airport. He'd wanted to let Mary know he was turning up. He didn't want just to appear unannounced at her door. He had phoned ahead to the safari place to tell them he was coming, but he had no idea whether Henrique, the guy he'd spoken to, would let him in when he arrived. He'd tried Mary several times, but she just wasn't answering her phone. He'd have to work it all out when he arrived. He would touch down in Cape Town at midnight, so he should be with her by around 3 a.m. Presumably, she'd be tucked up in bed at that time, and he could burst in and surprise her.

"Tell me some of the silliest things that have happened while you've been working as a ranger," I said, pulling the duvet over my shoulders and looking out into the sky, full of the brightest stars I'd ever seen. The lack of light pollution made them quite dazzling.

"Oh, I've seen everything," said Pieter. "I've had baboons open car doors and get in. Just once, but it was quite a shock for these four women sitting in the back. I had to jump over the seats and clamber into the back to shoo them out. They went pretty quickly, but it was all a bit alarming to start with."

"Did they leave the door open or something?" I asked.

"No, but you used to be able to open the doors from the outside...you can't anymore because of incidents like that."

"What's the worst thing people do?" "I guess it's two things - the first is to ask really stupid questions, the second is to be too brightly coloured and too noisy."

"Oooo...so even though I looked like I'd stepped out of the Victorian era, I was OK with my beige palette of clothing then?"

"You were perfect," he said. "It's the multiple neon colours that tend to cause the problems. And the noise that people make, honestly - when you've been out on a game drive for over two hours, searching an area where there was a recent leopard sighting, everybody is craning their necks, looking in all directions to get a glimpse of the animal, then - suddenly - the bloke in the row behind you bellows "LEOPARD OVER THERE" at the top of his voice. You swivel around, and if you're lucky, you'll glimpse a tail disappearing.

"Oh God, that would be a real pain," I said.

As Pieter picked up the bottle to refill my glass, I noticed that one of his fingers was shorter than the other. It looked as if the end had been cut off.

"What happened to your finger?" I asked.

"Ah," he replied. "That was the time I got too close to a lion. I was trying to pull a thorn out of its foot. I gently held its paw, but he turned and bit the end of my finger off."

"Oh no! That's awful. It must have been bloody agony. And you're miles from a hospital here. Where on earth did they take you? What did they do?"

"Nothing. I decided it would be OK, so for a few days I didn't get any treatment at all...I just hung out here with my finger all wrapped up, then I started to feel faint and shivery, and we thought I'd better seek treatment. By the time I did, the end of my finger was completely hanging off and couldn't be saved."

"Jesus Christ. You were lucky not to lose your whole arm."

"I was lucky not to die, to be honest. The lion would have killed a weaker person on that day." He looked so solemn as he spoke, then he smiled from ear-to-ear. "I'm sorry. That's a load of bollocks," he said. "There was no lion. I got completely hammered in the pub and cut it on a pane of glass."

"You rotter!" I said. "But, for the record, the first story's much better. Stick to that."

I looked at my watch. It was 1 am already. How had it got that late? Dawn must have come in and gone to bed, leaving us out on the balcony chatting away.

"Are you warm enough?" asked Pieter.

"To be honest, I'm starting to feel a bit chilly," I said. "Come on, let's go inside."

I followed Pieter into the room, where it was much warmer. We'd finished one bottle of wine, so Pieter grabbed the other one and the remainder of the food, and we sat on the soft carpet, leaning back against the bed, with our mini picnic laid out in front of us.

"Can a kangaroo jump higher than the Empire State Building?" I asked.

Pieter looked at me expectantly. "I don't know, Mary," he replied.

"Of course," I said. "The Empire State Building can't jump."

"Yep. That's the standard I've come to expect from you, Mary Brown."

"OK - another one. What did the elephant say to the naked man?"

"I don't know, but I dread to think," said Pieter.

"How do you breathe through something so small?"

"Oh dear. These are getting much worse. I'm going to need more wine if we're going to carry on like that. Want a top-up?"

"Yeah," I said enthusiastically, even though I'd already

had way more than I was planning to. I'd been determined to go to bed early and sober. Now I was at the stage where I couldn't be bothered to worry about it anymore. I felt invincible, as if I could drink as much as I wanted, and all would be fine.

"Why couldn't the leopard play hide and seek?" I said.

"Go on..."

"Because he was always spotted."

Dawn lay in bed, listening to the chatter from Mary's room. She was glad that Pieter and Mary were getting on so well. She felt bad about always videoing Mary and putting it up on the blog, but that's what she did. That's why she was here. That was her job. If she stopped putting funny videos on the blog, people wouldn't look at it, and the lovely life she'd built for herself through her blogging would be over in a heartbeat. She'd always done this when she'd been on holiday; it was just that she'd never been on holiday with someone quite like Mary before...someone who was forever getting herself into stupid scrapes.

She giggled to herself as she thought of Mary stuck in the tree. And to do it twice! It was the funniest thing. She could see why it had so many hits and bounced around on social media all afternoon.

THE UNEXPECTED ARRIVAL OF TED

"I've really enjoyed being here with you," said Pieter, giving me a friendly squeeze of the shoulder.

"Me too," I said. "You're really good company Pieter."

"Thanks," he replied. "I wish all women thought that...I seem to have absolutely no luck at all with the opposite sex."

"Whaaaaat?" I asked. "I mean - really? I don't believe that for a second."

"It's true," he said. "There's this girl I like, but I just don't think she's interested in me."

"What girl - tell me everything," I said.

"No, I can't."

"Well, if you don't tell me, I can't help you, can I? In any case, I'm going home tomorrow night - it's not as if I can do much damage between now and then."

Pieter raised his eyebrows and looked at me askance. "Not a day has gone by since you've been here when you haven't caused a whole pile of damage, Mary Brown.

You're very loveable, but chaos does seem to follow you around the place."

"I can't argue with that," I said, nodding wisely. "But I'm always chaotic and disruptive to myself. I'd never do anything to hurt anyone else. Not ever."

"I know, I know," he said. "I realise that. That's why I came around tonight - when I saw your video online, I knew that you would never have done the same to Dawn. I remember you deliberately didn't video her when she screamed at the cheetah. You're a lovely person."

"Well, if I'm so lovely, you can tell me. Come on, Crocodile Dundee - spill the goss..."

"OK," he said, laughing at me. "I like Cristine, but I don't think she's interested in me."

"Cristine?" I said. "Really?"

"Yes, why do you look so surprised?"

"Because I had no idea."

"Didn't you? But I've been really obvious. Rushing to help her out when she calls - only to find you stuck up a tree, helping her with all the oil barrels last night."

"That's not obvious at all," I cried. "You need to make it much more obvious. I bet she doesn't have a clue."

"Oh God - I hate all this," he said. "I wish I'd never told you now."

"Why do you wish you'd never told me? I can help," I said.

"I want to know whether she likes me," he said. I had to stop myself from explaining to him that every woman in the whole damn world probably fancied him.

"I'll find out," I said. "Leave it with me. I'll be subtle, I promise."

"Thank you, you're wonderful," he said, giving me a huge hug. It was a lovely big, warm embrace, but it was just friendly; there was no sense of romance or sexual interest... Just two people who had spent a lovely night chatting to one another and had become firm friends.

"I think you're pretty wonderful, too," I said, and he pulled me even closer to him.

As we sat in the lovely, warm embrace, bonded by mutual respect and a great friendship, the door suddenly burst open, and Dawn rushed in, her hair standing up on end and a look of utter horror on her face.

"Ted's here," she screamed. "The security guards just phoned through to say he's here. Pieter - you'd better hide, quick."

I looked up as Pieter disengaged from our warm embrace and threw himself under the bed. As he did, there was a loud knock on the door.

"God, he's here already," I said, opening the door cautiously.

"Hello, my beautiful angel," said Ted, wrapping his arms around me. "God, I've missed you. I just couldn't stay away any more... I wanted to see you to check you were okay."

"I'm absolutely fine," I said, my voice loud and high-pitched and shot through with panic.

"What's the matter?" he said. "You sound worried."

"No," I said. "I'm just excited. It's so wonderful to see you."

"I'll leave you to it," said Dawn, backing out of the room, and giving me a look which said 'Pieter's under the bed, your boyfriend has just arrived at the door, I don't know what to do, so I'll just get out of here".

Ted looked up as Dawn left, closing the door behind her. "I haven't seen you all week, you gorgeous woman. You look amazing..." As he spoke, he lifted my arms and removed my pyjama top, pushing me back towards the bed.

"Why don't we go and get some breakfast or something?" I said.

"Let's have breakfast later," he said.

He took his shirt off and began unzipping his trousers as he pushed me back onto the bed. He began kissing me passionately and urgently. I hadn't been to bed all night, I was half drunk and starting to feel exhausted, and now we were going to make love in a bed on top of Pieter. To say this holiday had descended into farce would be to totally underplay the madness of it all.

"You know I love you, don't you," said Ted. "Now let me put my hand on your little muffin."

He pushed me back onto the bed, and I swear to God I heard a squeal from beneath us. While Ted continued talking about my little muffin – his embarrassing pet name for my most private parts- he kissed me more passionately, removing all our clothes and beginning to breathe heavily and tell me how excited he was. All I could think about was Pieter lying under the bed. Ted pushed himself inside me, and I could feel the bed move and push against the wall. Neither Ted nor I was small; I was well aware that the bed would push down on Pieter as he lay beneath the springs. Ted began moaning and pushing harder and the bed rocked even more. Oh God, this was unbearable. Finally, Ted rose to a climax, grunted, roared, and squealed in delight. There was no way I was going to orgasm with Pieter under the bed, so when Ted touched me, trying to raise me, I held his arm away and held him in a warm embrace. "Just cuddle me," I pleaded.

"Are you sure, is everything okay?" he said.

"Everything is lovely," I said. "I'm so glad you are here, but I'm really hungry, let's go and get some breakfast. They have the best breakfast buffet here – it's brilliant. It's open from 2 a.m. for those on early safaris."

"Okay then," said Ted. He jumped out of bed, dressed, and the two of us left the room and walked down to the buffet bar.

Around 10 minutes later Pieter came wandering through the restaurant and said hello, introducing himself to Ted.

"You must speak nothing of what happened just then," I said threateningly when Ted had set off on a second trip to the buffet.

Pieter smiled broadly at me.

"Okay," he said. "You can rely on me... my little muffin."

HOMEWARD BOUND

Neither of us had slept the night before, but the walking safari was one of the week's highlights, so I didn't want to miss it. Pieter said it was no problem for Ted to come with us, so we headed off on the Land Rover together, with Chris, Patrick and Dawn sitting behind us. I could sense that Dawn wasn't happy about Ted being there. She wasn't happy that I had a boyfriend, I don't suppose. Though I was very glad that she had burst in last night to tell me he was on the way.

We had Cristine and Pieter with us for the walking safari because you're not allowed to wander out of the Land Rover with just one ranger to guide you. I knew that I needed to get Cristine on her own so I could find out how she felt about Pieter. After having sex on top of him this morning, that felt like the least I could do.

"Wow, look, elephants," said Ted. "This is bloody amazing. It's like Jurassic Park."

Ted's enthusiasm for the animals reminded me of my own enthusiasm on the first day. I'd kind of got used to them being around every corner now, but Ted was wide-eyed as he watched them.

"A baby elephant," he squealed. "Look."

"Shall we get out and go closer?" said Pieter.

He looked over at Cristine, who nodded and smiled. I knew instantly that she liked him...it was so obvious. Why hadn't I realised that before? Why couldn't he see that?

We all stepped out of the Land Rover. Ted helped me down so I didn't have to do my bizarre rolling routine, and we walked carefully towards the elephants. Honestly, it was the most amazing experience of my life. Cristine led the way, given she was queen of the elephants, and told Ted all about what emotional creatures they were and how she'd seen them cry and respond with real tenderness to their young.

I held back so I was walking with Pieter.

"Everything OK?" he asked.

"Fine," I said. "I'm sure that Cristine likes you."

"She does? How on earth would you know that?"

"I just do...feminine intuition. I can tell. You have to ask her out."

"No way," said Pieter.

"But - why?" "Because...I don't know, just because..."

"Just say to her 'do you fancy going out for a glass of wine tonight?' Just say it."

"Oh God," said Pieter, looking nervous at the thought of it. It was a very sweet moment; this big, strong man with huge shoulders and massive boots clutching a gun and looking terrifying but as nervous as hell about asking a pretty girl out on a date. I'd seen him charge in to break up a huge fight without a care in the world, but the idea of asking someone out had left him crippled with nerves.

"Maybe later," he said.

We caught up with the others, and Ted entertained Cristine with his terrible jokes.

"There was a Mummy Mole, a Daddy Mole and a Baby Mole. They lived in a hole in the country near a farmhouse. Dad poked his head out of the hole and said, "Mmmm, I smell sausage!" Mum mole poked her head outside the hole and said, "Mmmm, I smell pancakes!" Baby mole tried to stick his head outside but couldn't because of the two bigger moles. Baby mole said, "The only thing I smell is molasses. Get it? Mole arses... see!"

"Blimey, that's truly awful," said Pieter. "You and Mary were made for one another - your jokes are appalling."

"Oy," I said, prodding him in the side. "Go and talk to Cristine."

"OK," he said, terror written on his face. "I'll go and talk to her now."

The walk on the wild side was great fun...we saw tortoises, birds, flowers, plants, and elephants. We even found some rhinos that we tracked from a distance.

"We have to come back here," said Ted when we were back in the room and packing for our flight home. "Shall we start a blog or something...one fat couple? It might work."

"Ha!" I said noncommittally. I'd loved the holiday, but I think I might have had enough blogs for now.

Ted and I sat together on the flight home...in economy, of course, while Dawn trundled up to business class with a huge grin on her face. The whole thing had been a giant success for her; some brilliant, compelling videos on the site and loads more people signed up. Presumably, that would mean lots more free trips for her and more income from advertisers. The woman was a pain in the arse, but you had to admire her in many ways.

"All things considered, and bearing in mind that the whole world has seen your bottom, would you ever consider going on holiday with Dawn again?"

"No," I said.

"Even if it was a free trip to somewhere exotic?"

"No," I said with a shrug. "It's quite simple, Ted; I've realised that free trips, luxury, exotic surroundings, and all that are wonderful when you're with someone you love. Not so great when you're with a complete nutcase. Having said that, I met some amazing friends – Pieter was great, wasn't it?"

"Yes, he was," conceded Ted. "He's a nice guy, a bit too good-looking for my tastes, though."

Ted nudged me in an affectionate way as he said this.

"It must've been horrifying to be at home and see all those ridiculous videos appearing on the blog," I said.

"It was insane," said Ted. "I made the mistake of telling my mum and sister all about the blog, so they've been looking at it too. My sister wants to know where you got those lacy knickers from."

"Oh God, this is all getting worse by the minute," I said. "Dawn's nuts"

"Yep, she does seem to be. Do you think you'll stay in touch with her at all?"

"I don't think so, but then I didn't think I would stay in touch after bumping into each other in the garden centre, and we ended up on safari in Africa together, so you never know. I thought I should get her a nice present to thank her. I know she only invited me because I'm fat, but it was a hell of a trip in the end, wasn't it? An amazing experience and such an incredibly beautiful place. I'll just ensure I don't go on holiday with her again."

The air hostess appeared beside Ted and asked us to turn our phones off and put our tray tables up before the flight took off.

I checked my phone one last time. I had a text...from Pieter.

"Hey blondie - just wanted to say thanks for making the past week more memorable than any other week I've ever had. You're a very special lady...don't let anyone ever tell you otherwise. Pieter x PS I'm taking Cristine out for dinner tonight."

Yes. Brilliant.

As I was about to turn the phone off, another text popped across the screen. It was from Dawn.

"I've been invited on a cruise in three weeks' time," it said. "Do you want to come?"

Oooooo...a cruise. I looked over at Ted who was engrossed in his phone. I couldn't, could I? But then again...

"I'd love to," I texted back. "Count me in."

I switched off my phone and put it away.

"Everything OK?" asked Ted. "You look thoughtful." "Everything's fine," I said. "I've got one little thing to tell you, but let's get you a nice large gin and tonic first..."

LETTER FROM THE CAPTAIN

3rd Sept 2023

Dear Ms Brown,

Thank you for arranging to come on the 20-day Mediterranean cruise with Angel Cruises. We look forward to welcoming you on board and hope you enjoy the holiday of a lifetime with us.

The ship will leave Southampton at 5 pm (BST), and boarding will start at 2 pm. All the information about your cruise and the ship is enclosed, along with details about our on-shore excursions and events. If you have any questions, please do not hesitate to contact us.

We look forward to seeing you on 7th October.

Kind regards,

Captain Homarus *&* *the crew of The Angel of the Seas*

REPLY TO THE CAPTAIN

7th September 2023

Dear Ms Brown,

Thank you very much for your reply to my letter.

I can confirm that there is an 'eat-as-much-as-you-possibly- can' buffet on board, the bar is open all day and there is a mini bar in every cabin. We will make sure that it is stocked with plenty of gin and snacks, as you request.

We look forward to meeting you.

Kind regards,

Captain Homarus *& the crew of Angel of the Seas*

THE CAPTAIN RESPONDS

10th September 2023

Dear Ms Brown,

Thank you very much for your letter.

We will certainly ensure that there's a variety of snacks in the room, not just 'those daft peanuts in a tin'. We also take on board your point about leaving measly chocolate pieces on your pillow. If we wish to leave you chocolates, we will, as you suggest, leave you a whole box next to your bed and not in it.

We look forward to meeting you.

Kind regards,

Captain Homarus & the crew of Angel of the Seas

THE ITINERARY

20-DAY MEDITERRANEAN CRUISE

DEPARTURE: **Southampton**

First stop: Lisbon
Second stop: Gibraltar
Third stop: Tunisia
Fourth stop: Sardinia
Fifth stop: Malta
Sixth stop: Sicily
Seventh stop: Naples
Eighth stop: La Spezia
Ninth stop: Toulon
Tenth stop: Barcelona
Eleventh stop: Valencia
Twelfth stop: Southampton

MEETING CAPTAIN HOMARUS

The first thing I did was tell mum: "You won't believe this," I said, breathless with excitement, "I'm going on a cruise."

There was an overly long pause while she put down the steaming iron and worked out how to reply.

"A cruise? What - like a big boat?" she offered.

"Yep," I said. "A very big boat. It's got restaurants, a pub, a tennis court and swimming pools on it."

"OK," she said, looking at the basket full of crumpled clothes, then at me.

"Will you be gone all day?"

"It's a 20-day cruise, mum. I'll be gone for most of the month. Dawn invited me. Remember Dawn? The girl I was at school with who's now a successful blogger."

"Yes - of course I remember Dawn. You went on safari with her and it all went pear-shaped."

"Yep - that's the one."

"You wrote a blog called Two Fat Ladies and ended up stuck up a tree in your knickers."

"Yep - that's the one."

"And my bridge club was round here when I opened the blog up to show them, and they were treated to the unusual sight of your bottom as you clambered out of a tree while half drunk. Marjorie's never forgotten it."

"Yes, yes. No need to go back over all that, mum. Well, Dawn's invited me on a cruise ship now, and there are no trees on cruise ships, nor are there baboons, so I'm confident that there won't be a repeat of the knicker-wearing nonsense. It's going to be free because I'm her guest for the trip, and she'll be blogging about it. Dawn gets to take someone with her every time. I've had letters from the captain confirming it. It's happening. There's a massive 'eat all you can' buffet and everything."

"It's called 'eat all you want', not 'eat all you can' - you make it sound like some sort of competition. And you'll need to watch yourself with those buffets. You don't want to put on any more weight. You'll come back 10 stone if you're not careful."

I didn't want to point out that I was over 14 stone, so to come back 10 stone would be a very marvellous thing indeed, probably involving some sort of gastric bypass surgery along the way.

"Do you want to know what countries I'm going to?"

"Go on then," she said, and I listed the glamorous locations where the luxury cruise ship would stop. I mentioned Sicily and Barcelona, and she ironed dad's pants while I told her about Gibraltar and the tantalising thought of Tunisia and Lisbon.

"Pass me those shirts," she said.

"Mum, are you listening to any of this?"

"Yes, dear. Pass the starch as well."

She seemed more concerned with getting creases out of y-fronts and starching shirts than hearing about the glamour of life on the ocean wave, so I gave up and went to put the kettle on.

Two days later, she called me in a state of near hysteria.

"I'm calling from Walker & Sons - the travel agents on Barnes Road."

"Right," I said. "Everything OK?"

"Yes, I'm here with your Aunty Susan. We've been looking at the brochures for cruises. Goodness me, Mary Brown. They are lovely."

"I know. They are, aren't they?"

I was in Marks and Spencer at the time, looking at bright red, plunging bikinis and trying to summon up the nerve to go and try one on.

"They have theatres and ballrooms and EVERYTHING," mum was saying.

"Yep," I said, holding the tiny bikini up against my large frame and trying to ignore the distasteful glances from the assistants.

"Well, you make sure you have a lovely time, won't you. I've never seen anything like this. A pub on a ship! Is that even legal?"

"I think so" I said, putting the bikini back on the rack and picking up a sober, structured swimming costume that might actually fit me.

"I'll tell you all about it when I return."

"OK, dear," said Mum. "Do be careful though, won't you? You know what you're like. You'll have too many cocktails, trip over your flip-flops and fall overboard or something."

"I promise I won't," I said. "I won't wear flip-flops if there's alcohol around."

"Good girl," said mum. "You have a good time."

"I will," I said, putting down the swimming costume and reaching for an outsized kaftan. "Love you lots, mum."

So, all goodbyes had been said, three weeks had been booked off work, and I'd packed a colossal amount of clothing into a massive suitcase. Ted, my lovely, long-suffering boyfriend, had agreed to take me down to Southampton Docks, so we went bouncing into the car park in his dilapidated old Mini Micra. The car's not really stable enough for two adults, let alone two obese ones. I'd taken to wearing a sports bra and clutching my breasts on long journeys because the damn thing bounced so much.

Ted drove round the car park, directed by a series of men in fluorescent vests until he was shown a parking place facing the harbour. "Look at that!" he gasped, pointing to the ship before us. "Wow it looks impressive."

My goodness, it did. It looked amazing. The sun beat down on the sparkling water, and in the middle of it all was this incredible ship: *Angel of the Seas*...my home for the next three weeks. It was massive. MASSIVE. It demanded a full head turn to follow it from end to end. I don't know what I was expecting, but this was awesome.

I could hardly believe what was happening...it was a beautiful, warm, early summer's day, and I was going off on a Mediterranean cruise, and it was all free. Dawn had to be the best friend in the world. I mean - she was nuts and had been slightly uncomfortable company when we were on safari, but - a free cruise! I could put up with a bit of Dawn madness for that.

I clambered out of the car and felt excitement rush through me. This was just thrilling. I started to waddle off towards the ship at full speed until Ted stopped me.

"Haven't you forgotten something?" he said.

"Have I? My passport? Sun cream? Sun dresses?"

"No, a kiss. Where's my kiss goodbye?"

"Oh yes - sorry!" I said, rushing back, throwing myself into his arms, hugging him closely. "I'm going to miss you."

"Yes - I'm sure you will," said Ted sarcastically. "I'm sure you'd much rather be in the pub with me than exploring the delights of Tunisia and Lisbon."

"I'm not sure about that," I said. "But I wish you were coming with me."

"Me too," he said, stroking my hair tenderly. "I don't feel like we've spent any time together recently, what with you off on safari and me working so hard. Promise me we can see each other loads when you get back."

"I promise," I said. "And I'll text you and call you to let you know how it's all going."

"Make sure you do," said Ted. "I want to know everything."

"You will. I love you."

"I love you, too," said Ted, finally letting go of me and wishing me a bon voyage.

Bloody hell...it was all real - I was going on a cruise!

A HANDSOME CAPTAIN AND A MASSIVE BUFFET

By the time I stepped onto the ship, I was already head over heels in love with cruising. It's all incredibly easy. You check in quickly and wander onboard, unencumbered by any of your bags delivered directly to your cabin. Easy. None of the faff that's usually associated with international travel. No angry customs officials or mind-bendingly long queues.

There weren't endless shops at the departure point either, which was a blessing. I can't be trusted around those airport shops. I have more orange lipstick, glittery highlighter and green eyeliner from those things than I could use in a lifetime. The stuff you buy when you're all excited and waiting to go on holiday is the sort of stuff you would never normally go anywhere near. I have makeup that would look perfect were I ever invited to perform in the Mardi Gras or join Abba circa 1978, but it is entirely unsuitable for my life as a checkout girl at a DIY and garden centre in Cobham.

Anyway - all I'm saying is that it was a small mercy

that there were no shops to drive me wild, and it was lovely that it was so easy to board.

I stepped onto the ship to the sounds of a string quartet playing soothingly in the background. The captain was there to greet us, a strikingly handsome man with all the suave sophistication you'd expect of a man in his position.

"Good morning, Madam. Welcome to the Angel of the Seas. My name's Will Homarus," he said. "I'm your captain for this cruise."

"Good morning," I said back, curtseying slightly, which was highly embarrassing. Something about the uniform and the majesty of the ship made me behave as if I were meeting royalty.

Will was reassuringly good-looking. Big and manly, kind of swarthy, like he might be Greek or something. He certainly looked like he could save us all if things went pear-shaped.

"The boat's not going to sink is it? "I said because I habitually say ridiculous things to handsome men.

"No, you're quite safe," he said, smiling. I knew instantly that I would have to keep right away from this guy when I'd had a few glasses of wine or I'd be wrapping my legs round his neck and asking him to marry me.

"I'm Claire Oliver," said an attractive woman standing next to him. She was tall and painfully thin. I didn't want to talk to her. I was much happier talking to the Greek God with the hairy chest, but he'd turned away and greeted the next passengers: a rather dour-looking woman in a brown dress and an ancient man in a wheelchair.

"I'm the staff captain," she said. "Kind of like the deputy captain. We'll both be around the ship, so do talk to us if there's anything you need or if there are any problems."

"Yes, I will," I said, trying to catch the captain's eye, but he was crouched down, talking to the guy in the wheelchair, so I gave up and told Claire that 'yes, of course, I'll come and find one of you if I needed anything.'

I was very sure which one of them I'd be going to find, and it wasn't Claire.

A lovely young man called David showed me to my cabin, opening the door and leading me into a gorgeous room with two beds, a bathroom, and a joyous sea view. I rushed to the patio doors and flung them open.

"It's the sea," I said.

"It is," said David. "There's sea all around. Is it OK if I go now?"

"Of course," I said, slightly embarrassed that I sounded as if I didn't I understand how boats worked.

I texted Dawn when he closed the door behind him: "OMG. I've just walked into the cabin...it's bloody lovely...see you soon. M x"

Then I did what every self-respecting woman does in a situation like this: I opened the mini bar, pulled out a Toblerone and a mini bottle of gin and tonic and threw myself onto the bed to work out how the TV operated.

My God, the bed was soft...it was like lying in cotton wool. I snuggled into it and watched the video on the screen about life aboard the ship.

There was a beautician that looked amazing...like a proper New York spa. It even did Botox. I rolled over and peered into the mirror by the bed, holding my eyebrows up to see what I'd look like. Was that better? Or did I just look like a fat Chinese woman? It was hard to tell. Probably best not to take the risk, though. They did manicures and facials as well, which I definitely wanted to try.

Next, they showed the gym and fitness suite and the classes that took place every day. If I went to the gym every morning and did regular beauty treatments, I could go home from this cruise looking amazing, especially if I also had some sun on my skin. That would be great.

Then, the video moved to the buffets available for breakfast and lunch. My God! In an instant I knew that far from returning home having lost a few pounds, there was every chance I would return home 10 stone heavier. The meat. All the Chinese food. Ooooo...I just love Chinese food. And the puddings! Have you seen these buffets? Miles of tables groaning under the weight of all the food. On the video they showed a slim, young lady going to the buffet and helping herself to a light salad and a sliver of smoked salmon.

No woman can do that.

It's impossible to go to an eat-all-you-can buffet and return with a sensible plate of food. Whenever I'm confronted by them, I panic and end up with a plate of roast potatoes, chips, pasta, chicken in black bean sauce, cheese, prawn toast, fried egg and sprouts, or something...food that has no right to be sharing crockery.

The sight of all the food had made me a little peckish, so I finished my drink, slipped my shoes on and wandered out of the cabin. When I got outside, my case was sitting there with a little note on it, wishing me an excellent holiday. This was perfect...so easy and smooth. Three weeks of this and I'd return home totally relaxed and stress-free. Assuming, of course, that the rest of the holiday went as smoothly as this first day had.

I walked up to the buffet and saw Captain Homarus. He was putting a delicate collection of olives, little silver skin onions and some fancy cheese onto his plate. He must have been watching the girl on the video. I smiled at him and started placing items onto my plate in a similar fashion. As soon as he was out of sight, I'd start digging into the lasagne and make a serious dent in the chips.

"Do come and join me," he said, indicating the table by the window in the corner.

"That would be lovely," I said, thinking of the fried chicken and potato wedges I'd have to forsake. "I'll just get a drizzle of olive oil and I'll be right with you."

I walked the length of the buffet, picking at delicacies as I went; a spring roll went into my mouth, then a handful of chips. I grabbed a burger to eat while walking around. I bit into luscious beef while dropping two slivers of sun-dried tomato onto my plate. I don't know who I thought I was kidding. No sane person could believe that I ate in the way my plate indicated. I wouldn't be morbidly obese if my diet consisted of delicately flavoured olives and bits of tomato, would I?

Still, one had to keep up appearances. I took a glug of water to wash down the last of the burger, wiped my face, and headed to the corner table. But when I looked, he wasn't there. There were three people sitting there, chatting away.

Where was he? I have a terrible sense of direction and

wandered up and down the buffet that ran the length of the boat. Now I didn't know where to go. Which corner was he in? There were so many nooks and crannies. I walked up and down. I asked the chefs whether they'd seen him, but they shook their heads, I asked a couple of fellow passengers, but - no - no one had seen him. I was completely lost. In the end I had to get them to put a message over the tannoy for him to come and find me. By the time he reached me, I'd been gone for 20 minutes. He'd eaten his cocktail onions and had been sitting there patiently, wondering where on earth I'd got to.

"Sorry," I said, exasperated. "I got lost."

"No problem at all," he said patiently. "Come and join me." He was on the other side of the boat entirely.

I stayed with Handsome Homarus until I'd finished my food, then he excused himself and went back to work. The minute he was out of sight I loaded my plate with every different Chinese food on the buffet, and then I ate the whole plateful quicker than anyone has ever eaten a plateful of food in their life before and practically rolled back to my cabin, feeling like I might explode. I lay on the bed, poured myself another gin and tonic, wished I hadn't eaten so much and downed the drink to make myself feel better. Then I read my messages. There was one from Ted, wishing me bon voyage, and one from Dawn.

"Hi darling," it said. "Can you call me urgently?"

I picked up my phone and glanced at the time. It was 4 pm. We were setting sail soon. Where the hell was she? I dialled her number, and there was a terrible noise when she answered it.

"Dawn, it's me," I said. "Dawn, can you hear me?"

The noise stopped. "Yes, sorry - I was just getting a blow dry. How are you?"

"I'm fine, but shouldn't you be - like - on the ship instead of in the hairdressers?"

"Oh darling, I'm so sorry - that's why I was ringing - I can't make it. Something's come up. Could you write the blog for me?"

"Whaaat?"

"It'll be fine," she said.

"Errr...no it won't, because I'm not a writer. I've never written anything longer than a Christmas card before."

"You can do it," she said. "Just send me text updates with what's going on, and I'll load them onto the blog. No one will be any the wiser."

"OK," I said, struggling to keep the concern out of my voice. "So, I literally just send you texts with what's going on, and that's all I need to do."

"Yep," she said. "Simple eh?"

"Yes, that does sound quite straightforward," I agreed.

"Oh, one other thing," she added. "Don't tell anyone that I'm not there. Just pretend I'm in the cabin if anyone asks. OK?"

"What? I can't spend 20 days telling everyone you're in the cabin."

"Tell them I've just left, or I'm in the hairdressers or having a lie-down, or getting my nails done. Use your imagination. It'll be fine. Have fun. Just don't tell anyone that I'm not on the boat though, please or I won't get any more free trips."

Christ.

MEETING THE GUESTS

As the ship prepared to move out of the harbour, we were all encouraged to go onto the deck for a setting sail party. This event involved glasses of fizz, excitement, singing and flag waving - all of which I approve of entirely, so I was there like a shot. It was also a chance to get to know the other shipmates, so I wandered around, introducing myself and sending texts to Dawn, updating her on what was going on and who I was meeting so she could write about it in the blog.

"Pictures!" she texted back. "Send pictures."

"No one mentioned that," I replied.

"We need pictures, and videos are VITAL. The blog will fall flat, and no one will read it, and neither of us will ever get any free holidays if you don't send me videos."

Great. Now I had to be Steven Spielberg as well as JK Rowling. So much for a free holiday.

I held my phone up and took a video of all the guests singing and waving their flags, and then I moved it around slightly to capture the sight of Captain Homarus bending over to tie up his shoes. I confess I lingered on that shot slightly longer than was necessary but panned back out to take in the whole boat before he saw. "Video attached," I wrote, texting it to Dawn.

"Hot, hot, hot!" she replied.

"Thank you."

"Not you. The dude in the tight, white trousers."

"He's called the captain."

"Wish I was there," she typed.

"Glad you're not. I have him all to myself," I typed back, texting it to her with a still from the video of his manly bottom.

The downside of chatting to people was being forced to explain to them about Dawn: "No, I'm not on my own. I'm with my friend, but she's in the cabin, feeling unwell."

"Oh dear," they all said before asking exactly what was wrong with her.

"Just illness, you know," I replied vaguely, looking at them with great seriousness so they didn't probe further. What I lacked in medical nous, I made up for with steely gazing.

I sent Dawn another video of the ship leaving Southampton harbour and of all the happy cruisers cheering, waving and singing Rule Britannia and Land of Hope and Glory, and then I went back to the cabin to get dressed for the evening.

Cruise ships have very strict sartorial guidelines, as Dawn had been at pains to point out to me. Even on the 'dress down' nights, women tend to wear cocktail dresses. On the black-tie evenings, it's full-on long dresses, sparkly handbags, mink stoles and long gloves. I have all of these things...in case you were wondering. I LOVE getting dressed up. My stoles aren't real mink, and my sparkly shoes and matching handbag don't have a diamond on them, but I look the part all the same.

For that first evening, I went for a long red dress designed for a woman with a far smaller bust than I have. I rammed my assets into it and looked in the mirror. "Oh no," I thought. "All you can see is blonde hair, a red dress and enormous breasts."

Then I stopped for a minute and thought, 'No - that's a good thing. I will be very popular tonight if all you can see is blonde hair, a red dress and enormous breasts.'

The positive thinking (coupled with the gin) gave me a real confidence boost, and I walked down to the gorgeous, art deco-style dining room swaying with delight and swinging my hair back. I stopped for a gin and tonic at the bar first, and then sauntered over to the table at which I'd been told I was dining.

It turned out it was the captain's table which meant I'd be having lunch and dinner with Handsome Captain Homarus. Not a bad start to the holiday.

I glanced at the floor-to-ceiling mirrors by the table. I seemed to have 'dropped' a little in the walk over. I shoved my hand down the front and hitched up my boobs so they sat better in the dress, giving me a more attractive cleavage. I did this just as Claire, the deputy captain, came over to say hello. The wide-eyed look and little gasp she gave made me realise that I'd released a little too much flesh to the world. I looked down. Yep - It looked like two small bald men were trying to peek out of the top of my dress. I smiled at Claire and pushed them down again...kneading them as if I were preparing dough for the oven.

"This is your seat here," she said, politely ignoring the rigorous adjustments I was making and pointing to a chair on the other side of the table from her.

I stood next to my seat as other guests drifted over to join us. There was a couple called Edith and Malcolm who looked like they were in their early 60s. They were the sort of people who were very helpful in life. Do you know the type I mean?

You find them on every committee in every borough in the country...real salt of the earth types. Probably members of the tennis club and the church organising committee - she does the flowers and organises the summer fete, and he plays golf on Fridays. Nice people. Like my Aunty Susan. Nice, but not necessarily the sort of people you'd choose to join for dinner.

Next to me was the man who'd followed me onto the boat earlier - very, very old and frail and in a wheelchair. He smiled weakly and I bent down to introduce myself. He nodded like he couldn't hear me properly and said his name was Tank. An odd name, but quite nice for a little old man to be called something so powerful and evocative - I liked it.

Next to him sat the dour, plain-looking woman who'd pushed him onto the boat earlier. She had mousy hair which fell limply by her face, large, square glasses and was dressed in what looked like a uniform from the Brownies, or a nurse's outfit from years ago - like the sort of thing they wore on Call the Midwife. Her shoulders were massive - like an American Footballer's. Perhaps it was all that wheelchair pushing that did it?

"I'm Mary," I said, and she nodded without offering her name.

"How long have you known Tank?" I asked her.

"Tank?" she said.

"Yes, your friend," I indicated the man in the wheelchair. "His name's Frank," she said.

"Oh, sorry. I misheard." She looked at me as if I'd confessed to killing babies and chopping up kittens. Meanwhile, Frank smiled and nodded, not looking at me or anyone else. His red-rimmed eyes watered as he looked off into the distance. He was warm and friendly but not quite with it, somehow. Very different from the others at the table, most of whom seemed to have been invited because they were regular cruise-goers and knew the captain. They were raucous and lively and sharing jokes on the other side of the table. This side? Not so much. I looked at Frank while Frank looked down at his shaking hands.

"What made you come on a cruise, then?" I asked.

He smiled at me again, and the lady with the large shoulders and bad dress leaned over and fiddled with what I imagined to be his hearing aid.

"I can hear now," he said with a broad smile. "What were you saying, dear?"

"I just asked why you were on the cruise."

"Oh. You don't want to know," he said. "It's a very long story."

"Of course, I want to know," I said, but he just smiled at me and the lady next to him began feeding him. We fell silent as he chewed his food, and I began to eat mine. To be honest, I didn't much want to know. I was only being polite.

Once Frank had finished eating, the woman wiped his face gently. "Tell her your story, Frank," she said. "Tell her why we're on the cruise."

"I'm here because I'm off to Tunisia say a proper goodbye to two old friends...and then to Sicily to apologise to the family of the love of my life."

"Oh. Why do you have to say goodbye to your friends?" I asked.

"My friends died in the war. I fought beside them when they were gunned down on a rainy night. One guy died where he fell; the other died in a military hospital soon afterwards. I want to go back to where we lost them on that bleak hill on that bleak night and say goodbye properly, forever, before I die."

"Oh my God, that's so moving," I said, feeling tears in the backs of my eyes. "Moving and so sad."

"It was war," he said with a distant smile. "Sad things happened."

"And did you say something about the family of the woman you loved?"

"Yes, I need to make amends. I took her away from them in the dead of night. I need to go back and apologise, and hand them the letters from 70-odd years ago that were never sent. It's the right thing to do...I need to give them the letters."

"Come on, Frank," said the woman in the brown dress. "It's time for you to go to bed now."

"No, not yet," I said, now genuinely intrigued. "Can't

he tell me the story first? Tell me about the letters...I don't understand."

"In time, my dear," said Frank with a lovely, big smile. "I'll tell you everything. It's a long cruise. No need to rush things."

"Oh, but - I have no patience at all. Please tell me now."

"He will tell you everything, but not now," said the woman in the horrible dress, pushing the wheelchair away.

"OK," I said reluctantly, turning my attention to the glass of wine in front of me and the captivating smile of Captain H, but I couldn't stop thinking about Frank. What letters? What apology? It was so intriguing. And imagine losing your best friends like that. It was beyond comprehension.

EN ROUTE TO LISBON

Oh God. Oh God. It was so bright. Where was I? What happened? My head felt like it was spontaneously combusting from within. My tongue was so dry it was like I'd spent the previous evening licking the carpets. I couldn't have done that...could I? It wasn't beyond the realm of possibility; I'd had worse nights.

The light in my cabin was on full blast, and the sun was streaming through the window. It was bright enough to perform brain surgery. I crawled across the bed and lashed out at the lamp and the main light switch. I was still too drunk to execute any subtle manoeuvres, but eventually, after much swatting, the lights went out, and I crashed across the bed and went to sleep. When I woke up, it was 10.30 am.

There was just half an hour left before the sumptuous breakfast buffet became the sumptuous lunchtime buffet. I needed to move.

Slowly I stumbled out of bed and dressed myself rather like a toddler, picking the first top I saw in the wardrobe (green) and the nearest trousers (pink) with complete disregard for how they would look together.

I wandered cautiously along the corridor and took the lift up to the main deck. Every step made my head hurt more. I needed coffee...and food, but then I always needed food. I stepped out of the lift and saw a man standing with his back to me but with his reflection clearly visible in the glass in front of him.

Oh, my f-ing God, it was Simon Collins. Simon Collins!

It was like being shot back in time.

I reversed into the lift and pressed the button to the lower floor, pushing it a thousand times, urging the doors to close, but they were too slow - Simon looked up and saw me in the mirror in front of him; his eyes widened, his eyebrows raised, and he spun round just as the door was closing.

"Mary?" he said, with incredulity sweeping through his voice. "Mary? Is that you? Mary Brown. In the pink trousers?"

If I was surprised to see Simon, then he was a million more times surprised to see me...for the simple fact that I'd told him I had six months to live four years ago. I know, it's appalling behaviour but I'm rubbish at finishing relationships and I just came out with it.

I'd told Simon I no longer wanted to see him, adding, "it's not you, it's me." And he'd said, 'No, it's not Mary - that's a stupid thing to say - it's me. It must be me. If there weren't something wrong with me, you'd want to carry on going out with me."

Dear readers, I panicked at this stage and said, 'Yes - it *is* me...I've got leprosy.'

"Leprosy," he'd said, jumping back, his little face awash with concern. "Blimey, that sounds serious."

My lies kicked off more lies, and before I knew where I was, I was explaining that I was going off to Fiji in search of a witch doctor. I know - it was bizarre. I don't know what made me say it. I was in a panic because I hate upsetting people. I suppose I thought I could get away with it because Simon lived in Birmingham, where he was working at the university, so there was no chance of us bumping into one another. He called a few times to check I was OK, but I'd begged him to get on with his own life and leave me to my fate.

Now, here he was, on the bloody ship with me, and there was no way of me escaping.

I stepped out of the lift on the cabin floor, went back to my room and texted Charlie, my lovely friend who'd been in on the whole witch doctor thing (if memory serves me right, she'd jumped around in the background, making 'witch doctor noises' one time when he'd called and I'd pretended to be on a Fijian island).

"You are joking. That is hysterical," she said, rather unsupportively. "God, I wish I was there to see this. His face must have been a picture!"

"Yep. He did look very shocked," I said. "How do I get out of this?"

"Tell him you got better. Insist that the witch doctor performed his magic and the illness disappeared."

"Yeah, I could," I said. "Or I could just avoid him."

"Yeah - well, if you can avoid him - do that, but I don't fancy your chances on a 20-day cruise."

"Yeah," I said. "I'll try to avoid him, and if I can't, I'll go for the witch doctor line."

"Perfect," said Charlie. "What could possibly go wrong?"

I couldn't risk going back up to breakfast, so I had to miss it and wait until lunchtime (exactly 20 minutes, so it didn't involve my internal organs collapsing due to lack of nutrition or anything, but it felt quite a long time for a girl who likes her food), then I went back up on deck when I knew that breakfast was over. I used the lifts on the other side of the ship instead of risking exiting at exactly the point where I'd seen Simon earlier. I don't know why I did that; it wasn't as if Simon would have stood in that position all day, but it seemed safer to avoid going where I knew he'd been. I strode out of the lift and over to the buffet, avoiding looking at everyone in the misguided belief that if I didn't see anyone, no one could see me. It's a tactic used by every toddler who's ever played hide and seek.

Once at the buffet, I started loading chicken wings and nuggets onto my plate, and then noodles and curry sauce followed. I figured I was allowed to go a little bit mad because I hadn't had any breakfast. Also, I'd been drinking the night before, and every right-thinking person knows that a little indulgence is a must the day after massive drinking has happened. It's practically the only way to make yourself feel better again.

I wandered over to sit down when I caught sight of Frank and his nurse (I assumed she was his nurse, based on her dress sense and bossy attitude, but to be honest, she hadn't even given me her name, let alone her occupation).

"Hello, do you mind if I join you?" I said, giving them both a big smile.

"Of course not," said Frank, beaming. His craggy face came alive when he smiled.

"I was just hearing about you," he said.

"Were you?"

"Yes, the captain told me you were performing *YMCA* last night and doing high kicks to *New York, New York*. You were quite the party animal by the sound of it."

"Oh God, no."

"The captain said your Elvis impression was one of the best he'd ever seen."

"Oh, hell. Tell me about your evening, Frank. Let's not dwell on mine anymore."

"Well, it was a bit quieter than yours by the sound of it. No doing the can-can round the boat for me."

"Right, good. Glad to hear it."

"I don't think she wants to be reminded about last night," said the lady in the brown dress. "We all drink too much occasionally; the last thing you need is for someone to remind you of all the details of it the next day."

"Fair enough," said Frank, with a nod of his head. "That's a good point."

I smiled appreciatively at her. "I'm so sorry, I don't even know your name," I said.

"It's Janette," she replied. "You can call me Jan."

"I will. Thanks," I said, then asked: "Are you Frank's nurse?"

"No, I'm not," she said. "Not really. I am a nurse, but I'm here as Frank's friend. He knew my grandfather well, and our families have become best friends."

More and more people were coming along to the buffet, and I was sure I could see Simon in the group. Either that, or I was being paranoid. Too many people were wearing navy blue T-shirts and shorts...it would be very hard to avoid him when I couldn't pick him out of the crowd.

I looked at Frank, who was looking down at a piece of paper in his hands.

"What's that?"

"Irene," he said, lifting up the paper. It was a picture of a beautiful woman with dark eyes and raven hair set in an old-fashioned curl around her shoulders. She had a huge smile like a movie star.

"She was the love of my life," he said.

"Is this the woman you mentioned last night? The one whose family you are going back to find and apologise to?"

"That's right," he said. "You have a good memory."

"You were going to tell me why you have to go back there, do you remember? You said you would tell me the whole story. "

"Of course, I remember. Maybe I should tell you this evening, you must have things you want to do now. "

"No, please tell me now," I said. I had nothing else to do, and the thought of wandering around the boat had lost its appeal since I'd seen bloody Simon Collins. Frank squinted in my direction and began to talk. His voice was very soft; it was hard to hear everything he said. I moved in closer to him.

"I'll have to take you right back to 1942 if I'm going to tell you the story properly," he said.

"Suits me," I said. "You can consider me firmly back in the 1940s."

"Well, I was 19 years old, living in a two up, two down in Portsmouth, when I was called up to go and fight in the war."

"God, how awful. "

"No, not at all – I was thrilled. Especially when I was told I'd be going to North Africa with a group of other new recruits. I'd be joining the Eighth Army in Tunisia. The guys over there were known as the "desert rats". I'd heard about them on the wireless. They seemed incredibly glamorous.

"I'd never been abroad, let alone to a different continent. And my family were so proud that I would fight for the country. No one else in the family had ever been to war. My father was injured, so he missed World War I and always hated himself for it. Until his dying day, he felt less of a man because he couldn't fight.

"None of it was his fault; he'd had had an industrial accident and had lost a foot. He also had limited use of his hand, so he couldn't go to war. But he still felt terrible. I grew up thinking that if you were a proper man, you went to war and fought for your country. That's why it mattered so much to get the call-up.

"I was super excited the day the papers came and determined to make my parents proud. I didn't know, when I kissed them goodbye and headed off to war, that I would never see either of them again."

"Oh no."

Frank took a huge breath. "Yes, they were both killed in the bombings."

"Come on, Frank," said Janette. "Time to go now..."

"Noooo.... Stay and tell me what happened. Please, Frank, carry on. You've hardly started." "Later," he said as Janette started to push him away. "We have plenty of time, Mary Brown. Lots of time for storytelling."

FIRST STOP - LISBON

There was something both frightening and exciting about coming in to dock for the first time. We'd all become so friendly on board that it seemed odd that we would be mingling with other people who weren't part of our on-board community. It was also exciting...we'd been cooped up for a few days - it was time to see the world. A frisson of excitement filtered through the group as we all queued up like children on a school trip at the edge of the boat, looking out into the foreign port.

For me, it was a time of particularly mixed emotions because while it was great fun to be coming into port, I also reasoned that this was a time I was most likely to bump into Simon. That's why I had dressed incognito with a chiffon scarf over my head, entirely covering my hair and large sunglasses.

"You look like that actress...what's her name?" said one of the guys. "You know - the blonde one?"

"Grace Kelly?" I said. That was certainly the look I'd been going for.

"No, no - Rebel Wilson," he said. "You look very like her."

"Thanks," I said. "I was hoping I was channelling Grace Kelly."

"Nope. Rebel Wilson before she lost all that weight. That's who you remind me of.."

As people stood, looking across the sparkling waters into the harbour, there was murmuring and chattering about the day ahead and what joys it might hold. People were making plans for what to do. I had no plans at all. I just wanted to see as much of the city as possible and post some interesting items on the blog so that Dawn would think I was a perfectly acceptable stand-in should she ever find herself unable to make a luxury holiday.

It was odd to be facing the day in a strange city by myself, but I'd read about the extraordinary number of ice cream parlours, so I thought I'd probably be OK. One of the places was called Gelato Therapy, which seemed to be the best kind of therapy you could ever hope for.

We left the ship with strict instructions to be back by 5 pm, having been told colourful stories of people who'd missed the ship in the past and ended up having to take flights to the next port. Their woeful antics seemed so frowned upon that we all swore we wouldn't be one of those people who broke the rules. We were advised to take passports and any essential medications with us, though...just in case.

I left the ship and bid a fond farewell to handsome Captain Homarus, walking into the searing Portuguese sunshine with a huge smile on my face. It was surreal to be abroad when all I'd done was get on in Southampton, eaten a vast amount, drunk gallons and had a nice time, and now - ta-dah! – I was in a foreign place.

I walked off the ship with everyone else, clutching my map of Lisbon, and found my way to the narrow little streets leading up to the main road. It was very pretty: a cascade of houses rose up from the sea towards the castle at the top of the hill. From the beautiful blue waters of the harbour to the white houses with their caramel-coloured roofs all stacked higgledy-piggledy, interspersed with lovely cafes, bars and rooftop restaurants, it was beautiful. Lisbon has the sort of buzz that you always get in cities, but with the added loveliness of being by the sea. How many capital cities are by the sea? Not many, I bet.

I walked up to a café sprawled across a rooftop and took a seat, looking down on our ship, sitting there majestically in the harbour. I watched the line of passengers snaking up the side of the hill. The café was so pretty that lots of the cruise passengers decided to come in, and it was starting to feel a little like being back on the boat, I kept thinking that Simon would walk in, so I turned quickly to the leaflet that the events co-ordinator had handed out, showing all the things that were happening in Lisbon, and decided it was time to make a plan. It seemed that the best way to see the place was either in a -Tuk-Tuk or by doing a circle of the city on a tram. I'm self-aware enough to know that if I got onto a Tuk-Tuk, I'd break it, so I decided that the tram was the most sensible option.

I grabbed my bag and headed off for the tram stop.

According to the literature, there was one due in around 5 minutes.

Once it appeared, I clambered on board, took a seat by the window, and enjoyed the view as the tram snaked its way through the harbour streets, bouncing around on the rough, uneven roads and squeezing between large trucks that had no place to be out on these tiny, narrow lanes.

The tram turned up a hill dotted with houses in a range of chalky pastel colours.

"Well, this is nice," I said, muttering the words out loud by mistake.

"It nice is yes," said a guy behind me. I swung round and found myself looking straight into deep brown eyes.

"Are you Portuguese?" I asked.

"Yes, I live Lisbon all life."

"All life?" I replied. " Oh, you Lisbon long time live."

I do no know why I thought mimicking his Pidgin English would somehow make me easier to understand, but I did it all the same.

"You are film star, yes?" he said.

I smiled at him warmly. "Thank you. No, I work in a gardening centre in Cobham."

"I have not seen this film," he said. "I will go."

"No, I work in a garden centre in Cobham. That's what I do."

"Yes, I always want to meet film star. I will watch all your film. What your name is?"

Now, come on, you must accept that I tried to correct him. I tried to make him understand that I wasn't an international celebrity. I told him twice that I worked in a garden centre, but he didn't understand me. Hell, I was miles away from home… one would know.

"My name is Rebel Wilson," I said.

"Well, I am Ernesto. It is nice to meet you Rachel."

"No - Rebel. My name is Rebel," I said, and then I went back to looking out at the views, examining a large black and white painting of a woman's face on the side of a building. Suddenly, I felt my new friend by my side.

"I sorry, can I get picture with you, Rebel?"

"Of course," I said, adjusting my head scarf and posing next to him for a selfie.

"I will show you castle?" he said. "We get off here and I show you castle."

"No thank you," I said. "I'm going to stay on the tram." "Yes, I show you castle," he said again. I seemed to have acquired a tour guide, but I wasn't really in the mood for old buildings; I wanted to hit the shops.

"I have to be back on my ship at 5 pm," I told him. "So I have no time to see the castle."

"You have a ship! A film star ship."

"Um, well, not really mine. It's the big ship in the harbour. Lots of people are on it...not just me."

"OK," he replied as the tram stopped at the castle. "I go now." He stood up and began backing away from me, bowing slightly and holding his hands in prayer.

"I've just convinced a Portuguese guy that I'm a famous film star," I texted to Charlie.

"Was he blind?" she texted back. I need new friends.

After a few hours strolling through the streets, buying a new handbag and some candles and trying and failing to fit into a cream linen dress, I walked down the hill back towards the ship, loving the feeling of the sun on my skin as I walked.

The sight of the gorgeous white houses with their caramel-coloured roofs hit me again, and the beautiful blasts of pink flowers all set against the bright blue of the sea. I felt quite excited that I would be seeing Frank again. I hoped he'd been OK on the ship without us all. He'd said he was too exhausted to get off and would stay and make the most of having the whole place to go swimming and relax.

As I walked to the ship, I saw dozens of people lining up waiting by the passenger entrance. Why couldn't they get on, was something wrong?

Then there was a shout.

"There she is!"

I looked up and saw Ernesto, running towards me followed by cheering crowds of people.

"Rebel, Rebel, Rebel," they shouted excitedly. "We love you, Rebel Wilson."

There were cheers and screams and begs for autographs and selfies. I looked up at the ship and saw passengers on board, looking down, wondering what was going on.

I felt my cheeks scorch scarlet as Claire came towards me. "Everything OK, Mary?" she asked.

"This Rebel Wilson - famous American film star," said Ernesto.

I looked from him to Claire and back again, unsure what to say.

"Well, Rebel has to come on board now," said Claire.

"I will go see new film," shouted Ernesto.

"We all go see Garden Centre in Cobham," said another voice.

"Good luck," they cried as I followed the incredulous Claire onto the ship.

"Well that sounds like it was an adventurous day," she said. "I hope you had a lovely time in Lisbon and weren't hassled by all your fans too much."

"A lovely day," I replied.

"I'm glad," she said.

And though every fibre of her being must have been dying to ask what on earth was going on, professionalism won the day, and she wished me a good evening and a pleasant dinner and strode off across the ship, the chants from my new fan club, and cries of 'we love Rebel' still audible as she went.

EN ROUTE TO GIBRALTAR

"Hey Frank, Frank," I said as I saw my nonagenarian friend after dinner that evening. I raced up to him at such speed that Janette looked genuinely frightened. If Frank could have seen further than the end of his nose, I suspect he would have looked frightened too. As it was, he just sat straight-backed, staring into the distance as I ran towards him.

"Hello," I said warmly. "It's me - Mary."

Ah, Mary. I heard all about your intriguing day over dinner. Didn't you convince half of Portugal that you were a famous film star?"

"Yes, something like that," I said.

"I don't think it was Mary's fault," said Janette kindly. "I was speaking to the captain earlier. A load of people just decided that she looked like a film star and began running around after her. Not her fault at all."

"Ahhh. Look, don't tell anyone else, but it was my fault. The truth is that I told a guy on the tram that I was Rebel Wilson. God knows why...I regretted it as soon as I'd said it. I certainly didn't expect them to chase around after me and ask for autographs, but it was all my fault. I feel like such an idiot. I'm always doing things like that, Frank. Always getting myself into a complete state."

I looked over at Frank, and he smiled broadly, his shoulders shaking slightly as he laughed.

"Always a joy to meet someone who doesn't take life too seriously," he said. "Your generation can be so serious about the most trivial of things. I've never understood why. Go tell 'em you're Rebel, whatever her name is, if you want to. Tell them you're the Queen of Sheba if you want. Life's supposed to be full of surprises, Mary Brown. Don't let anyone tell you otherwise."

"Yes," I said with a smile. "And when the psychiatric nurses come to take me away, I shall say that it is all your fault."

"Of course," said Frank. "Just blame me. I'm too old to go to jail."

"Can you carry on the story you were telling me earlier? You know...about you going off to war."

Frank laughed to himself. "Are you sure? You don't want to spend half your time talking to an elderly man."

"I'm fascinated. Please tell me everything. PLEASE."

"OK," said Frank, smiling and shaking his head. "I can't remember where we got to. Did I tell you about Jim and Tom?"

"No. Who were they?"

"OK. Let me take you back to November 1942," he said, his voice soothing and calm. "Close your eyes for a minute and think about it. I was just a teenager, and I'd received my call-up, and within a few days, I was on a military flight to Tunisia. In my newly acquired uniform, I sat there surrounded by complete strangers. I couldn't believe what was happening. Before that, I'd worked on the fish market. I'd never been out of the county."

I adjusted myself in my seat, taking a gulp of gin and tonic and resting my feet on the small, glass coffee table in front of me. I closed my eyes.

"OK, I'm there," I said. "I'm on the plane with you."

"Most of the men on the flight with me were older," he continued. "They had been serving for a couple of years and were being redeployed. I felt like the only one going into combat for the first time. I was so much younger and much more inexperienced than the others. It was like they had known a world that I knew nothing of.

"Then I got chatting to two guys, they were called Tom and Jim. Great guys. Like me, they were off to war for the first time. They were a bit older, but not much. Tom was from Birmingham, and Jim was from Slough. Very funny and entertaining on the journey out there they were. Full of mischief. I guess it was what you'd call gallows humour...all of us trying to cope with what might lie ahead, but it was humour all the same. We quickly became close friends."

Frank stopped to take a sip of his drink, which had been poured into a plastic beaker to make it easier. He lifted the bright blue cup with his shaking hand, and Janette rushed to help.

"We all arrived safely, and I remember walking out into the furnace. I'd never felt heat like it before...this burning, intense heat that seemed to blast itself into us. Then, we were taken for a briefing session before being handed weapons and equipment. I'd had a few basic training sessions in England before leaving, but I didn't know what I was doing. When I look back now...I was just a kid. I knew nothing. Nothing at all.

"I remember one time, after we'd been on the move for a while without seeing anything, we were walking across the sand and saw a plane overhead. Jim thought it was a German bomber, so we all jumped into a ditch nearby. We didn't realise that the ditch was full of stagnant water. Nor did we realise that it was a US plane, so there was no need to have hidden at all. We looked up, and all the other soldiers were standing, looking down at us. They had more experience; they knew a US plane from a German bomber. We stank after that for days and days because it was hard to wash. God, we stank.

"I remember the first people we came across were Arabs sitting on their camels and making their wives walk by their sides. Tom made the Arabs get off and put the women on the camels! He was a big lad, Tom, you wouldn't argue with him.

"The Arabs were nice guys. We got to know them fairly well before we got into serious combat. We learned to respect the local culture. We struck up friendships with the Bedouin. They were the salt of the earth. They were generous and polite to a fault.

"When we were in camp, though, I felt useless. I was good for carrying and fetching things, but Tom was a carpenter, and Jim was a chef, so they had proper skills. At one point, Tom created this latrine for us that was a work of art. It was 100m from the main tent lines and faced toward the Atlas Mountains. The only trouble was - the loo got used a lot by a lot of blokes and one day, the main supporting beam gave way with a mighty crack, there was a loud howl, and Jenkins rushed out with his trousers round his ankles. The whole thing had broken. We were back to using holes in the ground after that, but it had been nice while it lasted.

"Me, Tom and Jim laughed all the time, and we went everywhere together, like brothers we were. That was before the fighting started. Do you have any relatives who fought in the war, Mary?"

"No," I said. "No, I haven't."

"Good. I'm glad. War is terrifying. Worse than you can possibly imagine. Don't let anyone tell you otherwise. Don't let puffed-up army generals convince you that war is good for anything, don't let politicians who want to make a name for themselves incite conflict. No one who fought on the western front or went through what we went through can look at their medals without weeping. War is messy and solves nothing. Nothing."

There was a pause, and I wasn't quite sure what to say. I desperately wanted him to carry on with his story, but I didn't feel it was appropriate to hurry him when it was so difficult for him to talk about it.

"Lots of the guys perished; one was right next to me when a bomb blew him to pieces in a second. I saw him explode. Can you imagine what that's like? The noise from the shells and bombs was deafening. Most nights were lit up with gunfire. We were dive-bombed and machine-gunned by Stukhas, 13 of our lads killed, ten wounded.

"Jim, Tom and I stayed tight as anything through all

this. We'd seen so many people die and been forced to grow up so fast. It helped that we looked out for one another. Then one day we walked to the hills of Tunisia. It was a hellish journey. We joked about there being pretty girls at the top and flagons of ale for everyone.

"Our mission was to capture Longstop Hill. If we succeeded, it would open up the road to Tunis. We trudged up the slopes of the hill in blinding rain. All you could hear was "slop ... slop" as each foot was lifted from the mud. There was so much noise from bullets; it was dark, and the sheeting rain made it impossible to see anything. You'd hear cries as your colleagues were hit. Many of the wounded sank into the mud and died. The rain and wind muffled the cries of the dying. We got to the top, and there was no sign of Jim or Tom. I ran around screaming for them, crying their names, but it was no good.

"Then two lads appeared carrying Jim; he was badly injured. He'd tried to save Tom, but it was no good. Tom had been hit and collapsed into the mud and died. We got Jim to an MDS - a Medical Dressing Station – but it was too late. He clung on for a few hours, then died. He looked me in the eye and said goodbye."

"Oh no," I said. "Oh God - this is awful. You lost two friends on the same night?"

"I did, dear," he said, his voice croaking with pain. "And Jim turned to me as life slipped away from him and said. 'Look after my wife for me, won't you, Frank? Keep an eye on her. Will you? Please say you will."

"Of course, I will," I said. "Jim, I promise you." Then his eyes closed, and he died.

"Frank, I can't imagine what it must have been like to lose a friend like that. When I think of my friends and how much they mean to me...it's heart-breaking."

"It was very difficult," he said, staring off into space into an imaginary place that he seemed to escape to so frequently. "I need to go back to see where I lost them...one last time and to say goodbye properly. Janette will be there with me. It'll mean so much to both of us."

"I suppose you want to go because you've heard all the incredible stores over the years," I said to Janette.

"Yes, and because Jim was my grandfather," she said.

"Oh my God! That's so lovely," I said. "How did you two end up meeting?"

"I kept my promise to Jim. I went and ensured his wife was OK, and I got to know his family and helped look after them."

"Oh, how wonderful," I said, settling into my seat and curling my feet beneath me. "Tell me more."

"Frank's tired now," said Janette, protectively.

"I promise I'll tell you more tomorrow," said Frank as Janette stood up and prepared to push him away. "I haven't told you about Irene yet. We'll do that story tomorrow."

"Yes, please," I said, shouting after him. "Please tell me all about it tomorrow."

SECOND STOP - GIBRALTAR

Cruising has messed with my internal clock. I went to bed early last night and was up early this morning - most unlike me. As the sun rose, I was to be found standing on deck in a large sunhat and dark glasses to watch as we travelled down the south coast of Spain towards the Straits of Gibraltar. It was quite chilly that time of the morning and not at all bright, so the sunhat and glasses were entirely unneeded, but I felt they offered me an appropriate disguise should Simon saunter on deck. I was astonished that I hadn't bumped into him but quite sure that a meeting was inevitable, and I had to always be on my guard.

I WAS STANDING NEXT to a guy called Malcolm as the ship sailed along. He'd been on my table on the first night, a wiry man with a warm, friendly face. He had been talking mainly about politics, so I hadn't engaged much with him. I don't know much about politics, only that Winston

Churchill was a large man who smoked large cigars, Donald Trump was a giant, orange loon-bucket, and that having a strong view about Margaret Thatcher is compulsory. You must love her and think she was the greatest Prime Minister ever, or you must loathe her so much that you can't bear to hear her name.

"One of Britain's last remaining colonies," said Malcolm as we drifted along. I tried to look interested in his words, but it was hard. "British colonies," he said, shaking his head. I shook mine too because I didn't know what to do.

"How is your friend?" he asked. "Still not well enough to leave the cabin?"

"No, she's going to stay in there for a little bit longer...until she feels stronger."

"Goodness," he said. "How awful for her - missing all of this."

"Yes, absolutely," I said. "I've been telling her all about it." "Very good. Lots of pictures for her to see?"

"Yes, that's right," I said.

"Would you like to join my wife and me today as we look around?"

How do you answer a question like that? I did not want to spend the day with him or his wife – a wide-eyed woman with mad frizzy hair and the look of a woodland animal that had just emerged blinking into the sunlight.

The only thing I'd really learned about the two of them was that they loved talking politics, were frantic about cleanliness, and spent their whole time wiping down surfaces. I just didn't think we'd get on at all.

"I'd love to," I said warmly. "Thank you very much for asking."

Then I stomped back to my cabin to get my things, feeling very cross for not being able to think up a reason on the spot why I couldn't go with them. I ate a packet of crisps and an odd-looking chocolate bar that I thought was a Twix, but when I bit into it, I realised it wasn't (it was runny caramel with bits of nougat and raisins in it, but I ate it anyway). Then I felt doubly annoyed with myself - first for getting pushed into spending the day with the woodland creatures, then for eating all the snacks in the fridge after enjoying a massive buffet breakfast. If I carried on eating like this, the damn ship would sink beneath my weight.

It was quite an easy walk into town from the port, even for a hugely overweight woman in white Capri pants that were at least two sizes too small (I had bought the size 16s convinced, I mean CONVINCED, that I would lose weight and fit into them but here we were a year later and they were no more able to fit me than they were able to fly to the moon).

We walked along, passing a small statue in the middle of a roundabout which gleamed in the morning sunshine as if it were made of fire. It was quite breathtaking.

"Would you mind taking a picture of me?" I asked, reaching out to give my phone to Mary. "It's very straightforward - just an iPhone...you press there."

But Edith looked very embarrassed. "I'm sorry, we don't do that," she said. "Germs."

"Don't do what?"

"Touch other people's phones."

"Right, OK," I said, walking over to the statue and preparing to take a selfie. "I'll do it myself. I'm fine with my germs."

This day was going as well as I thought it would.

"Don't take offence," she said. "Nothing personal."

But it was hard not to take it personally when someone point blank refused to touch something that belonged to you in case you infected them.

Once I'd got my selfie, we walked across the square to Main Street, where there were lots of bars and restaurants.

"Shall we stop for a coffee and work out what to do next?" I said, but I knew what the answer would be.

"A lot of these cafes are quite dirty," said Edith. "And the coffee on the ship is free; let's wait until we get back before we have coffee."

I tried to be understanding, but this was bonkers.

"I might just get one to take away," I said, more to assert myself than because of any overwhelming desire for coffee. It was very much the Malcolm and Edith show, with me just tagging along behind. It was all making me feel very uncomfortable. I would get coffee whether they approved or not.

"Right, where shall we go next?" I said, leaning on the side of the coffee shop and sipping a ridiculously strong, piping hot coffee I didn't want. It was so incredibly hot already. The last thing I needed was coffee with the consistency of gravy. Also, my white trousers were killing me. I'd undone the button to breathe, but they still hurt. Edith wore tennis shorts and a Fred Perry t-shirt with a sun visor. Her legs were the colour of mashed potato; she looked like she'd never been exposed to the sun before, but she looked fresh and comfortable. I found myself wishing I was dressed like her, and I bet no one had ever wished that before.

Edith produced a map and a tourist information leaflet about Gibraltar.

"Right, here we go," she said. "Gibraltar has a population of around 30,000 and is a tiny 2.6 square miles so it's easy to walk around."

I wanted to point out that nowhere was easy to walk around in these trousers, but that seemed churlish. I looked down at the map, at where Edith had her finger pushed into our current location...

"We thought we'd just head up the Rock of Gibraltar, walk around and see the wild monkeys," said Edith. "I've brought some food from the buffet for a picnic lunch. I'm not sure we'll have time to do much else before we're due back on the ship."

I longed to come up with an alternative suggestion, just to be awkward - this is what having too-tight trousers does to a woman. But I couldn't think of a better plan, so I acquiesced.

"Yes," I said, following behind them, feeling like an angry teenager. I wished I hadn't worn the white trousers, wished it wasn't so hot, and wished I hadn't eaten so much at breakfast.

Despite all my reservations, Gibraltar was really good fun in the end. Edith and Malcolm were nice people. Their obsession with cleanliness was bordering on insanity, but I learned to see the funny side and mocked them gently as they wiped everything down and spritzed their hands constantly.

Most importantly, I saw the monkeys - the best bit by far. They were everywhere...everywhere - scampering around the place, not like the big baboons I'd encountered on safari, which had left me terrified and climbing a tree to escape - these were friendly, perky little things. I loved them. I loved them so much that I didn't want to leave them, so I stayed and had a picnic lunch instead of heading for a restaurant as I'd planned to. While we dined on bread, cheese, crisps and dips, I told them all about Frank.

"What an incredible story. I have to say we've enjoyed spending the day with you," said Edith, as she attempted to pack away the remains of the picnic while I tried to eat it from out of her hands as she did so.

"Thank you for having me," I said, trying to take a handful of crisps from the bowl as she put them into a carrier bag for disposal. "It's been nice to get to know you."

"Right, enough of this, back to the ship," said Malcolm, standing up and offering me his hand. If I took the hand to help me up, I would pull Malcolm down on top of me, so I was forced to pretend I hadn't seen it, then roll onto my side and clamber to my feet.

"Let's go," I said, charging towards our floating hotel.

CAPTURED BY THE GERMANS

"Hello sir, what a pleasure," I said to Frank as I took my seat next to him at dinner that evening. I'd explained to the captain that Dawn had a terrible migraine, so she would stay in the room. He'd offered to send someone in to check on her, but - as usual - I reassured him that she just needed to rest and that she would be much better off if we all left her alone.

"Such a shame that your friend is unwell," said Frank.

"If I tell you a secret, will you promise to carry on with your story over dinner," I whispered.

"Oh, how intriguing," he replied. "Of course."

"Well, Dawn's not actually with me on the ship, but she doesn't want me to tell people that she's not here, so I'm kind of just saying that she's ill all the time. It's bloody nuts."

"Ha, ha," said Frank, with a smile. "Lots of very 'nuts things' seem to happen around you. I like it!"

"All well," said voices behind me. It was Malcolm and Edith. "I hope you don't mind us intruding, but Edith wanted to meet Frank," said Malcolm. "We loved your story about him earlier."

I made the introductions and explained to Frank that I'd been telling them about him.

"Frank's about to carry on with his story, aren't you, Frank?"

"May we stay and listen?" asked Malcolm and Edith in unison, sitting at our table. "Is that OK?"

"Of course," said Frank. "If you want, but I'm sure there must be other things you want to discuss."

"No, no. We want to hear about the war," I said, and then I turned to Malcolm and Edith: "So - just to recap - he lost his two great friends - Tom and Jim - in Tunisia while trying to capture Longstop Hill. Now - what happened next?"

"My, my, you've been listening," said Frank. "That's cheering for an old man to hear."

"Of course, I've been listening," I said. "It's amazing."

"Well, I suppose I'd better carry on then, hadn't I? OK, we managed to capture the hill position, and the British army marched into Tunisia...it was a very special, very important victory, but I was numb. I felt that nothing in my life would ever be the same again, and in many ways, I was right...it wasn't.

"Everything felt flat and colourless after that. Nothing had quite the same meaning for those days, weeks and months after I lost my friends.

"The battalion headed for Sicily after Tunisia, and I went with them, feeling weary and worldlier than I should have been at that tender age. The seventh and eighth Army combined forces and headed through Sicily towards Corleone. Joining two battalions meant we weren't being properly led - officers vied for position, and the whole thing was a bit of a shambles. The lack of proper leadership came to a head one day when we came up to a river, and no one really knew what they were doing. While we were waiting to cross it, some of us were captured by the Germans."

"Oh no," I said. "After you'd been through so much."

"Well, yes, and I just didn't care anymore because I had been through so much. We were rounded up and put into an army vehicle, and all I could do was to hope that my death would not be too painful. Nothing mattered, nothing at all. Then one of the lads nudged me.

"Follow me," he said. He'd seen a gap we could escape through so we all filed out.

"But as we were escaping, the Germans saw us, and it was mayhem - we all ran off in different directions. I ran down an alleyway and straight into a Sicilian man standing by his car at the front of a small, white cottage. I looked at him, desperation sweeping through my eyes, as German voices filled the streets behind us. He hid me behind his small garden wall and stood over me; that man was Antonio Catania - he saved my life.

"The Germans took a cursory look, but when they found no one there, they gave up and left. I told Antonio I would never be able to thank him enough, and then he invited me back to his house.

"Come, have food," he said. "My daughter will tend to your injuries."

"I looked down to see I was bleeding all down my arm. I had no idea what or how I'd done it.

Once we got into his house, he called for his daughter. I stood in the hallway, desperate not to drip blood on the polished wooden floors when I heard footsteps on the stairs. I looked up and saw her...the most beautiful woman I'd ever seen. Irene. She looked like a movie star. Like Sophia Lauren. Have you heard of her?"

"No," I said. The name wasn't even familiar.

"Look her up," said Frank. "A beautiful Italian actress who was the spitting image of my Irene.

"I stopped in my tracks when I saw her and wiped my dirty hand against my trousers before shaking hers. She had these tiny hands, so soft and delicate. "Hello, I'm Irene Cantania," she said in her lovely Italian accent. For the first time since I'd lost Jim and Tom, I actually felt something. Like life wasn't pointless after all. Like there was someone here who moved me, who mattered to me."

"Oh, that's lovely," I said. "Really lovely."

"Beautiful," chorused Malcolm and Edith.

"It was," said Frank. "It was very lovely and very beautiful, but it was also quite complicated because she had a brother - Alberto - who'd fought with the Germans against us Brits, and although Italy had changed sides and were fighting with us against the Germans by the time I got there, it was tough."

"What do you mean - Italy changed sides - is that true, or are you joking?"

"No, that's true. Didn't you know that?"

"Er...no," I said.

"They changed sides just months before I arrived at the house. It was very difficult. Her brother had fought against us and had lost good friends to Allied guns. British soldiers had killed people in Alberto's battalion. How was he supposed to welcome me into his home?

"Hostility and anger were bubbling away, and real resentment towards me from him and his friends. I wouldn't have stayed more than one night because it was awkward, and I knew I shouldn't be there...I should be back with my guys, but I was quite badly injured, so I stayed longer.

"And I wasn't in any rush to leave because I had fallen hopelessly in love with Irene, and I knew that Marco Vellus, a local boy, wanted to marry her. I was determined that before I left, I would make her mine. Marco was a friend of her brother's...the whole family assumed they would get married.

"It was very difficult. But all I cared about was that in the middle of it all was me and Irene - two people who fell for one another despite all the difficulties. We couldn't help ourselves.

"We got on so well. It wasn't like it is now - we didn't jump into bed together or do anything other than sit and chat, but it was enough for me to know that she was the woman I wanted to marry.

"Irene was tending to me daily - my left arm had slivers of shrapnel in it that are still there today, and I had badly cut my face, arm and leg. Her father was as kind as he could be, but he knew my presence was tearing his family apart. He told me that I needed to leave. I nodded, thanked him for everything he had done, shook his hand and told him I would leave that night.

"I left, under the cover of darkness, heading towards Salerno where my battalion was based. I swore to Irene that I would be back soon, and we would marry, and I would give her the life she deserved. She cried when I left and begged me to come back soon.

"When I left that night, I felt like I had something to fight for, something that was worth staying alive for. I headed for Salerno to rejoin my battalion, feeling like a different person from the one who'd left Tunisia weeks earlier. I'd been devastated by the death of my two friends and was feeling helpless and hopeless. Now, I felt desperately sad about losing my friends, but in their name and for Irene, I would fight on. There was so much that I wanted to live for. For the first time in my young life, I was in love."

LIFE IN A POW CAMP

"Can I interrupt," said Captain Homarus, leaning over to check that my glass was full of wine. "You do know you have a fan on the boat, don't you?"

"A fan?" I said, scrunching up my face in disbelief.

"Yes. A guy called Simon," he said you used to go out together and you became very ill and moved away. He hasn't seen you for ten years, and now you're back, looking lovelier than ever."

"Oh God, no. To be honest, I've kind of been trying to avoid him."

"Oh," said the captain, tapping the side of his nose. "I'll tell him I haven't seen you then."

"Thank you," I said. "That's really kind of you. The relationship ended because we weren't suited."

"And because you were seriously ill, according to him."

"Yes, sort of."

"Who's that?" asked Frank.

"Oh, there's this guy on the ship I went out with years

and years ago. It's so embarrassing; he's turned up on the ship and keeps trying to talk to me."

Then I whispered: "To be honest, we used to go out together, and I wanted to get rid of him. I told him I had leprosy; isn't that awful? Now he's wondering how on earth I recovered so well."

Frank roared with laughter while the others looked on, startled by the strange noise he'd just made.

"I'm trying to avoid him, but I'm bound to bump into him at some stage."

Frank smiled at me while I spoke. "I'm sure you'll be able to talk your way out of it," he said.

"I'm not so sure," I said. "But enough about me and my stupid mouth. Tell me about you. What happened next?"

"Well, the story takes a bit of a sad turn," said Frank.

"No," we all chorused. I'd forgotten that Edith and Malcolm were still sitting there. They were leaning in, with their elbows on the table and their faces in their hands, like little children listening to bedtime stories.

"Blimey - really? It gets sadder? This is already the saddest story I've ever heard."

"I never made it back to my battalion," said Frank. "I was captured again before I reached them. If I had got there, I would have seen there was a letter for me saying that both my parents had been killed. Their lives were taken from them in a moment when a bomb dropped on Portsmouth and destroyed our house."

"Oh no, I'm so sorry."

"I wasn't the only one who this happened to...when you go away to war, you assume you're the one in danger, but there was as much danger for those left behind, and many soldiers returned home, thinking the worst of the war was behind them, only to discover that family back home hadn't been as lucky.

"Anyway, as I said, I didn't know about this at the time because before I could make it to Salerno, I was captured again, but this time there was no escape - and I was sent to Poland to a Prisoner of War camp called Stalag 8a."

"Oh no, how awful. Why Poland? Were they on the German side?"

"No, far from it - the Germans had occupied them. The Nazis controlled the country at the time, so took prisoners of war there."

I'd read about POW camps at school. I remembered that they sounded like hell on earth.

"What's got everyone so animated," said Captain Homarus, pulling up a chair next to us.

"Frank is telling us about his time in the war. He was captured by the Germans and sent to a Prisoner of War camp."

"Goodness, Frank. How fascinating. Mind if I listen in?"

"Of course," said Frank, smiling to himself as his entourage grew.

"Conditions were tough; rations were meagre. It was hard work," he said. "Doing heavy labour while you were weak from hunger was very difficult. You see images in every war film of men escaping from prison camps, but the truth is that everyone was much too exhausted to escape, and those who got beyond the wire ran the very real risk of being shot. Escape never felt like an option.

"You're so weakened when you're locked up like that.

The Germans didn't heat our cells, and it was freezing. Night times were difficult. You got to the stage where you'd wake up so cold you were glad just to be alive.

"Daytime wasn't much fun either, I have to tell you - surviving on a daily ration of hot water and barley porridge is tough. I was so skinny. There was nothing of me. It was a horrible, dark, difficult time in which I became convinced every day that I would die.

"I stayed in the camp until the war's end when Russians rescued us. It was May 1945. I've had a great fondness for Russians ever since. I was weak, dirty, cold, and hungry; they looked after me. I was taken back to Italy and reunited with my battalion. That's when I was told about the death of my parents."

"Oh, Frank," said Captain Homarus. "Your parents were killed in the war?"

"Yes, they were."

"As soon as I was strong enough, I went to collect Irene - the woman who had kept me sane as I'd been starved, beaten and freezing in the POW camp. I planned to propose to her and take her back to England."

"Ah, good news at last," said Edith. But Frank was looking down at his hands.

"When I got to Sicily, I discovered that she was engaged to Marco," he said.

"Noooooo," we all chorused.

"Blimey, Frank, when are you going to get a break? This is insane," I said. "Please tell me that's a joke.... I can't bear it."

"No, not a joke...far from a joke," he said.

"Frank needs to go to bed now," said Jan. "He needs to

get a good night's sleep; tomorrow, he will be going to Tunisia to say goodbye to Tom and my grandpa."

We all looked at one another, bereft that the story had to end at this point.

"Just a little bit more," I tried.

"Not tonight," said Janette, and she stood and began pushing Frank away.

"Good luck tomorrow," I shouted, and I saw him nod as she pushed him away through the dining room and out of view.

DRAMA IN THE THEATRE

I watched Frank and Janette go, Captain Homarus returned to work, and Edith and Malcolm headed to bed. I thought about everything he had said. It was hard to imagine what he had been through... what traumas and difficulties he must have endured. It was kind of weird that someone alive today had been through all that. His experiences felt like they should be trapped in the pages of a history book, not living in the memory of that lovely, softly spoken man.

I left the table and wandered through to the bar area. It was very busy, and getting busier all time, with couples in their finery coming in after dinner, and groups of newly-established friends gathering at tables. I didn't feel like going back to the cabin just yet, so I took a seat on a bar stool.

"Everything OK, Madam," said one of the crew, seeing me sitting alone.

"Yes, I'm fine," I said.

"Can I get you anything? A drink?"

"I'll have a gin and tonic please," I said. I didn't particularly want a drink, but turning one down was beyond me.

The waiter brought me my drink and I suddenly felt quite lonely, and a little lost. I seemed to be the only person sitting on my own. I'm usually good at making friends but it felt like everyone else was in a couple, and quite settled in their own company. It didn't feel like I could go charging up to them, introduce myself and sit down. I sipped my drink and decided to walk around for a bit, then head to bed.

I wandered through the small art shop where people were browsing and commenting on the art and how much they liked it. The only thing that stood out to me was a bronze sculpture of a ballerina. I thought it would look nice in my flat. I turned it over in my hands; it was cool and heavy. The price tag underneath said £3600. Whaaaat? Who would pay that for a sculpture? I wouldn't pay that much for a car.

How did these people have so much money? How did they make it? I walked out of the shop and past the pub, which was playing some sports match that had everyone cheering wildly.

Next to the pub was a small theatre I'd seen earlier in the day. It looked prettier at night, lit up and with people dressed up, sipping champagne in the boxes and settling down to watch a play. I fancied going in, but I didn't want to see some desperately dull play by some worthy, philosophical type – I just wasn't in the mood.

"What's on tonight?" I asked the guy on the door.

"It' a medley of songs and dance routines...just a load of fun," he said.

"Oh, that sounds perfect. Do I need a ticket or anything? Or can I just come in?"

"Just come in...you're more than welcome," he said. "Take a seat anywhere. It starts in five minutes."

I settled into a seat by the gangway and sipped my gin while waiting for the curtain to go up. People continued to come into the theatre, and the gentle murmur of voices soothed me as I sat there in quiet contemplation. I couldn't remember the last time I felt so relaxed.

The lights began to dim, and I looked round to see how full the theatre was....and that's when I saw him. Shit! Striding into the theatre alone, dressed up to the nines in his tuxedo...Simon. Oh my fucking God. It was definitely him... there was no doubt about it. I recognised how he pushed one hand deep into his pocket as he walked. The slightly mechanical movements...like a giant puppet master was controlling him. There was always something so unnatural about him. I dropped my head so he wouldn't see me and sunk down in my seat. There was no way I could leave without him seeing me, but – at the same time – there was every chance of him seeing me if I stayed where I was. I had no idea what to do.

I glanced over to see where he was sitting, and I'm sure he saw me. He did a dramatic double-take just as the lights went down. Christ, what now? There was a door to the right of me that was marked 'authorised personnel only'. Under the cover of darkness, I sneaked out of my seat and peeled the door open, sneaking through it into a corridor full of dancers. There were dancers everywhere dressed up in fabulous sequined leotards and feather headdresses.

"You're not dressed," said a man in a tight blue catsuit.

"What the hell?"

"I know. I'm late," I said, shuffling from foot to foot, afraid to announce that I wasn't in the cast in case he made me go back through the door.

"Damian....one of the larger dancers here needs dressing," said the man, wiggling off towards the stage while two wardrobe assistants grabbed me and began undressing me. There was a great deal of sighing and muttering as they surveyed the racks of clothes for something for me to wear. I tried to insist that I could just sit in the dressing room and didn't have to be dressed up at all, but this clearly wasn't an option.

"With four dancers ill, we need everyone we can find on stage tonight."

"Right, OK," I said, as they wrapped me in blue sequined robes and pinned my hair up, attaching feathers and jewels. It looked quite good by the time they'd finished. So good that I completely forgot that there was no way I could go anywhere near the stage for the simple reasons that (a) I couldn't dance and (b) I didn't know any of the choreography.

"This way," he called.

I could hear that the performance had begun, with loud music hall songs being belted out on the stage, and the sound of footsteps as the dancers tap danced through their routines.

"You're on next," said a behind-the-scenes assistant, leading me through to the edge of the stage. The headdress was so bloody heavy. I had no idea how I was supposed to dance in it.

"Good luck," said the guy, pulling back the curtain a little for me to go on. "When they sing 'arimbo, arimbo' that's when you pull off your top to reveal your tasselled nipples."

"That's when I what?" I said, regarding him with a mixture of alarm and confusion.

"Go!" he said. I strode onto the stage, trying to keep my head upright so the damn headdress wouldn't come tumbling off and trying to do some sort of steps that could be described as being dance-like. The guy in the blue catsuit looked at me like I was insane as I danced around on the spot, clicking my fingers and stamping my feet while all the other dancers moved together in a lovely rhythmical dance that they had clearly been practising for months and which I could in no way hope to pick up.

Then, it happened. "Ariba, Ariba!" came the shout, and four dancers pulled off their tops. I just looked at them... wide-mouthed and disbelieving. I turned out towards the crowd and saw Simon. His eye caught mine, and he stood up.

"Oh my God – Mary Brown – it's you. It's a miracle!" he shouted. "I thought you were dying of leprosy."

"No, I'm better," I shouted back as the headdress slipped over my eyes. "The leprosy has all gone."

GYM BUDDIES

I woke early the next morning and stretched out across the bed. It was so comfortable I didn't want to move. The sun was streaming in through the balcony windows where I'd forgotten to close the curtains again. I looked out across the white pillow towards the ocean, and then I saw it – a bright blue feather lying next to me along with a sprinkling of glitter – and all the horrors of the night before came bounding back to me.

Juan Pedro, the head dancer, had been hysterical afterwards – laughing uproariously when I told him of my conundrum and that I wasn't a dancer at all.

"No! Really? I couldn't tell," he said, mimicking my little solo dance routine and the look of fear on my face when he'd shouted 'Ariba.'

"I particularly liked the stamping," he'd said, and the way your eyes moved upwards towards the headdress all the time because you were sure it would fall off.

"It's hard work," I'd said. "Dancing and holding the

weight of that thing on your head...I have a new respect for dancers."

I told him all about Simon and my efforts to avoid him, and he laughed a lot at the fact that, far from managing to avoid Simon and keep the whole thing quiet, I'd been forced to address it in a packed theatre and announce from the stage, while dressed in glitter and feathers, that I used to have leprosy.

"You must see the funny side," he insisted. I wasn't sure I did, but I was confident everyone else would.

Now it was morning, and my head hurt, and it was only 6 a.m. There was no way I would get back to sleep, so I climbed out of bed and decided to go up to the gym and do a workout before breakfast. A 'wake up workout' session occurred at 6.30 a.m. If I did that, I could justify going completely nuts at the buffet later. So, off I went onto the top deck to find the workout class.

I walked into the glass-panelled room to find Juan Pedro sitting there, legs akimbo, stretching out.

"Ah, you're doing this class as well are you?" I asked.

"I'm taking this class, darling," he replied. "I hope you're ready to work hard."

"No, not really," I said. "Especially not after last night's extravagances."

"It'll do you good...it'll help get the booze out of your system. Also, I hear it helps to do lots of exercise if you've suffered from leprosy."

"Stop it," I said, nudging him playfully.

There were six people in the class – three of them were dancers from last night – lithe, slim and gorgeous young men, the other two were called Bob and Doris and looked about 75. I fancied my chances of being more able than the elderly couple but considerably less able than the dancers.

The music struck up – loud drumbeats that rocked through me, making my hangover feel instantly about five times worse.

"OK, and marching on the spot," said Juan Pedro. "Lift your knees as high as possible; come on, I want to see those knees up by your shoulders."

I did my best, though I have to report that my knees were nowhere near my shoulders. Still, I had a light sweat and was quite enjoying it. That's when Juan Pedro put down steps in front of us and said that we'd do a step routine for the second half of the class.

He had us stepping on and off the steps at high speed, kicking out and lifting her arms.

"Don't worry if you get lost – just keep going," he said in an encouraging voice, so I gleefully stepped on and off the step, waving my arms, completely out of time with everyone else in the class.

Afterwards, Juan Pedro came up to me and put his arm around me.

"Well done," he said. "You kept going all the way through."

"Thanks," I said. I was proud of myself too. I can't remember the last time I did an exercise class like that and kept going. "I really want to try and lose weight, but it's so hard when you love food."

"Yes, and these ships are a menace with all those buffets," he said. "They're impossible to resist."

He tapped his rock-hard, not-an-ounce-of-fat-stomach as he spoke as if to illustrate how much weight he'd put on.

"There's nothing there," I said, rubbing my own stomach and seeing how it rippled wildly like it was a separate entity entirely. Like a man made of jelly was lying on my tummy.

"You keep up the exercise, and that will go in no time," said Juan Pedro. "You just need to cut back on the food a little, and exercise a bit more – it's not rocket science...none of it is difficult, you just need to make a promise to yourself to take your health seriously from now on."

"I think I will," I said, standing up and wiping the sweat from my brow.

"Good," said Juan Pedro. "Fancy breakfast?"

Going down to breakfast with Juan Pedro was great, and it made me realise how much I don't like being on my own... how much I like to have company. I live on my own, but I'm at work a lot of the time, and when I'm not, I either have Ted round, or I'm at his. Or I'm out with friends. I never spend a lot of time alone.

The only downside to going to breakfast with Juan Pedro was being so restrained. Having had a conversation with him about how I wanted to lose weight, it felt all wrong to pile my plate high with pancakes, syrup and croissants. But – and this is what people don't understand about fat people – I can't not have those things. If I don't have a pancake and syrup at breakfast, I'll feel awful and deeply deprived all day, and it will play on my mind until I cave in and go to a sweet shop and eat everything they've got.

I walked to the buffet, piling my bowl with melon and pineapple, and then shoved a couple of pancakes into my mouth while still there so Juan Pedro wouldn't be able to see.

I grabbed a pancake, lay it on my hand and dribbled maple syrup into it before rolling it up and pushing it into my mouth. Then I returned to my seat with my little bowl of fresh fruit salad.

"Well done," said Juan Pedro, looking at the food I'd selected. "That's brilliant. It can be so hard to eat sensibly with so many unhealthy options on offer. That's really good."

So, I ate the lousy pieces of pineapple and melon and took his praise on board. "Thank you, Juan Pedro," I said, the taste of delicious pancakes and maple syrup still strong in my mouth. "Thank you."

"Listen, do you fancy spending the day together in Tunisia? Walking around on your own won't be much fun."

"That would be lovely," I said. "If you don't mind..."

"Mind? I'd love that. Any woman who will rock up and join a dance troupe with no dancing experience to escape from a boyfriend whom she told she had leprosy is my kind of woman. Especially if that woman then proceeds to stuff her face with pancakes and pretend only to eat two small slivers of melon for breakfast. Perfect."

DRESSED UP IN TUNISIA

I'd arranged to meet Juan Pedro on deck to head into Tunis together and explore the sights. I didn't know quite what to expect, but he was good fun and - much as I loved Frank's stories of wartime love and loss - it would be good to have a light-hearted day of fun and frolics with a nutter like Juan Pedro.

"Coming then?" he said, appearing beside me in an odd but strangely flattering clothing combo - skin-tight jeans that were ripped both at the knee and alarmingly close to his crotch, along with a shirt with ruffles down the front of it and a very fancy, patterned, shiny blazer. His hair was combed back.

"Glad you made an effort," I said.

"Well, I'm glad one of us did," he retorted, looking me up and down.

"Cheeky hound. It's not easy to be glamorous when you're nearly 15 stone."

Juan Pedro laughed. "You're not 15 stone," he said.

Actually, I am. But I didn't want to push the point, so I took it as a compliment and smiled at him.

"I bet I could get you a fabulous outfit today," he said. "I could make you look gorgeous."

Dear readers, I should have realised this wouldn't end well. You only had to look at Juan and his bright, shiny blazer and skin-tight, ripped jeans to see that his idea of 'glamorous' would be entirely different from mine. I wanted to look like Grace Kelly; he was clearly going to dress me like Danny Le Rue. But all of those thoughts didn't enter my head. All I heard was, 'I can make you look gorgeous' and I thought 'I'd like that,' so off we went, into Tunis, with Juan talking about the lovely, native dress and describing something called a sefsari - a gorgeous huge scarf he wanted to buy for me. He told me about dresses lined with rhinestones. "A gorgeous bodice studded with crystals would be wonderful," he said.

"Bodice? Have you seen the size of my breasts?" I replied. "There aren't enough crystals in the entire world..."

We decided that a stop in a lovely Turkish cafe was called for before we began our shopping expedition, so we wandered into the first one we came to and ordered drinks.

"Not too strong," I said as Juan Pedro raised his eyebrows. "You might be in the wrong place altogether if you want weak coffee, doll," he said. "They take it strong and dark here."

The coffee came as predicted - tiny cups full of wildly strong coffee that was undrinkable.

"Mmmm..." I said. "Mary loves hot tar in the mornings."

There was an added bonus with the coffee when I stirred it because it had this sludge at the bottom - like the stuff you get on the floor of a river bed.

"Fancy another?" said Juan.

I pushed my cup over to him. "Have mine," I said. "I can't do it. The taste of it is making me want to cry."

I looked at the map on my phone as we talked. I'm a terrible map reader, but I hoped to see roughly where the town centre was. As I scanned across it, I saw a sign for Longstop Hill.

"That's where Frank's going," I said, pointing it out. "You know Frank - the old guy on the ship...in the wheel-chair...he fought there in the war and two of his friends died. He's going back to say a final goodbye to them."

"Really?" said Juan. "I know all about the battle of Longstop Hill."

"No, you don't." It seemed very unlikely that Juan Pedro would know anything at all about battles fought in the Second World War

"I do," he insisted. "It was a crucial battle. When they took control of the hill, they could go straight into Tunis."

"Yes, that's right. That's what Frank said." I looked at Juan, amazed.

"I took a group of vets out there. They had fought there too and wanted to go back to see it," he explained.

"Gosh, you must tell Frank tonight," I said. "He'd love to hear that."

"Of course," said Juan. "How interesting that he's come back to see it too. It sounds like it was hell up there. The guys I took up had lost friends - they were hit and fell and died in the mud."

"That's what Frank said. That's how he lost one of his friends, the other one died just after they got him to safety."

"Awful," said Juan. "You couldn't imagine any of that if you look at the hill now. It's grassy and pleasant, with goats roaming over it. There is a new road through the Kasserine Pass - the only sign of the war is when it runs past the rusted ruins of tanks. Farmers find shattered helmets in the fields occasionally, but that's it. There's no doubt, though - the landings in North Africa and the Tunisian campaign were vital in the final surrender of the Germans. Frank played an important role in securing our freedom today."

There was a moment of solemnity as we both looked down in quiet contemplation, and then Juan spoke: "So, shall we use that hard-won freedom by going shopping?"

"Yes," I said. "Let's go shop."

We pushed our chairs back from the table, and Juan leaned over to touch my arm. "One condition," he said. "Whatever outfit we buy for you this afternoon, you must wear at the dinner this evening."

"Done," I said, with staggering naivety, and we wandered off, arm in arm, to the shops of downtown Tunisia.

THE FINAL PART OF THE STORY

"No, "he said. "Go back and put the gold chains on."

"But I look ridiculous with this much jewellery. "

"No – you look very glamorous with this much jewellery. "

I walked back into the changing room and looked at myself in the mirror. My arms were full of gold bangles, I had a dress on which was deep pink cotton on the top and had puffy sleeves and a fitted bodice which fell from the waist into a skirt shot through with gold thread. Over my head, I had a pink scarf studded with crystals and gold necklaces were tied around my forehead with these gold discs dangling down. I had similar necklaces around my neck...lots of them. My upper body was so heavy I could barely stand straight.

Juan was unperturbed by the pain I was in. "No pain, no gain," he said. "You have to suffer for your art. It looks really good; I don't see what the problem is. "

I looked back into the mirror. "You don't see what the problem is? I look like a gypsy."

"You don't look like a gypsy; you look like a very glamorous Tunisian woman. Trust me," he said. "When you wear this to dinner tonight, everybody will think it's amazing."

"I'm not wearing this to dinner tonight, absolutely no way," I said.

"That was the deal," said Juan. "You promised me that if I got you into a glamorous outfit, you would wear it for dinner tonight. "

"Yes, but I didn't realise I'd look so bloody ridiculous."

"You don't. You look glamorous and gorgeous, and you're wearing this tonight."

To say that people looked at me with shock in their eyes when I walked into dinner back on the ship that evening would be to understate the impact I had. Elegant women wandered all around in black column dresses, cream sun dresses and stylish party dresses, and in the middle of it all was me - a woman of nearly 15 stone dressed head to foot in pink with huge gold jewellery dripping from everywhere. I had more jewellery on me then everybody else on the ship combined, and there were a lot of women with a lot of jewellery on.

I'd had a gin and tonic in the cabin to take the edge off it, but the edges were still very much there as I walked onto the dining floor and I caught up with Juan who continued to say how great I looked.

In front of us I could see Frank, sitting alone at a table with Janette. I desperately needed to talk to someone non-judgemental, so I headed over there, dragging Juan with me and telling him he needed to meet Frank so they could talk about Longstop Hill.

"Good evening," I said.

Janet jumped when she saw me.

"I thought you were an exotic dancer then," she said. "I thought you were going to give Frank a heart attack."

"No, it's just me. And this is Juan," I said, jangling as I made the introductions. "He dragged me around Turkish boutiques today, telling me he'd make me look me glamorous, but I feel like a complete idiot."

"You don't look like an idiot at all. You look beautiful," said Frank.

"Thank you," I said. The fact that he was almost blind made his compliments less reassuring, but it was kind all the same. "How was Longstop Hill today?"

"Moving," said Frank, nodding his head. "It was very moving. Quite difficult at times, but I'm very glad I did it."

"I found it moving too, and I never fought anyone or anything in my life," said Juan.

"You were there today?" said Frank.

"No, I went a few weeks ago. I took a group of Vets. They said the same. Very difficult but very, very worthwhile."

"Yes, the memories have never faded, so it wasn't like I went there, and the memories suddenly came pouring back, but being there did cut through me a bit, and made me think of all those brave young men who died. That was very difficult."

Janette and I sat and listened awhile while Frank

talked through the day. I jingled and jangled every time I nodded my agreement, and Janette looked at me sternly as if my musical accompaniments were somehow lessening the impact of the story.

"Listen, it's incredible to meet you, Frank, but I'm going to have to head off to dance practice. We've got a show later. Will you come?"

"I won't. I'm exhausted after the trip today, but thank you for asking. Good luck!"

"Thank you," said Juan, blowing me a kiss as he walked away.

"He seems like a nice young man. Is he your boyfriend?" asked Frank.

"Er....no, I'm pretty sure he's gay," I replied. "Anyway, he wouldn't be my boyfriend if he was the straightest man in the world. He's made me look a complete fool. I've dressed like a gypsy thanks to him."

Frank just smiled and shook his head. "You look adorable."

"I look like mad gypsy Rose-Lee. People will be asking me to read their fortunes."

"Nonsense," said Frank, with a smile. "You look perfect."

It was a kind remark, but I was well-aware that he was almost blind.

Over dinner that evening, Frank and I resumed our chat, with Frank picking up where he'd left off...arriving in Sicily to discover that Irene was engaged.

"I felt as if my insides had been churned out," he said. "I didn't even try to see Irene; as soon as I heard the news, I turned and walked away."

"No! Why didn't you try and find her and persuade her? She probably got engaged to him because she thought you weren't coming back...you were away so long. How could you just walk away?"

"I didn't want to spoil her happiness; if she chose him, then who was I to ruin it for them? Remember, her father had saved my life, and her family had been incredibly kind to me. I didn't want to make life difficult for them at all. I just turned and walked away."

"And what did you do then? Where did you go?"

"I left and got the boat back to England, but I couldn't stop thinking about her. I got home, and that's when I realised how much she mattered. Nothing was there; my family had been wiped out, and the house was boarded up. I was offered temporary accommodation but decided to travel to Slough to fulfil my friend's dying wish to take care of his wife."

I noticed Janette smiling as Frank spoke about Jim's wife.

"It was lovely to meet her. What a charming lady. Elizabeth was her name. She was standing there with a little three-year-old girl called Linda at her feet."

"Linda was my mum," said Janette. "Dad never found out that mum was pregnant. He never knew he had a daughter."

"Oh no, that's sad," I said.

"It was a difficult time for mum, but Frank really looked after them. He moved them into his mum's old house as soon as that was repaired and took care of them."

"And your grandma helped me too," said Frank. "It was

Elizabeth who forced me to go to Sicily and try to win back Irene's heart.

"I got a boat back a week later and talked to Irene. She was astonished to see me. I'd been away so long she assumed I'd been killed. We talked for hours, and I told her I loved her. She said she loved me too, and we decided to run away together. It wasn't a brave thing to do, and it wasn't fair on this family who'd cared so much for me, but we ran away in the night, leaving a note for her parents and one for Marco.

"We settled in England, and she never went back. I know she missed her home and her family. She wrote to her parents and went over to visit them secretly, but never saw her brother ever again because she was worried he would come over to England and find me if he knew where we were.

"I need to go back to the house in Sicily to see who is there and to apologise for everything that happened. Those guys saved my life. They were kind, decent people. I need to see them again, just to say I'm sorry about how I took their daughter away from them. Even if everyone I knew is dead, I want to apologise to anyone there who knew Irene and explain why we ran away; explain to Alberto why she never stayed in touch.

"She wrote letters to Alberto and I thought she was sending them, but after her death, I found them in a vanity case; she'd not sent them because she was worried he'd come and find her."

"Gosh, what does Irene think about you going?" I asked.

"Irene died four months ago. She'd been very ill. She

passed away peacefully. I'm hopelessly lost without her. I miss her terribly. I need to do this for her. I do hope we find the cottage. We will, won't we?" he said.

"We will. I promise we will," I said. And suddenly I realised that I would be going with him to Sicily and that I had to help him find Irene's relatives.

JUAN'S COMING TOO

I didn't see Frank much over the next couple of days after hearing the rest of his emotional story on the boat. His journey to Longstop Hill had exhausted him so he stayed on board, mainly in his cabin, being looked after Janette, while the boat stopped first in Sardinia, then in Malta. I explored them both with Juan Pedro. But I couldn't stop thinking about Frank's tale.

"Hey Juan Pedro," I said as we both sat there, sunning ourselves on the deck one day. "You know Frank - the old guy in the wheelchair who went to Longstop Hill?"

"Yeah," he said without moving his tanned face from its position, staring up into the sunshine. "Nice guy. I liked him."

"I'm going with him for the day when we get to Sicily - he's going to try to find the cottage his wife lived in when he first met her. He stole her away from her fiancé just after the war. He wants to go back there and make amends to anyone who's still there. He still feels bad that Irene was forced to abandon her family."

"Blimey doll. I doubt there'd be anyone there now that was alive then."

"Well, Frank's still alive, so there could be."

"True darling," said Juan. "I suppose it's worth him trying."

"Did you hear about the letters he has...letters that Irene wrote to her brother to explain why she'd left and updating him on her life and what was going on? She wrote hundreds and never sent any of them. After she died, he found the letters in her vanity case with a note saying, 'Frank, I'm sorry - I never sent these - I was worried about Marco finding our address and coming to hurt you. I'm sorry."

"Good grief, doll," said Juan, turning slightly to face the sun. "We're in the middle of a Sunday afternoon rom-com; you know that, don't you? Hugh Grant is going to show up any moment."

"Haha. Very funny. It does seem like that. I've been writing all about it in the blog I'm doing for Dawn and apparently, it's got quite a big following back home...loads of comments and tonnes of likes."

"My God. They are going to make this into a film. We'll get back to Southampton and a film crew and director will be waiting there. Who's going to play us? I was thinking maybe Johnny Depp for me and Jennifer Lawrence for you. What do you think?"

"Yep, I'll go with that," I said. "It would make a brilliant film - Frank's story is so amazing...I just love him. I think he's one of the kindest, warmest and most friendly people ever. Considering what he's been through, you think he'd be wary and guarded. I mean, he can hardly see, he's got shrapnel inside him still, his wife's just died, and yet he's lovely and friendly. I have to help him find that cottage...I'm so worried about the effect it will have on him if we can't find it."

"We will. I'll come with you," said Juan. "I've been to Sicily a few times before; I might be able to help."

I smiled to myself at the thought of us: me - this extra-ordinarily overweight woman, Frank, a 96-year-old widower and Juan Pedro, a flamboyant Spanish dancer - all trekking around looking for a house from the 1940s while being watched by a slightly angry-looking nurse in a brown dress.

"Yes, you should come," I said. "I'll talk to Frank - you should definitely come."

OFF TO SICILY

Finally, the day arrived. I stood on deck as the boat docked in Sicily - looking out towards the cluster of houses nestled in the hilltops in front of us. The thought of tracking down Frank's relatives made me tingle with anticipation. It would be so amazing if Marco and Alberto were still alive and Frank could meet them, shake hands and hand over the letters. I knew how much it would mean to him to make amends.

I looked up to see Janette pushing Frank towards me; he was sitting in his wheelchair looking incredibly dapper, dressed in a brown three-piece suit that looked like it came from the 1930s, along with very shiny shoes. In his lap, he carried a hat and a cane. Like the suit, they looked like something out of a 1930s musical. We were just a burst of incidental music away from a chorus of singing in the rain.

"Wow, Frank," I said. "You look amazing."

"Well, I thought I better be prepared for anything. This

is how Irene loved me to dress, so I thought it's how I should dress today."

"It's very hot out there, though," I said. "Are you sure you won't be too warm like that?"

"I have tried telling him," said Janette, with her hands on her hips. "But he won't listen."

"I can handle a bit of heat," said Frank with a shake of his head, as if to indicate that his past involved more discomfort than a warm suit on a hot day could ever threaten.

"Howdy!" came a shout from the other side of the deck. I looked up to see Juan Pedro walking towards us, dressed like something out of a gay pride march. He was wearing rainbow-coloured trousers in some sort of shiny material that gleamed as he walked, along with a flowery, Hawaiian-style shirt in orange with red and white blossom on it. On his feet were these odd kind of winkle-pickers in a glittery material. He was carrying a man bag made of lime-green, crocodile material. Now, I love unconventional people, I'm all in favour of people who don't look strictly normal, but I couldn't imagine what Frank would make of him, and I was slightly worried since this was very much Frank's day, a day on which we had to all behave in a way which wouldn't alarm or frighten him.

"Good lord alive," said Janette, seeing Juan Pedro close up.

"Frank, remember Juan Pedro?" I said.

"Very nice to see you again, son," said Frank, reaching out a trembling hand. Juan Pedro shook it and patted Frank on the back.

"Frank, I hope I can help locate your wife's cottage today. If there's anything I can do, or - Janette - if you need any help pushing the wheelchair or anything, you just shout, and I'm here for you. "

"Thank you, that's very kind," said Frank, and I was reminded that Frank couldn't see enough to judge Juan Pedro on his appearance. Just like he couldn't see how fat I was or how dull Janette looked, none of that mattered. He was just judging us on how we behaved and treated him and each other. It gave me a shot of warmth and reminded me that what matters is not how you look, but how you behave, how you treat people, and how kind you are. I felt a tear come into my eye and instinctively hugged Juan Pedro, and Janette. Juan Pedro seemed delighted, Janette seemed alarmed, I was determined by the end of the day she would've softened a little bit and realised that we all just wanted to help.

Janette, being the only sensible person in the party by a considerable margin, was given the job of carrying the maps and all the information that would help us track down where Irene had lived and where we might start to find her family.

"In this part of the world, people tend to live in the same house much more than we would in England," said Frank. "Houses are passed down through generations. It's not uncommon for children to live in the houses their grandparents and even great-grandparents bought."

"Great. Then let's hit the road."

"Absolutely," said Juan Pedro. "Follow me."

So the rather odd party of an enormous fat girl in loose-fitting separates, a man in rainbow-coloured trousers carrying a lime-coloured clutch bag, an elderly man in a wheelchair dressed as if he'd just dropped in from the 1930s, and a rather stout and unsmiling nurse in a starched brown dress, all headed off into Sicily for the day. It was, I admit, hard to see how this was going to work out well.

EVERYTHING'S CHANGED

We walked up to the main square and jumped into a cab. Well, I say 'jumped' - that's a bit of a lie...what with the wheelchair being folded up and Frank being manually lifted in, and me unable to get the seat belt around me, and none of us speaking a word of Italian...it was all rather a palaver if I'm honest, but we struggled on board, and off we set. Janette clutched the modern-day map and handed me the map from the 1940s to look after.

Frank entertained us with his wartime stories.

"We were called the D-Day dodgers, you know," he said.

"The what?"

"Well, D-Day took place while we were in Italy. Lady Astor said that we were in Italy to avoid D-Day. If she'd seen what we'd been through, she would have realised we'd all much have preferred to be at D-Day. We sang a song to take the mickey out of it all; let me see whether I can remember it...it's to the tune of Lili Marlene. Here we go:

'We landed at Salerno, holiday with pay,
Jerry got the band out to help us on our way.
We all sang songs, the beer was free.
We danced all the way through Italy.
We were the D-Day Dodgers, the men who dodged D-Day."

We all applauded heartily.

"Here is the place," said the driver. "Corleone."

Frank looked through the window, and his face fell. We were relying on a 90-odd-year-old man to remember the place from 70 years ago, and he clearly didn't recognise anything at all. The two maps looked vastly different, so it wasn't hard to see why he was confused.

"Come on, let's get out and look around," I said, trying to fake confidence.

I looked over and caught Janette's eye. I knew exactly what she was thinking...we had no way of knowing how we would do this, but on the other hand, we simply had to do it. We couldn't let Frank go back to England without finding the cottage, saying his goodbyes and handing over the letters. He was an old man - he might never get this chance again.

We walked over to a small wall.

"Let me have a look at that," said Janette, and I opened up the map from the 1940s while she unfolded the current map. We laid them both out in front of us, across the wall.

On the 1940s map, there was hardly anything - just a handful of houses and shops. Irene's cottage was circled. The modern-day map featured a new road system, roundabouts, motorways and loads of houses, shops and offices that weren't there before.

"It looks to me," said Janette. "As if the cottage has gone."

"Really?"

"Yes. Look on this map - see that small hill there, well, that must be here on the modern map."

She pointed at the two maps, and I saw what she meant.

"Yes," I said. "Look - there's the church spire. It looks like the cottage was there - I pointed to where it should be...it was now a cafe next to a garage."

"Really?" said Juan. "You reckon it was turned into a cafe?"

While Juan came over to investigate the map, I went to see Frank. He looked exhausted and sad, sitting there, barely able to see, listening to us talking about how the cottage - his only link to his wife's past - had disappeared.

"Come on, let's go and have a cup of tea," I said, seeing his face brighten up. "We'll go to that cafe over there while they are messing around with the maps, and I'll get myself on Google to see what I can find."

"Good plan," said Frank. "I don't know about Google, but tea is an excellent idea."

We sat at a rickety old table, and the others joined us. Juan had pulled out a pen and was jotting down numbers.

"Are you doing your tax return?" I asked.

"Map coordinates," he replied, tapping the side of his head. "Right, OK. Got it."

"Got what?"

"These are the map coordinates of the cottage we're looking for." He pointed to the map from the 1940s with the cottage marked on it. "And this is where the coordinates fall on this map."

We all looked down. Juan was pointing to the cafe.

"The family must have sold the cottage to a developer who built this cafe," said Janette, scratching her head and looking at the map.

Frank looked up and around the cafe as if hoping to see something that would remind him of the past.

I called the waiter over and asked him, in my best Italian, whether this used to be a cottage. It was no good; my broken Italian and his lack of English were getting us nowhere.

"Wait minute," he said, rushing into the back of the cafe and emerging with a very handsome young man.

"How can I help you?" he said in near-perfect English.

Janette clapped her hands together in relief. She repeated our questions, laying the maps out on the table. The guy looked through them and confirmed that this was the spot we were looking for, but it was never a cottage.

"My parents owned this cafe when I was born, so it's been a cafe for a long time," he said. He shouted out in Italian to his mother, who came out and stood next to him, looking at the maps and chatting to him in Italian.

Then she called someone's name, and a man came in from the kitchens in a white overall.

"My parents say that they bought this cafe 20 years ago. It was already a cafe when they bought it," said the young man.

"Damn," said Juan Pedro. "No cottage here?"

"No cottage," they confirmed.

"But it does look like the right area, doesn't it?" said Juan. The young man nodded as he studied the two maps.

"Let me try another tack," said Juan, beckoning over the English-speaking man. "Do you have any documentation from when you bought the cafe? I wonder who sold this property to you. Maybe we can track them down?"

"I will take a look," he said.

The man disappeared for so long that we thought he wasn't coming back, but to our delight and surprise, he re-emerged with a piece of paper, the purchase agreement from when they bought the cafe two decades ago.

"My mother keeps everything," he said.

The name of the person they had bought the cafe from was Monsieur Dalmeny.

"I've never heard of him," said Frank. There was an address next to it.

"Do you have a phone number?" I asked. "No phone number here," he said.

"OK, then, we'll go there," I announced, standing up. I was conscious that we didn't have much time if we were going to get back to the ship by 5 pm.

"Your best bet is to head on the main road. Where is your car?"

"We don't have a car. We'll need to get a taxi," I said.

"No problem," said the man. "I will take you there."

"Really? That would be amazing. Thanks so much," I said, and the four of us climbed (Janette), waddled (me), sashayed (Juan Pedro) and were lifted (Frank) into the car, and the man, who we discovered was called Andreas, dropped us at the end of a pathway which led to the house of Monsieur Dalmeny - the man who'd sold them the cafe.

"Thank you so much," I said. "You've been very generous. Can I give you some money?"

"No, not at all," he said. "I'm just helping. Here is my number...please call if I can do anything else."

So, there we were, wandering down a path to knock on some stranger's door and ask them what they remembered about when they sold a cafe.

The house was quite plush, much posher than the other houses in this heavily rundown part of the country. Two goats wandered outside one of the houses, and children's toys were scattered on the lawns, but the bigger, more imposing house had none of the paraphernalia of family life dotted around the place. It gave the feeling of being totally empty.

I knocked. The four of us stood there in silence. I knocked again. Still nothing.

Damn.

It was hard to know what to do next. We were starting to run out of time, but I knew just how much Frank wanted to track down anyone related to the family that he felt he had let down so many years ago.

"I'll put a note through the door and see whether they respond to it. I'll put my phone number on, and they can call me when they return."

"It's 3 p.m.," whispered Juan Pedro. "We're running out of time here."

I knew he was right. We needed to be back in the vicinity of the boat by 5 o'clock in order to make sure we had enough time to sort Frank out and get onto the ship before it left at 6 p.m.

"We're going to have to go soon, aren't we?" I said. Juan Pedro nodded gently.

I turned to Janette: "What do you want to do?" I asked.

She agreed that we should start heading back to the ship and that Frank would have to send the letters once they'd tracked the family down. Janette leaned over to talk to Frank. He wanted to pass the letters on personally and talk to the family himself, but he knew there was no time today to do that.

"Let's go," he said, his voice barely a whisper, and I felt like we'd all really let him down. I just hadn't thought about how difficult it would be, how much everything would have changed, and how hard it would be to find anyone who knew Irene's family, let alone know where they were now.

To add to our woes, it turned out that getting a cab back was easier said than done. I rang the number for the taxi company and was told by a surly Italian that it would be half an hour before they could get one to us.

"Okay," I said. "But we're heading back to the dock to get a ship, so it can't be any longer than that. Will it definitely be here in half an hour?"

"Yes it will be," confirmed the cab lady.

We sat down on the edge of the grass and talked about how we must all work together once we got back to

Britain to try and locate this family. I looked at my watch. It had been 40 minutes, and there was no sign of the cab. I rang the company again, and the woman assured me it was 10 minutes away.

"It's 10 to 4," said Juan Pedro.

"I know, but what can I do? Shall I try calling Andreas at the cafe and see whether he can take us back to the harbour?"

"Yes, do that. If we miss this ship, I'll be shot," said Juan. "I'm supposed to be dancing in the razzmatazz ball tonight."

"We won't miss the ship. It will be tight, but we will get there," I said with a ridiculous amount of confidence, considering there was no sign of a taxi anywhere, and I was struggling to get through to Andreas.

An answerphone came on, and I left a message, explaining we were the guys he'd given a lift to earlier, and we were stuck. We waited another 30 minutes - no cab, no reply from Andreas. It was almost half past four, and the journey would take at least an hour. Unless the cab came within the next 15 minutes, we were in serious danger of not making the boat.

Finally, finally, a cab came around the corner and we clambered on board. I tried to tell the driver how much of a rush we were in, but he didn't seem to understand.

"Don't worry," he kept saying as we drove at unbelievably slow speeds through the narrow roads, coming up against obstacle after obstacle...there was far more traffic than there had been on our way up, which slowed us down considerably; there were animals in the road as they were being taken from one field to another, then, just as we thought we were there, a diversion which cost us 15 minutes.

We arrived near the docks at five to six. While Janette got the wheelchair out of the car and put Frank into it, Juan Pedro and I ran as fast as we could towards the ship, hoping to alert them to our presence and encourage them to wait. But it was no good. When we reached the boat, out of breath and dishevelled, it was 6.15, and our floating hotel was pulling out of the harbour. On the deck, many of the crew and passengers were gathered. Captain Homarus and Claire were there, along with Simon, waving furiously and shouting my name.

"Mary, Mary," he cried. "Get on the boat."

"How in God's name am I supposed to do that?" I said. "Swim out to it?"

I glanced at Juan Pedro. "Shall I?" he said. "Maybe I should swim to it to save my career."

"No, you nutter," I said. "Look how far it is now. Come on - let's go and find Frank and Janette."

So, the two of us walked back towards our 96-year-old friend while a man I once dated for a few weeks screamed at me. "You must get on the boat". "You've only just recovered from the leprosy. Make sure you don't get ill again. Get on the boat."

"Leprosy?" said Janette.

"Long story," I replied.

AWOL FROM THE SHIP

Just to recap...there was an ancient man in an ancient suit, a nurse in a brown dress, a fat lady in sandals that were hurting her feet and a spruced-up Spanish dancer - all standing on the quayside with no provisions and no luggage while the ship they were meant to be on sailed away.

"Well, this is turning into quite an adventure, isn't it?" said Frank with a smile.

There was no doubting that.

"The good news is that we have another day in Sicily to find the Corleone family," I said. "I suppose that counts as good news, doesn't it?"

"Yes," said Janette. "Let's look on the bright side; that's very good news, isn't it, Frank?"

I glanced down at our elderly friend; he looked exhausted.

"Let's find a hotel as near as possible to where we were earlier," said Juan Pedro. "You Google the area, Mary, and see whether you can find a hotel anywhere, and I'll ring some of the guys on the ship and see what's the best thing for us to do now. The ship goes to Naples next. Maybe we should spend the morning tracking Irene's family, then head to Naples and get on the ship when it docks there?"

"Yes, good plan," I said, feeling a little more relaxed now that there was a plan of some kind, even if it was a plan that involved a trek across Italy with a wheelchair-bound nonagenarian.

Juan Pedro picked up his phone to call people on the ship while I found a couple of hotels near the cafe, and left messages on answer phones.

"We are okay," said Juan Pedro with a huge sigh. "They said getting to Naples tomorrow would be quite simple, and we can jump on the ship there. It leaves at 6 pm again, though, so we must be there this time."

"Great," I said, just as my phone rang. "Oh good, this will be the hotel now."

"Hello, Mary speaking."

"Hello," came a rather gruff voice. "Is Dalmeny here. You put note about buying the cafe under my door. You said someone from the cafe have senting you?"

"Oh yes! Thank you so much for calling back. We want to come and talk to you about it."

"Okay, come now," he said. "I am in house."

"Great. We're on our way."

I hung up, explaining to the group what we would do, and calling for a taxi once more. If we could sort this out tonight, it would make getting to Naples tomorrow much easier. Things were starting to look good. This time the taxi came very quickly, and we clambered on board. Once we were in it, my phone rang. It was Andreas from the cafe returning my call.

"Don't worry, everything's fine," I told him. "We don't need a lift anymore, and things look really good. I'll let you know how it all goes."

We reached the house, and I was awash with positive feelings. The goats still grazed outside the neighbouring houses, as Dalmeny stood in the doorway of his superior abode. He was a large, heavily built, bearded man with hands the size of laptop computers and as hairy as a bear's. He invited us in, and I explained what we were trying to do and showed him the map – both the one from 1940 and the current one. He put on his glasses and looked carefully from one map to the next and agreed that it looked as if the cafe was currently where the old cottage used to be.

Great, I thought. He agrees with us, he's going to help us.

"I can't help you," he said.

Brilliant.

"Why not?" asked Juan.

"I know not anything for cafe," he said.

"Is there anyone who might know?" I tried. "We're really keen to get someone to help us. I'm trying to track down the Corleone family – Alberto Corleone?"

"I don't know them. Maybe my mother know. Come back tomorrow," he said.

"What time will she be here?"

"Maybe come back middle of day," he said.

"Okay. We have to be in Naples by 5pm though," I said. "Is there any chance we can come earlier perhaps?"

"No, she not earlier," he said.

"Is there any way we can call your mum?"

"Tomorrow," he said. "My English not good. My wife here tomorrow. Her English good. My mother will know, my wife will help," he said

"OK. And when will your wife be here?" I asked.

"Middle of day with mother."

It seemed fairly conclusive that we couldn't get any more information out of them until midday, so we wended our weary way out of the house, past the goats and onto the main road. Luckily, he was able to point us in the direction of a local bed-and-breakfast. By the time we arrived, Frank was exhausted, so he and Janette went up to their rooms. Juan and I were also exhausted but decided it would be much more sensible to sit up drinking beer all night instead of going to bed. So, we sat outside in the warm evening air, drank beer, ate bread-sticks, and tried to make sense of the whole thing.

"We have to find this cottage, Juan," I said. "You saw Frank's face today - he looked destroyed. We have to find it. How has no one heard of this family? I thought it was a tight-knit community?"

"They might have moved out years ago, though. They could have moved 50 years ago for all we know."

"Yes, I guess," I said, looking at Juan. He didn't look quite himself. "Are you worried about what the captain will say when we get back to the boat tomorrow?"

"I will be shot," said Juan dramatically. "You wait and see...they will shoot me like a dog because I missed the ship."

He grimaced as he wiped bread crumbs off his shiny, rainbow-coloured trousers and shook his head with an artistic flourish. "I have to be there tomorrow. I am leading the cha-cha-cha in the evening. Who will do it if I'm not there? I can't see Captain Homarus doing it. Can you?"

"You won't miss the boat tomorrow...everything will be OK."

THE LONG-AWAITED MEETING

The next morning I awoke, bursting with energy, and walked down to breakfast, utterly determined that we would find Irene's relatives if it were the last thing we did. I arrived in the breakfast room first and was instantly dismayed by the food on offer. I'd been so spoilt on the ship with luxurious buffets every day that seeing a plate of pastries and rather mouldy-looking cheese made me feel quite unwell.

Still, I had to keep my strength up, so I managed to force three croissants down me, along with coffee so strong it made me shoot up out of my seat. By the time the others arrived, I had discovered they had pain au chocolate around the other side and was burrowing my way through those.

We headed off at 11.30 a.m. to go back over to the house. I'd called a cab, and we assembled, ready to climb in and begin our day's searching.

"This is it," I said to Frank. "I'm confident we'll find Irene's relatives today."

Despite a long night's sleep, he still looked exhausted. I noticed he hadn't eaten anything at breakfast. I knew we could do with getting him back onto the ship as soon as possible.

We were back at the big house by 11.50 pm and were let into a much noisier home than the one we'd visited the day before. Children played on the lawn outside, and a baby cried upstairs.

"My wife soon back," we were told, and we set ourselves down in the kitchen while our host went to see the baby.

By 12.30 p.m., we were becoming a little worried.

"My wife is come 2 p.m.," he said.

"Oh no," I said, trying not to catch Juan's eyes. I'd promised him we'd be back on the boat by 5 p.m., but that would be impossible the way things were going. In the end, we heard a key in the front door at 2:30 p.m., and a small, slim woman with long, wavy brown hair walked in. She didn't look unlike the picture that Frank had shown us of Irene, and for one almighty moment, I thought that she might be related, and we might sew up this whole mystery once and for all. It turned out that she wasn't in any way related to Irene, and it was pure coincidence that she vaguely looked like her.

"Clutching at straws, darling," was how Juan described it.

She was helpful, though, and had all the paperwork, which showed that she bought the cottage from Alberto.

"Irene's brother," said Janette, breathlessly, leaning down to explain to Frank.

"I remember that he was selling it because his parents

had died, and he was living in his wife's parents' old house or something like that," she said.

"Have you got any details about where the man you bought it from was living?" I asked. Holding my breath for the answer.

"Yes – it's here," she said. I'll write it down for you."

In a beautiful italic script, she wrote down an address. It was about half an hour away.

"If we go there, we will miss the flight," I said, and I heard Juan emit a small shriek, like the sort of noise you hear when air is escaping from a tightly pulled balloon. I decided to ignore it and look at Janette.

"Let's stay in Sicily for another night, then go straight to La Spezia tomorrow, missing out Naples completely," I said.

"OK," said Janette. "If that's OK with you two?"

"Oh, fine, no problem at all with me," said Juan. "Don't worry about the cha-cha-cha or the ballet spectacular."

I elbowed him in the ribs to silence him.

"Let's book back into the bed and breakfast," said Janette.

"Sure," I responded. "We'll go back there so Frank can have a lie-down, and I'll ring the phone number on the sheet, and we'll head off to see them later this afternoon."

It seemed that finally, finally, we were getting closer to Irene's family.

We said our goodbyes and thanked them very much for their help. When I looked down at Frank, he looked nervous.

"Everything OK?" I asked.

"Everything's fine, dear," he said. "I'll be glad when this

is all done, though. It's been a long time since I saw her family. A very long time."

As we headed out into the bright sunshine, I realised what a difficult thing this must be. I'd appreciated how important it was but didn't realise how difficult. Frank was about to confront issues that had lain dormant for decades. I smiled at him and called the number on the sheet, bracing myself for the sound of Alberto's voice...Irene's brother...the man they'd had to flee Italy to avoid.

Rather anti-climatically, it went straight to answer-phone. I couldn't leave a message because I had no idea how to begin describing what was happening, and I had no idea whether he spoke any English at all.

"I'll just keep trying," I explained to Frank. "Don't worry - we'll get hold of them and we'll go and see them."

Then I turned to my panicking dancer friend, "Juan - do you want to ring the guys on the boat and explain that we'll be there tomorrow evening instead?"

"Sure," he said with a shrug. "That'll be a nice, easy call to make."

Juan walked off, pouting and sulking, and the rest of us waited for a taxi on the edge of the road. I wish I'd known about all this before I left England. It would have been so much easier to get on the main computer at home and start searching than sitting on roadsides in Sicily trying to get a signal in the blasting midday sun while waiting for taxis.

It would also, with hindsight, have been much easier to have hired a car.

In the end, it was the next day before I got an answer

on the phone. I'd paced around all evening, reassuring Juan that he wouldn't lose his job and reassuring Janette that we would find the relatives and Frank would be able to hand over the letters. I'd been updating the blog with all the ins and outs of our battle to find the cottage, and Dawn - who never issues an iota of praise to anyone, came back to say how much she loved the updates. It was a bright moment in quite a tense few days.

When I finally got an answer on the phone the next morning, I was relieved that it was a young-sounding man who spoke English. I explained, as best I could, who we were and what we wanted, and he replied that he had heard of Irene and he knew the story of her running away with Frank. He said his name was Louis, and he was Alberto's grandson. I smiled from ear to ear. We'd found them.

"I will get my mother," he said.

A lady called Gisella came to the phone and said she was Alberto's daughter.

"Irene was my aunt," she said. "She wrote to us all the time; we heard from her on birthdays and at Christmas, but we never saw her. I never, ever met her. While my grandparents were alive, she visited them but that was it. It would be lovely to meet Frank...she wrote about him so lovingly in her letters."

"One final question," I said. "Is Alberto still alive?"

"Yes," she said. "He is in a nursing home. I will take you to see him."

"Oh, my Goodness," said Frank when I told him. "Oh, my goodness. We've done it. We've found him. I'll get to talk to Alberto after all these years."

Visiting time at the nursing home was in the mornings. I tried explaining that we'd come so far to see him, but it was no good. We would have to stay another night in Sicily, miss out on the Toulon stage of the trip and rejoin the cruise in Barcelona. It was the only way. I looked over at Juan.

"That's the Viennese Waltz gone then," he said. "And someone else will have to judge the grannies' tap dance competition. And I'll need to buy clothes. It's getting ridiculous."

"Yes, we can go shopping this afternoon, buy some new clothes, then go and visit Alberto tomorrow morning before heading for Barcelona. You'll need to let them know on the ship, though."

Juan looked ashen at the thought. "They'll tie me up and beat me til I'm dead," he said. "Or they'll roast me alive and put me on the buffet table."

"No, they won't," I said. "They'll be mildly pissed off, then get over it."

Juan made the call.

"No," he assured them, for the third day in succession. "We will not miss the boat in Barcelona. I promise you." Then he put the phone down and smiled at me. "He said your blog's very good. They are keeping up with our progress through that. I must take a look at it when we get back on board."

"Oh good," I said, remembering that I'd described Juan's clothing in great detail and diarised all his pouting, huffs and stomps off to the corner when he didn't get his own way. To be fair, though, I had also said how kind, warm and generous he was and what a credit to the cruise company. Hopefully, he'd focus on those comments and not dwell on my descriptions of his vile trousers and ridiculous green handbag.

The next morning, we all assembled dressed in '*I am love Sicily*' t-shirts for breakfast. There were no clothes shops nearby, so we were forced to buy the only T-shirts the gift shop had. Mine was turquoise, Frank's was white, Janette's was navy, and Juan's was yellow. We looked like Sicily's entry for the Eurovision Song Contest when we walked next to one another.

"It would be bad enough if they said, 'I love Sicily'," said Janette. "But to say 'I am love Sicily' is just ridiculous."

"Oh God," cried Juan. "I hadn't noticed that."

We headed for Frank's daughter and grandchildren's house, and Gisella took us straight to the nursing home. She explained that she and her children had moved into her mum and dad's house with them. "We needed to look after Dad," she explained. "He fell apart a bit when mum died."

"I know that feeling," said Frank, and Janette touched his shoulder gently.

The nursing home was cramped and stuffy, and like every other building housing lots of people, it smelled faintly of cabbage.

"Reminds me of school dinners," said Janette as we walked along the corridor towards Alberto's room.

"I couldn't call him to tell him we were coming because he's not really up to using the phone," said Gisella. "I'll go in first and explain."

"Of course," said Frank. "Don't want to terrify him."

We watched as she knocked gently and then went into

his room, talking in Italian. None of us could speak the language, but we heard her say 'Frank' and 'Irene' in the midst of the unfamiliar, foreign words.

"He says to come in," said Gisella.

I glanced at Janette, and she smiled as she pushed the wheelchair through the door. I wasn't sure whether to follow or stay where I was, so I opted for following.

"Shall I come in?" asked Juan.

"Yes," I said. "Let's support Frank."

Inside the room was a desperately thin old man. He was scrawny and pale as he lay back on the sheets.

"You haven't changed a bit," said Frank.

"You neither," said Alberto in a strong Italian accent but very clear English. "Just the same."

Then the two men laughed. Last time they'd seen one another they had been soldiers; strong, young men in their prime.

"I've waited all these years to apologise to you," said Frank. "What I did...it was terrible. Taking your sister away with no explanation."

"It wasn't terrible," said Alberto. "We all understood. You made Irene so happy. How could I be angry?"

"How do you know I made her happy? We all lost contact."

"My mother showed me all the letters that Irene sent. We knew she was well looked after...we knew she was happy with you, so we were happy too."

"Irene wrote to you, too, but never sent the letters. She was so worried that you would come over to England and find us in those early years when we were settling down to our new life together, so she just kept them all. I found them after she died. I'd like you to have them."

Janette opened the bag and handed the piles of letters to Gisella.

"I'll read them to you," Gisella told her father.

"Yes, please," said Alberto, his voice very weak. "How lovely of you to bring them after all these years."

"What happened to Marco?" asked Frank.

"He ran off with another local girl as soon as Irene had gone. He got her pregnant and left the area, leaving her alone to bring up the child. No one heard from Marco again. Irene made the right choice in you, Frank. Marco was no good; I think we all knew that deep down. Thank you for looking after her."

Frank wheeled his chair close to the bed and reached out to take Alberto's hand.

"Thank you," he said. "Thank you for your strength, and thank you for not being bitter. Irene was my life. We were very happy; thank you for understanding."

Alberto smiled and closed his eyes.

"He's tired now," said Gisella. "We should go."

We all left the room except for Frank, who stayed a moment longer before following us.

"Thank you all. Thank you so much," he said, tears streaming down his face. "I wish I'd come here years ago with Irene. I feel like a weight has lifted off me."

FACING SIMON

"We are in Spain. Viva L'Espania," said Juan Pedro, mincing off the plane like he was walking on stage. "Everyone - follow me."

Janette raised her eyebrows and signalled for me to go after him. She would wait until the airline staff brought the wheelchair to them so that Frank could be taken off.

"See you out there," I said.

I caught up with Juan Pedro to see him pouting into the frosted glass windows. "My lips have shrunk," he said.

"No, they haven't," I replied. "Maybe your brain has shrunk, but certainly not your lips."

"Oy!" he said, interlacing his arm through mine like we were two teenagers in an American soap. "I think we should go clothes shopping. Spanish clothes are the best."

"Yeah, no native dress, though. I'm not looking like an idiot again."

"OK, we just go to fashionable modern shops then."

"I'm not going to Zara, though," I said. I knew Zara was Spanish, and I also knew that their clothes were evil.

Even their XL was about three sizes too small for me - it was the most depressing shop on earth.

"No Zara," he reassured. "We will go to a fabulous designer market. You will love it. It's full of gays."

"Oh great," I said. "I'm glad you think I'd love that. What do you think I am - some sort of fag hag?"

"Why yes - but not any sort of fag hag. You are MY fag hag."

"We need to wait for Frank, though. I don't think he'll want to go clothes shopping in a gay designer market after everything he's been through, but I want to ensure he's OK."

We waited for them to appear. "Frank's exhausted, so we're going to head straight back to the ship," said Janette. "We'll catch up with you two later."

"We won't be long; I'm exhausted, too," I said.

"Whatever you do - don't miss the ship again," said Janette, and they headed off.

"I think Frank might be one of the nicest people I've ever met," I said to Juan, and he smiled in reply. "A very, very cool man," he agreed, then we went shopping.

I followed Juan around like a little puppy, weaving in and out of the racks behind him while he picked out clothes he thought would suit me. "Right - boyfriend jeans - you need these," he said. "We also want some skinny jeans, and I think some cropped white jeans would look good."

He called over the assistant, who he knew by name. The two of them talked together, looking over at me, before the lady returned with armfuls of clothes.

"Right, follow me," said Juan, leading me towards the

changing rooms with his clothing haul. "In you go...tell me what you think."

I slipped the boyfriend jeans on first; they were lovely, quite loose-fitting and comfortable, as well as looking good. "You know your stuff, don't you?" I said.

"This is coming as a surprise to you?" he replied sarcastically.

"Try the white jeans on. I know you won't like them because they are tight-fitting, but they are more stylish than those awful ones you had the other day. These ooze style, and you can wear them with either flats or high heels."

With everything I tried on, I emerged from the changing room to comments, prodding and, on a couple of occasions, a round of applause from Juan. We were making quite a commotion in our matching Sicily shirts, but it didn't seem to matter. Juan had this effect on everyone; everywhere he went he was the centre of attention without ever seeming to try.

"Will you try those skinny jeans on with this white shirt?" asked Juan, handing a soft white shirt to me.

I put the white shirt on and tucked it into the jeans, slipping on a pair of high heel boots that Juan had suggested. I looked in the mirror and even though I felt uncomfortable in tight jeans, given the size of my massive bottom, I looked good; much better than I usually do. I walked out of the changing room, spinning around in front of Juan.

"You look very beautiful," said an English voice. I looked up, and right in front of me, staring straight at me, was Simon.

"Hello," I said, flustered. "Let me introduce Juan."

Juan put out his hand and gently shook Simon's.

"I'm going to get jumpers," he said, running off to the other side of the store.

"Sorry we haven't had the chance to talk properly," I said. "I wanted to come and explain...I recovered from the illness. I'm much better now."

"I can see that," said Simon. "I'm so relieved. I always wondered what happened. It's good to see you looking so well."

"Thank you, you too," I said. "We should catch up for a drink later when we're all back on board."

"Sure, I'd like that," he said. "I've been reading your blog. Frank sounds amazing. Will you introduce me to him later?"

"Of course," I said, looking across the rails and seeing Juan ducked down, hiding behind the bikinis.

"Well, see you later then," said Simon, and he wandered off.

"Come back here now," I shouted over to Juan.

"Sorry - but you needed to talk...you can't just ignore him all the time."

"No, I know – well, we've talked now. I told him I recovered from leprosy, and he was very pleased."

"Nutter," said Juan. "Absolute nutter."

By the time we returned to the ship, I had seen nothing of Barcelona bar the biggest indoor market ever - it was astonishing. I had bags full of clothes, plus a pair of earrings that Bet Lynch would have thought too garish and a pair of pink boots that I knew I would never wear, but with Juan there, egging me on, it had seemed such a good idea.

Juan was in his element...trying loads of things on - coming out of the changing rooms, spinning around and pouting like a model. He had about three bags of clothing; all sold to him at bargain prices because of his astonishing ability to haggle.

Much to the captain's delight, we FINALLY boarded the boat, and I headed straight for my cabin - collapsing onto the bed with exhaustion. It had been the most draining experience - physically and emotionally. I could only imagine how Frank must be feeling.

I'd kept the blog up-to-date throughout the trip...I just needed to add a final update to the story then I could have a quick sleep before supper.

I sent several texts to Dawn, showered, and lay back on the bed. I'd taken a few pictures while out and about in Sicily, but fewer than I had on other days because it was such an intensely personal crusade for Frank. I didn't want to be intrusive; Frank didn't deserve that.

I decided to go onto the blog to see how it all looked on there and whether there was any reaction from anyone.

I called up the site and waited for it to load. My God! There were loads of responses. Thousands of people had been following Frank's story. The whole thing was astonishing. Even an MP had commented.

"Our war heroes are very special people indeed. They should be honoured."

There were hundreds of messages underneath the MP's.

"Help them get home!" said one. "Send the army out to help him find the cottage!" said another. "Knight him!"

It had never occurred to me before that the blog might have been a good way of summoning help. When we were wandering helplessly through the Sicilian countryside, it would have been useful to know that thousands of people were following us, willing us on.

I felt too wide awake to sleep, so I decided to get ready for dinner nice and slowly, really taking my time. I slipped on the huge earrings, looked in the mirror, realised I looked completely ridiculous, and took them off again. Then, finally happy that I didn't look insane, I went out to join the others in the bar. I'd been told that we all had to gather for 7 p.m. that evening, and when we met, I would understand why.

I wandered into the bar area, and as I walked in, everyone cheered and clapped. Juan walked in next, and they cheered him as well, and when Frank and Janette came in, there was the loudest cheer I'd ever heard. It was like being at a football stadium or something. People were clapping, banging the tables and cheering like mad.

"Frank, Frank, Frank," they chorused.

Frank and Janette stood in the middle, looking utterly confused.

"What's going on?" Frank asked.

"They are cheering us for our expedition and cheering Frank because he's so incredible," I said.

"How did they know about our expedition? Did you tell them?" asked Janette.

"No, I assumed you had," I said.

"No," said Janette. "It must have been Juan." We both looked at him.

"Not me," he said.

"Ladies and gentlemen, can I have your attention?" said Captain Homarus. "You've all given the most tremendous welcome to Frank, Juan, Janette and Mary, and I'd like to say just a few words. You've managed to miss the ship three times; you've caused mayhem and great worry and panic here..."

Everyone laughed as he spoke.

"But we have been following the blog and are overwhelmed by Frank's story. We've learned all about your incredible war service and how you lost your friends at Longstop Hill; we've heard about your life as a D-Day Dodger and evading capture once, only to be captured again and be forced to spend two years in a horrific Prisoner of War camp. And we've heard about Irene...the amazing woman you loved so much. Irene must have loved you a great deal too, Frank, to have left her family like that. I think we all understand why you wanted to return and find her family, and we're so glad you found them and that all is well. You are an amazing man, and we'd all like to raise our glasses to you."

There were tears in Frank's eyes, and his hand shook as Claire handed him a glass of champagne. He raised the glass slowly and sipped it, putting his hand out to shake Captain Homarus's hand and waving his thanks to the assembled throng.

"Tell me - what is this 'blog'?" he asked.

"Well, Frank, a blog is a story that someone called Dawn has written about you - to tell the world about your incredible life and the incredible journey you have just been on."

"Who is Dawn?" asked Frank.

"I think we all know that Mary is Dawn," said the captain.

"No - Dawn's in the cabin," I started saying.

"No, you're the one who's been writing this wonderful blog, and you're the one who deserves all the praise."

"So, I didn't manage to convince you that Dawn was in the cabin, then?"

"No, of course not. We knew she wasn't on the ship because she never checked in."

"Oh."

"The blog's great. You're talented," said the captain. "Shall I escort you into dinner?"

"Gosh, thank you," I replied.

VALENCIA WITH JUAN

Another day, another amazing city...the last stop on the cruise. It was incredible to think it was all coming to an end. It had been more astonishing than I could ever have imagined.

We pulled into the port of Valencia, and Juan Pedro raised his arms triumphantly. This was his home city, where he had grown up and learned to dance before his burgeoning profession took him to Paris, New York, and the open seas as head dancer on the cruise ship.

He had promised to take me around his city and tell me all about it...unveil all the hidden treasures that normal tourists never saw..., but when I met him on the deck, he seemed unusually pensive and not as exuberant as I was expecting.

"Everything OK?" I asked.

"Well, yes," he said, but it didn't sound as if everything was OK.

"You sure?"

"Everything is fine, but when I come to Valencia, I

always think of Javier. He was my one true love. He was a great dancer. We performed together for Ballet Valencia, and I haven't seen him in years. Last time we met, we made out up against the wall outside the men's toilets. It was wonderful."

"Yeah, it doesn't have quite the romance of Frank's story, does it?"

"It was romantic in its own way," he says, with an extravagant toss of his head. "Maybe I will pop into Ballet Valencia, and if he is there, I will say hello; if not, it was not meant to be."

"Sounds like a good plan. What shall we do first?"

"In Valencia? Why – first we eat."

It turned out that Valencia was the perfect place to have a day to wander around. We spent an hour or so exploring the old town before lunch in Casa Montana - one of the oldest restaurants in Valencia. We ate in the busy front bar, lined with wine barrels, and enjoyed big fried anchovies, brown broad beans stewed with chorizo, roasted piquillo peppers stuffed with béchamel and tuna, and jamón ibérico. I wanted fries as well, but Juan said that was tacky. Coming from a man in tight leather trousers that finished halfway up his calf, I wasn't sure whether that was a compliment or an insult.

After lunch, we went to the cathedral, which was just mind-blowing. We saw San Vincente's withered left arm and two Goya paintings, one of which showed a horrifying exorcism and which Juan seemed particularly fond of. He remembered going there as a schoolboy and being mesmerised by it. The guide told us that the windows were made from fine alabaster because Valencia's light is too dazzling for glass. I know this all sounds a bit 'touristy', but I enjoyed every minute.

We went into Ballet Valencia, but there was no sign of Juan's lover – apparently, he had gone on tour with the company to New York.

"I will see him there," said Juan.

"Yes, I've heard the walls next to the men's toilets are nice there," I said.

We then wandered down to the beach for a little siesta - lying on the sand and looking up at the blue skies.

"I don't want to go home," I said.

"Then don't," he replied. "Get a job on a cruise ship and tour the world with me. We'll have the best time ever."

"No - I need to go back. My boyfriend, my mum, my dad, my job..."

"You hate your job," he said.

"Well, that's true, but I have to do it, or I won't be able to afford to eat...and I do like to eat."

"Ha, you're a nutter. Come and live on a cruise ship, and you'll have all the food you could ever want."

As Juan spoke, I heard my phone ring in my bag.

"Hi, Mary speaking," I said.

"Mary, it's Janette here. Are you on the boat anywhere?"

"No, I'm lying on the beach with a ridiculously skinny gay man called Juan. Why? Everything OK?"

"Not really," she said. "Frank's been taken ill."

CONCERNED ABOUT FRANK

Juan and I leapt to our feet, grabbed our bags and raced like lunatics through the streets of Valencia, back towards the harbour and onto the ship. The boat was eerily quiet while it was in port. Everyone was making the most of the sunshine and the markets in Valencia. Everyone, that is, except for Frank.

I ran onto the deck and bumped into Claire. "Where is Frank?" I asked.

"Come with me," she said, leading me to the medical rooms.

"Just wait here a minute." She disappeared behind a closed door, and I heard voices, and then Janette came out.

"What is the matter? Is he okay?"

"He is fine; I think he's just exhausted," said Janette. "I was worried about him when I called you because he seemed extraordinarily weak. I sometimes forget how old he is; our trip took it out of him."

"Oh goodness, I feel terrible," I said. "We shouldn't

have traipsed around like that; I just wanted him to be able to put his mind at rest and hand over the letters."

"Absolutely," said Janette. "Please don't feel bad; what we did was amazing. I know we've made him a very, very happy man. He's just tired now and needs to rest."

Captain Homarus walked into the room and looked at me quizzically. "Have you come to see a doctor?" he asked.

"No, just checking up on Frank."

"The doctor says he needs to rest; I suggest you give him a few hours and maybe come down later if you want to see him. at that stage, the doctors will know what is going on. "

Janette and I walked out of the small surgery, back to the medical clinic, and out onto the main deck where Juan was waiting for us.

"Why didn't you come in?"

"I hate doctors," he grimaced. "They make me feel ill. Just can't stand them... The smell, the noise, the white coats..."

"There were no white coats, just Captain Homarus, who told us to come back in a couple of hours."

"OK," said Juan. "When you go back, make sure you say hello from me. I promise you - I can't go down there, doctors give me the heebie-jeebies."

"OK, OK," I said. "No need to go down there then."

I turned to Janette: "Do you fancy getting off the boat for a bit?"

I knew that all she'd been doing was looking after Frank; she might fancy an hour in Valencia before going down to see him again.

"I'd love to go out and buy some new clothes. I thought

you looked amazing after Juan took you shopping," she said.

"Whaaaat? Really? Are you taking the mickey?"

"No - really - those bright colours and that incredible jewellery. I'd love to dress like that, but I lack confidence."

"Then I shall take you shopping straight away," said Juan. "You see, Mary - this is a woman who knows good taste when she sees it."

"That would be great," said Janette. "I can't leave the ship though...I have to be here in case anything happens to Frank."

"I'll be here," I said suddenly. "I'll stay on board, and if anything happens, I'll phone you straight away."

"Are you sure?" asked Janette.

"Of course, I'm sure," I said. "Perfectly sure...off you go."

Once they had disappeared, I went back to the medical centre and made sure the doctor had my number in case anything happened; then I strode out onto the deck to sit in the sunshine for a few hours and enjoy a gin and tonic.

HOME SWEET HOME

I popped back down to the medical centre later in the afternoon, but there was no news; Frank was stable and sleeping soundly. He wasn't in any grave danger, but he was weak, and the doctor planned to get him straight to Southampton Hospital when we arrived back.

I went back up to my cabin, texted Janette to update her and did some updates to the blog; then I dressed in a simple black evening dress and went and sat in the bar before dinner, hoping to see Juan and Janette.

Now, when I say 'hoping to see' - it turned out that it was impossible not to see Janette. She walked into the room with all the style and glamour of Elizabeth Taylor in Cleopatra...and almost as much eyeliner.

She'd been transformed. Sure, she was completely over the top because Juan was styling her, but she looked magnificent. I felt dowdy by comparison and vowed to sneak back to the cabin and put more makeup on before dinner.

"You look sensational," I told her, hugging her.

"Thank you," she said, she was beaming. "I love this outfit...I'm chuffed. Isn't Juan amazing?"

"Don't talk about him like that," I said. "He'll get an even bigger head - we need to be bringing him down, not talking him up."

Dinner was called and the three of us sat together, hoping to sit alone and chat about Frank and everything we'd been through, but it was impossible. The entire ship was aware of Frank's illness. Concern and kindness had driven them to join us to enquire about him.

Our dinner was punctuated by the arrival of guests offering to help in any way they could and offering their good wishes.

Arriving back in Southampton was a bitter-sweet moment. I was looking forward to seeing Ted again, and I was looking forward to seeing my friends and telling them all about my adventure, but I would miss these guys. It was strange to think how close we'd all become. I knew we'd be friends forever.

Frank was taken off the ship and put into an ambulance, moaning that he was absolutely fine, and this was just a fuss about nothing, and how he fought in the war and didn't need all this namby-pambying.

"Bye lovely," I said, hugging Janette and giving Juan a huge squeeze. "Let's stay in touch - OK?"

"Definitely," they agreed, and I strode back through the car park to where I could see Ted: lovely, kind Ted, waiting patiently.

"Hello there stranger," I said, giving him a big kiss, and loving the way he lifted me up into the air. "How are you?"

"I'm much happier now you're back," he said. "Come on; let's go home...I want to hear all about it. By the way - do you know that t-shirt makes no grammatical sense at all?"

"Yes, I know," I said. "But I love it – it reminds me of the most amazing time ever. Come on, I'll tell you all about it."

It was three days later when the call came through. I was back at work, stacking bags of compost in the outdoor plant section when my phone rang.

"Frank has died," said Janette, her voice croaky with pain and choking back tears. "He passed away peacefully in his sleep."

It was horrible news, but at least Frank had died knowing that he'd made peace with the world, and now he was reunited with Irene. I hope he died knowing how much he affected my life and how much it meant for me to me to be with him on his Sicilian adventure.

Of course, I went to the funeral and met his friends, who had all heard about our exploits in Sicily. Back at Frank's house, after the funeral, we raised our glasses and toasted the lovely man with a rendition of the song he'd sung to us on that crazy afternoon in Sicily:

"We landed at Salerno, holiday with pay,
Jerry got the band out to help us on our way.
We all sang songs; the beer was free.
We danced all the way through Italy.
We were the D-Day Dodgers, the men who dodged D-Day."

. . .

RIP Frank

I WANT TO BE A YOGA LADY

"Oh Charlie, I don't know what to do," I said. "My life's falling apart."

I was standing in my friend's doorway a few weeks after returning from the cruise, clutching a bottle of wine and wearing a look of dismay and disbelief.

"Oh blimey, what's happened?" she asked, ushering me inside. "Nice tan, by the way."

"That's kind of the problem," I attempted to explain.

"What? The tan is the problem? Doesn't look like much of a problem to me. Wine?"

"Yes, please." I followed Charlie through to the kitchen while I explained that I had a lovely tan because of the cruise, and I was missing everyone from the boat, especially Frank.

"Why did he have to die?" I asked plaintively.

"Because he was very old?" said Charlie.

"I know, but he was incredible. The whole cruise was amazing. Everything about it was fab except that I put on so much weight. Those buffets are incredible."

"I've heard about the buffets," said Charlie.

"There's food everywhere on the boat. I put on 10lbs. Ten bloody pounds."

I usually laughed and joked to hide my embarrassment, but I was genuinely concerned about this recent development.

I had been doing so well with my weight loss until the cruise. When I went to Fat Club, I lost a stone and a half at the beginning of the year. I felt amazing. But then I started to get a bit bored of it all and found I was eating more, which led to me not caring as much, and the weight piled on. Now, I was well over the 15-stone mark and felt devastated.

Charlie sighed and shook her head. "Well, you'll have to cut back, won't you," she said.

"Cutting back is for someone who's a couple of pounds over fighting weight, not for someone who weighs more than a mini metro," I said.

"You don't weigh more than a car," she replied. "Cars are really heavy."

"**I'M** really heavy," I responded.

"You need to do some exercise," she said. "Come and join me on my training runs."

"Mate, you're training for a half marathon. I can't walk across the room without panting like a chain-smoking pensioner. Running with you will end up with me in an ambulance on the way to a lung transplant."

"You should try one of the classes at my gym; you might like those...there are loads and loads of them," said Charlie.

"Like what?"

"Well – there is Zumba?" she suggested.

"What on earth is that? Zumba sounds like the name of the leader of a Nigerian tribe, not an exercise class."

"It's a dance class. Look..." she reached for her laptop and called up 'Zumba'. Loud music burst through her computer as energised, young, fit women in various shades of brightly coloured Lycra danced, pranced and jumped around on the screen while a wildly enthusiastic instructor shouted at them. They just kept moving, dancing and spinning, hollering and shrieking. They seemed much slimmer and fitter than I was.

"I would rather sit there with a Stanley knife cutting the fat off my body," I said to Charlie. "Is this an American thing...this Zumba business? I can't imagine anyone with British blood doing it."

"It's great fun; the classes are always packed out," said Charlie. "You should try them. They might look scary on the screen, but when you're there, and the loud music plays, you'll find you enjoy it and get fit without realising you're exercising."

"We both know that is a complete lie. Are there any other exercise classes?"

"Yes, there are the traditional classes like aerobics and step."

"No," I said before she had barely finished the sentence. "I tried those when I was 5 stone lighter and hated them. Step is just ridiculous. Thirty fully grown women stepping on and off a bit of plastic that's been put in front of them to trip them up. No thank you. Anything else?"

"Maybe aquarobics will be for you?" said Charlie. "It's

a gentler exercise. You don't know how hard you're working at the time because the water supports you, but you feel it the next day. Also, you are in the water, so you won't get injured. It might be a nice introduction to getting back into exercise."

That did, indeed, sound like a rather nice way to lose weight.

"Call it up," I said to Charlie, and she keyed aquarobics into Google and called up a video of a class.

Now, maybe I was overly fussy, but the image that greeted me, of ageing ladies in swim caps waving their arms in the air while a tinny version of Madonna's *Into the Groove* screeched in the background, didn't seem like a wholly worthwhile use of anyone's time.

"Is this a class for old people?" I asked.

"Well, it's a gentle exercise class, as I said, so obviously, it's bound to attract older people, but you get young people doing it too, and it is a tough workout. "

I looked again at the women in their swim hats...wrinkly faces looking out from beneath flowery plastic headgear. I didn't think it was for me.

"Anything else?" I ventured, realising that Charlie was going to get fed up very soon.

"I don't know...there are spin classes, but they are hard-core; you sit on a bike for an hour cycling furiously, sweat flying everywhere; I don't think you'd like them."

"Nope, that doesn't sound like my sort of thing."

"What do you think is your sort of thing?" Charlie asked.

"Lying on my back and pointing my toes occasional-ly?" I suggested.

"I know!" shrieked Charlie all of a sudden. "I know what you should do to get yourself back into exercising slowly."

"And this involves lying on your back, pointing your toes occasionally?" I said.

"Pretty much," said Charlie, tapping away into Google.

Onto the screen sprang a lovely image of lots of people lying down while the instructor told them to breathe in deeply and then breathe out again... Breathe in, and breathe out again. I could do that!

"This looks perfect," I said. "What the hell is it?"

"Why," said Charlie with a flourish. "This, my dear friend, is yoga."

On the screen, they continued to lie there while the instructor issued gentle commands about breathing and stretching. All the women looked slim, toned, happy, and deeply relaxed while the lovely instructor talked kindly to them.

"Where do I sign up?" I asked Charlie. "I want to be a yoga lady."

TACKLING THE TREE POSE

At work the next day, I couldn't stop thinking about our conversation. The more I thought about yoga, the more it seemed like it would be the answer to all my woes. One session of lying on the floor in attractive yoga pants and a funky t-shirt would act as a panacea - somehow transforming me...through osmosis or something...into a beautiful, slim and lovely woman who was relaxed, flexible and serene at all times.

The more we'd sat there last night, watching videos while eating crisps and drinking wine, the more converted I'd become to life as a yogi. It seemed like the key to body transformation. A bit of chanting, some toe touching, and a new leotard and I, too, would look like those wondrous women in the videos. I could hardly contain my new-found enthusiasm for the world. The only mystery was why on earth I hadn't done this years ago.

I had memorised some of the poses they'd done in the class on YouTube, and as I watered the geraniums in the garden centre (I work here; I'm not just randomly going around garden centres watering the plants or anything), I tried to think of the poses I'd seen. There was the downward dog which was pretty much the position I ended up in when I tried to pick something up off the floor when I was drunk. It's one thing bending over when you're drunk and slim, quite another thing bending over when you're drunk and 15 stone.

The women in the video had done things like headstands and bridges, which I knew would be entirely beyond me. It would take a crane to get me up there and 20 highly qualified medical professionals to get me safely down afterwards.

Then there were positions that I probably couldn't do at the moment but with a little instruction and some concerted effort, I thought I'd probably be able to do at some stage. One of those was the tree pose. For all you yoga virgins out there, this is when you stand on one leg and put the sole of your other foot on the inside thigh of the leg you are standing on. You start by putting the foot on the inside of your calf, then the knee, then the inner thigh as you progress, then - ta da! - you have your foot flat on the inside of your thigh, right at the top, and you are doing a tree pose.

I looked up...no one was around, so I put down the watering can and decided to give tree pose a go. I balanced on one foot...not all that simple when you're a larger lady, and attempted to place a foot onto my inner calf. Gosh, much harder than it looked.

I moved nearer to the wall so I could reach out and hold on if I felt myself falling. I tried again. I stood up straight and tried to ground myself, then I slowly lifted my right leg, and attempted to put my foot on the inside of my calf. It was hopeless. I felt myself fall as soon as I took one foot off the ground. How could I be so unbalanced?

Right, one more try...I lifted my leg slowly and, trying to ignore the wobbling, put the sole of my shoe onto the inside of my calf. I lasted about a second before I felt myself start to fall. I moved my arms around to try and balance myself. Still, it was no good. I pitched to the side and reached up quickly, intending to lean on the wall, but I was falling faster than I realised, so I made a grab for the nearest thing - a luscious, flower-filled hanging basket that Maureen had spent all morning designing and planting.

I went flying to the ground, one arm windmilling furiously, the other one still clinging to the basket. I hit the ground first and the basket came crashing down on top of me - mud and pansies everywhere and me in the middle, lying on my back.

I wiped the dirt out of my eyes and looked up...there was Keith, my boss, along with Sandra from indoor plants and Jerry from the carpentry section. They were all struggling not to laugh.

"Are you OK?" asked Keith, while the other two bit their lips and choked back their amusement at my plight.

"Yes, I'm fine," I said. "Absolutely fine. I just tripped on some dirt. People need to make sure they clean up after themselves. Someone could really hurt themselves when there's dirt lying around." I wiped the mud off my face and lifted the lovely little flowers off my uniform.

"What were you doing?" asked Jess.

"Just watering the plants," I said.

"We were watching you on the CCTV cameras in our break," said Jerry. "Were you trying to be a flamingo or some- thing? You kept standing on one leg, it was very weird."

"If you must know, I was practising yoga," I said, rolling over and clambering onto my feet. "That move I was doing was called the tree pose."

"Oh," they said, simultaneously. And Keith added: "Well, as long as you're OK. We need to get on, Jerry."

The two of them wandered off, laughing, and leaving me with Jess.

"Do you do much yoga?" she asked.

"I do," I replied. "And I'm going to be doing much more in the future. Though not at work, obviously."

"No, best not destroy any more hanging baskets," said Jess, crouching down to collect the flowers that were strewn all around. "My friend is brilliant at yoga. She's really strong and flexible and says 'Namaste' all the time."

"Yes, like me," I said, nodding as I spoke.

"I think it's amazing that you do yoga. Good for you. Shall I stay and help you clear all this up?" she asked.

"No, it's fine. I can do it. Thanks Jess. And - Namaste."

"Namaste to you too," she replied.

ALL BOOKED UP

Charlie rang at lunchtime. "Slight problem," she said.

"Namaste," I replied.

"What? Anyway, I've been looking at yoga classes at my gym, and you have to do the beginners' course first before you're allowed to go to the normal, timetabled classes."

"Oh, OK, I'll do that then," I replied. "To be honest, a beginners' course wouldn't be a bad idea, I have a feeling it's harder than it looks." I omitted to tell her that my initial experiences with tree pose had left me covered in mud and pansies and the laughingstock of the shop. I still had soil down the front of my uniform, but she didn't need to know about that.

"Yes - I agree. The trouble is - the next course is in January, and it's already fully booked and with a six-person waiting list. The course after that is in April. Shall I book us onto the April one?"

"No," I yelled. "I don't want to wait til then. It's October now. I plan to be eight stone for Christmas. Is there anything else we can do? I want to learn how to do the tree pose."

"The tree pose? Really? OK, well, there are a few options...we could go to a different gym, join up, and see whether we could do a yoga course there, but all the other gyms in the area are expensive."

"Yeah, I'm not all that fond of doing anything really expensive, and you want to stay at Palisades while you're doing your marathon training, don't you?"

"Yes, ideally," replied Charlie. "There is something else we could do though. We could go on a yoga retreat where they teach you all the basics, then when we come back, we could go along to lessons and tell them we've done a beginners' course, so they'd let us straight on. That would be much quicker."

"That sounds good," I said. "Kind of yoga cramming for the weekend."

"Yeah, I think so," said Charlie. "There's a course this weekend at a place called Vishraam House in the New Forest. Two nights stay...beginners' yoga."

"Let's do it," I said boldly. "Come on, let's get onto this course and into Lycra."

"Maybe I should come around to yours tonight and we'll look through it properly, then book it if you think you fancy it. You know - if you think you're up to it."

"Up to it? I think yoga is going to be the making of me," I said. "Just you wait."

Charlie came around at 7 pm that evening, and I had to unravel myself before answering the door. I was trying the tree pose again, but this time I was using a pair of tights to lift my foot into place while leaning against the wall. Even with the help of the prop it was proving quite a task. My hands were sore from pulling on the tights and my foot wouldn't go into place.

"Come in," I said, still with tights in hand.

Charlie gave me a book about yoga. "For you," she said. "Keep it on your bedside table."

She glanced at the underwear in my hand, but I couldn't summon the words to explain, so I sat her down and began finding out about yoga weekends.

"Show me the retreats then," I said, and I thought how grown-up Charlie and I seemed looking at the images of health, fitness and good living on the screen. All the holidays we'd ever been on before had resulted in hospital visits, altercations with the police, and huge amounts of drinking. This time it would be altogether different.

"Here we are," she said. "Look - there are various different types of courses...you can specialise in different yogas...there's Ashtanga - isn't that the one that Madonna does? And I think Hatha yoga is the Megan Markle one. I don't know which one is better? And what's this Bikram Yoga? Hang on, isn't that the one that Pippa Middleton does?"

"I don't know," I said as I looked down the list...there were so many. "Aerial yoga? What the hell is that?" I asked. Charlie shrugged. We didn't really know what we were doing at all.

"Look up aerial yoga, I have to know," I commanded. For some reason, when it came to any sort of research or planning, it was always Charlie sitting in front of the screen, and me barking orders.

"Oh blimey. Very 50 shades of grey," she said, turning the screen round so I could see. There were lots of people hanging from the ceiling by ropes, with little hammocks at the bottom. They were pulling themselves up the ropes and rolling out of the hammocks. It looked fraught with danger. If the thing took my weight in the first place it was sure to be impossible for me to get in and out of it.

"Na," I said, and she nodded in agreement.

"Oh, how about one of these?" she said. She had pulled up a list of general yoga courses where you did all the different yogas on one weekend instead of having to specialise...they came in beginners, intermediate and advanced.

"Here we go," said Charlie. "A basic introduction to all the different types of yoga as well as meditation, mindfulness and clean living."

"Sounds like us," I said. "Oh, but how about this one?"

Below it were the more advanced courses including one called 'guru-led advanced course.'

"Stick it in the basket. I want a guru," I said, clicking on it and adding it into out virtual shopping bag.

"Oy, stop it. I don't think either of us is ready for an advanced course," said Charlie.

"OK - gurus next time," I conceded, and we booked ourselves onto a beginners' course for the weekend by emailing a woman called Venetta.

"I'm quite excited," I said. "It's run by someone whose name sounds a little bit like an ice-cream...that has to be a good thing, surely."

"Definitely," she agreed, with a small squeal. "This could be really good fun. I hope I don't make a fool of myself."

"Oh come now, Charlie," I replied. "We both know which one of us is more likely to make a fool of herself."

THE LAST SUPPER

In the lead-up to the course, I thought it would be wise to try and start living the life that I would be required to live on the retreat. I couldn't go from full-blown Chinese takeaways and large glasses of sauvignon to slices of air-dried mango, chakras and finding my inner goddess. I needed to ease myself into the new lifestyle gently, so I vowed to try and eat as healthily as possible in the few days before we left.

I started making changes on Thursday morning, the day before departure. I had a mug of hot water with a squeeze of lemon in it. It was supposed to curb my appetite and remove the yearning for a fried breakfast and loads of mid-morning biscuits. It tasted so awful that I could barely drink the stuff. I only had a couple of sips and knew that if I were to have any chance of finishing it, I'd have to add sugar, which would completely spoil the whole point of doing it in the first place.

Instead, I sipped green tea and ate slices of apple. Christ, it was dull. I phoned Charlie.

"This is shit, isn't it?" I said, looking at the limp pieces of peeled apple lying pathetically on the plate in front of me.

"Yep," she said. "But just imagine - we'll get used to healthy eating and return completely transformed. Just try to keep going...it'll do you the world of good. I'm about to have some grapefruit."

"Ahhh..." I said. "That's the most evil of all the fruits. To be honest, I don't know how it has the audacity to call itself a fruit. It's awful stuff."

The whole day was ruined by the thought lingering in my head that I wasn't allowed to have anything nice to eat and that I would be hungry all the time. My breaks weren't any fun, and lunchtime was pointless. Chicken salad? I mean - what's the point? Where's the warmth, happiness or joy derived from chewy poached chicken and a collection of garden leaves?

I got home that evening and slumped on the sofa, feeling out of sorts and slightly angry with the world. Ted, my boyfriend, was due to be coming around for the evening because I wouldn't see him for the next few days, but I couldn't face company, I felt all empty inside. I'm not sure whether anyone who doesn't overeat could ever understand this, but I felt horrible without being able to eat food that filled me up and made me feel all warm and lovely inside. All irritable and like there was no point to anything. The whole world felt prickly. I was unbalanced and cross. I told Ted I had a headache and sat on the sofa to spend the evening feeling sorry for myself.

I know this sounds pathetic, but it was so horrible being hungry. I felt so deprived, which led to loneliness and sadness. The lack of food seemed to signal a lack of comfort and warmth. I started to think that my life was not worth living...in my mind I began to question my job, my boyfriend, my friends and my family.

Eating isn't just about putting food inside me, it's about nurturing, warming and comforting myself and stopping myself from feeling sad and lonely. And - I know what you're thinking - I should address the things that were making me feel sad and lonely rather than just eating myself into an emotional slumber, but doing that would take months of self-analysis and confrontation with my darkest fears. Whereas a cheeky chicken and black bean sauce would take half an hour to arrive, and I'd feel great. That's why - at the end of the day - whenever I felt low, I always ate.

And it was very easy for me to justify overeating to myself. When I couldn't think of anything else but being full of lovely, tasty food, I could easily convince myself that eating obscene amounts was actually the best thing I could possibly do.

On that warm evening, I picked up the takeaway leaflet and told myself that this was the last chance I had to eat a big meal, and it would be a good thing if I ate well tonight because it would make me more committed, and give me the strength to throw myself into the weekend ahead.

So, I ordered the food and felt almost drunk and helpless with anticipation while I waited for it to arrive. The ring of the bell sent electric pulses of joy through me, and I practically danced to the door to collect the food. I had chicken and black bean sauce with egg fried rice, and I ate all the free prawn crackers that came with it. I loved eating when there was a lot of food. When I started picking at the food and could see there was absolutely loads more to eat, it gave me a real thrill.

The food was not quite the same without a couple of glasses of wine, of course, so I did that too. I'm like an animal when I eat. It's always better to be alone when I get the real hungers. I poured myself another large glass of wine, feeling drunk on food and alcohol and completely relaxed like I'd just had that drug you have before an anaesthetic...the one that knocks you out a bit and makes you feel drowsy without rendering you completely unconscious.

There were crumbs all over the place, and I'd managed to get dribbles of black bean sauce on my sweatshirt, but that didn't matter; they could be cleaned. All that mattered was that I felt relaxed and happy, and lovely. I just wanted to lay there and bask in the loveliness for a while. I knew I'd feel rotten later...really low, disappointed in myself, and frustrated at my lack of willpower, but I'd deal with those feelings when they arose. For now, it was all about the feelings of light-headedness, satisfaction and warmth. Mmmm...

When I woke the next morning, the memory of what I'd done hit me in an instant. Shit, I'd had a huge takeaway and a bottle of wine the night before. Damn. I'd bought lemons and apples and all sorts of healthy food so that I wouldn't be tempted over to the dark side, then I'd gone and bloody ordered a takeaway.

I'd just have to try and be good this weekend to make

up for it. I sat up in bed and saw the yoga book perched on my bedside cabinet, waiting to be read.

I turned to the section by a woman called Rachel Brathen. In it, the woman was describing all sorts of thoroughly awful things that had happened to her when she was younger. She wrote about how she was drinking too much and being sick and how her life was totally out of control...then she found yoga, and everything came together for her. She felt peace at last. A lovely, warm feeling ran through me as I read the words and absorbed her philosophy.

"There is no need to change your habits to make space for a yoga practice," she wrote. "Start practising yoga from where you are today, and let the practice change you. The more often you come to the mat, on your own or in a class, the easier it will be to make healthy decisions throughout the rest of your day. When you're listening more to your body, you'll find that it's not as difficult to eat well. With awareness of your body, you'll find it easier to stay away from sugar or alcohol or whatever it is that you're looking to remove from your diet. Or perhaps you will realise that the foods you're eating are just fine, nothing to obsess over at all! The bottom line is that you will be more conscious about how your body feels and how sensitive it is to what you put in it, maybe that the second helping of food didn't make you feel better after all.

"When we live more in the body and less in the mind, those choices that were so overwhelming before become easier to make. I know that when I really listen to my body, it very rarely wants two huge helpings of food. If I reach for more, it's probably because I'm busy talking and socialising or I'm feeling emotional. If I stay mindful, I'll be able to tell when I'm full. Much of what we eat in a day is simply a result of boredom. I'm not promising you'll stop wanting dessert or wine or all the good things that come with life just because you start practising yoga. You'll simply be more receptive to what your body wants and needs. And this is the very first step to healthy you."

I wished I hadn't eaten all that food last night. I wished I could think of other ways to cope when I was overcome by this emotional hunger that seemed to suck me into it, so that I had no control over myself. Sometimes the feeling was so overpowering that I felt I had no choice but to eat. Perhaps yoga could help me find a balance. Find peace? It was certainly worth a try.

A MUD BATH IN THE CHICKEN COOP

"I can't quite believe we're doing this, can you?" Charlie said, as I slid into the car next to her and made a token effort to put the seat belt on, knowing there was no way on earth it would go around me. I squeezed, pulled, and then dropped it, letting it fall by my side. Luckily, her's wasn't a bleeping seat belt. Those cars that start beeping at you when you can't do the seat belt up are a pain for anyone over about a size 18. The damn car can bleep as much as it wants, and the seat belt won't go around me, however much noise it makes.

"I think this weekend might be good for us," I said. Charlie raised her eyebrows in amazement. "You know, I read the yoga book you gave me, and it all sounded great. This woman was writing about how much it had helped her spiritually, and I thought - this weekend could be life-changing. It could be the time I get myself sorted, get myself together and really clear my life out. You never know.

"Well, let's hope so," said Charlie. "I can't say I'm

feeling as positive. I hate being hungry, and I think they only give us tiny portions. I'm worried it's going to be hard to concentrate on the yoga and do well at it when we're hungry all the time."

"Well, yes, I'm not great with hunger either," I said. "I did treat myself to the most enormous takeaway last night."

"Whaaat? I thought we were trying to detox yesterday so we'd be ready for today."

"I know, but I just couldn't. I feel so miserable when I'm hungry."

"You're gonna be great company at a bloody detox yoga weekend then, aren't you?"

We drove along in silence for a while.

"So, how much food do you think we'll get at this place?"

"I don't know, but all the comments on the website say that it was a great place except that they were all starving the whole time."

"Oh God, this is going to be horrible, isn't it? I'm dreading it now. I don't mind eating healthy foods, if we have to, but I don't want to be hungry. Should we get some snacks just in case it gets desperate?"

"We're supposed to be detoxing," said Charlie, admonishingly. "Maybe we should try and do it by eating their food and see how we go?"

"Really?" I replied, looking over at Charlie. "OK, fine. If you think you can survive for three days on half a cashew nut and a teaspoon of peach extract, I'm sure I can, too. "

"Oh, sod it," she said, veering across two lanes of

traffic and into the service station. "Let's get some nibbles so we have supplies in our bags in case things get desperate. As you say, we don't have to eat them all, do we?"

"No, it will be useful to have them, just in case we want them."

"Yes."

We decided that I would be in charge of snack purchasing, so Charlie put petrol in while I went inside and filled up with crisps, nuts, rice cakes and a couple of bottles of wine...just in case. It was all very naughty, but if we didn't eat it, we could easily bring it back with us.

I got back to the car with my bag full of goodies. Charlie was in the shop paying for petrol. I plonked the bag in the boot. Then I panicked...what if we weren't supposed to take snacks with us? I had a big suitcase with me with lots of room, so I decanted half of the goodies I could fit into my case. I shut the boot and got into the car.

"Right, where are we going?" Charlie asked as she took her seat beside me.

"I don't know," I said. "You're holding the map."

"I can't drive and look at it; you'll have to read it."

"I'm rubbish at anything map-related," I said. "We'll end up in Norfolk."

"No, we won't, and we'll have the sat nav on; we just need to keep an eye on the map as well because the instructions from the centre say that it is quite hard to find."

"OK," I said.

"Did you not get any snacks in the end?" Charlie asked.

"Yep, just a couple of things. I put the bag in the boot."

"Great. OK, let's go. The location is plugged into the sat nav; you have the map - we're sure to be OK."

I should point out that no one in the history of the world has ever said that my map reading would mean us being ok.

Still, Charlie seemed convinced, and we settled into driving along the pretty country lanes, guided by the satnav. I sat back and relaxed, wallowing in the tranquil sights as we moved further away from home and closer to our weekend rural retreat. The sun's rays reached through the windows as we drove along, caressing my face and arm. It was lovely.

"Right, this is where I could do with your help," said Charlie. I was half asleep, enjoying the gentle motion of the car, when I was brought joltingly back to reality.

"I think there is a left turn coming up...this is the one that their website said wasn't recognised by satnav. It's called Farm Gate Road."

"I'm on it," I said, peering out of the window in search of the road.

"Can you not see it on the map?" said Charlie.

"No, I can't do maps, I don't understand them."

"Oh God," said Charlie. "Well, have a look out of the window and see whether you can see it. I'll drive really slowly.

So, we trundled along the country lanes at a ridiculously slow speed with a very, very fat lady hanging out of the window looking for the road, while clutching a map that would easily have told her where it was.

"Here, look," I said, spotting a small side road that appeared to lead up to a farm. It had a gate about 20 yards along it. "This has to be Old Farm Gate Road. It has all the ingredients."

Charlie slowed and looked at the road, then at the map.

"It does look like it," she conceded. "It leads to an old farm, and it has a gate. What other clues could we ask for? Yay! I think we've found it."

Charlie indicated and pulled into the lane, stopping just before the gate. I clambered out of the car and waddled over to it, unlatching it and holding the gate open, bowing down to Charlie with a flourish as she drove through. I returned to the car, and we drove around the corner. As soon as we drove to the other side of the house, there was a great big flutter as hens and chickens flew up everywhere. Peacocks came striding up to the car, and geese began to make the most horrific crying sound. Charlie jumped on the brake.

"Fuck," we both said as the animals made a colossal noise, screeching and screaming and flapping all around us.

"Reverse...let's get out of here," I said.

Charlie was just sitting there. I couldn't understand it. "Let's go," I said. "This is the wrong place. This is the farmer next door. He's mentioned in the booklet they get all their fresh produce from him."

"I know we're in the wrong place, but I can't start suddenly reversing, or I'll crush half a dozen peacocks."

I looked in the mirror at the birds gathering behind us. Charlie was right...there were birds all around the car now.

"OK, look - don't panic - I'll get out and shoo them out of the way, then you reverse. OK?"

"You're going to shoo them away? What are you, all of a sudden? Some sort of champion ornithologist?

"I don't know what that is, and I've no idea how I'm going to shoo them away, but I'm willing to try. Are you ready to reverse when I give you the signal?"

"Yes," said Charlie.

"Right, OK."

I clambered out of the car and found myself ankle-deep in mud. It was like thick chocolate sauce. I pulled my foot out and moved slowly to the back of the car, taking off my hoodie and waving it in the air.

"Shoo, shoo, shoo," I cried. "Off you go, birds, off you go. And you, peacock - be away with you. Go, go." I clapped my hands ferociously, and they ran, flew and quacked away.

"OK, go," I shouted to my get-away driver, and Charlie put her foot down hard on the accelerator. The car growled but didn't go anywhere.

"Take the handbrake off," I instructed.

"I haven't got the handbrake on. The car is stuck. I can't move it at all. It must be because of all the mud."

"Oh God."

I could see two figures in the distance, walking through the field towards us. One of the guys was waving a stick in the air. He was clearly ranting at us, presumably telling us to get off his land and to stop petrifying his birds.

"Right, strategic thinking," I said, trying to sound like I

had half a clue what I was doing. I should point out at this stage that I don't drive and know nothing about cars. Still, in the absence of anyone else's advice, mine would have to do.

"OK, I'll try pushing the car," I said, wading round to the front. I now had mud all over my pale pink jogging bottoms, and my beautiful new trainers were completely covered. You couldn't see what colour they were (pink, in case you were wondering).

"Are you ready?"

"Yes," said Charlie, pressing her foot down hard on the accelerator. I pushed with all my might, and mud splattered everywhere. I could feel it in my hair and on my face. There were chickens and hens all over the place, all clucking and making the most terrible row.

In the distance, I could hear the farmer shouting. "Get out of there. What do you think you are doing? Get out of my hen coop."

Oh, Christ, the car wasn't going anywhere, and the angry-looking men were getting closer.

"Let's try again," I suggested, with one eye on the fast-approaching men and the other on the peacocks who kept striding confidently behind the car.

"Are you ready?" I asked and primed myself to push with every fibre of my being.

"Go," I said, and Charlie reversed the car. I pressed my whole body against the bonnet and pushed with all my might; the car skidded a little, then flew backwards, and I went with it, landing with a heavy thump. My lovely pink and white yoga kit was now covered in mud. There was mud on my face and my hair, feathers stuck to me, and chickens looked at me distastefully as they clucked and ran around.

"Quickly, get in the car," said Charlie. I clambered to my feet, sliding in the mud as I attempted to run towards the car. I finally made it over to the passenger side and joined her. I was filthy from head to foot; stray feathers had nestled in my mud-coated hair. I could taste mud and see it lying on my eyelashes. I'd never been so filthy in my entire life; I was caked in it.

Charlie reversed out and onto the road. She stopped for a moment so I could shut the gate. The trouble was that the men were getting closer, and their voices were getting louder.

"They'll shut the gate; let's just go," I said, slinking down into the seat. "Go, go, go..."

Charlie raced away from the farm as if we'd just done a bank robbery or a drugs deal.

"I don't know where to go now," she said, but a minute later, there was a very clear road sign on the right.

"Farm Gate," I shouted, and Charlie threw the car across the road and up the narrow lane leading to Vishraam House.

We drove along in silence. It was a long, gravel drive with pretty pink flowers in pots all along it until the driveway opened out and there, in front of us, was a magnificent country house - a lovely white building with turrets and a huge oak door. It was stunning.

"Wow," said Charlie, stopping next to the half a dozen cars parked outside. All the other cars were super expensive looking. Charlie pulled into the space in the middle of them, and we stopped for a moment to admire the views.

On the right of the house, there were horses and cows in the fields. On the left, near where all the cars were parked, there was a meadow full of wildflowers.

"Just look at that," I said, sweeping my mud-drenched arm across to indicate the bucolic scene. There was a gorgeous lake with trees on either side and lovely, colourful plants and shrubs. I once went on holiday to Corsica, and this reminded me of that place - just bliss, utterly idyllic.

"I can't wait to see what the house is like," I said to Charlie.

"I bet it's amazing," she replied. "I'm so excited now. This weekend is going to be brilliant. Just one problem."

"What's that?"

"You. You're covered in mud. Just look at the state you've made of my car. You can't go into her house like that."

"I'll have to," I said. "I can try to wipe some of the mud off on a towel, but what else can I do?"

Charlie was looking down towards the lake. "You're going to have to go in there," she said.

"No way."

"You can go in, quickly wash the mud off, and then dry yourself. You'll be in there for five minutes, and you'll be clean. What other option do you have?"

"But it will be freezing," I said.

"If you're quick, you'll hardly notice it, she said.

"Hardly notice what? The freezing cold?"

"Yes - it's probably lovely and refreshing when you get in there."

"Yeah, sure," I said. "Why don't you come with me if it's so wonderful?"

"Because I'm not filthy," said Charlie. "Just go in there and wash it off. You could've cleaned yourself in the time you've been sitting here talking about it. We've got towels in our bags; just go and do it."

"I don't want to," I said, looking down at the cold-looking water. Yes, it was very pretty and would look lovely in a photograph, but I didn't want to go *into* it.

"Just go," said Charlie. "You have to, or we'll have to sit here all day. You can't go in there like that."

Just as Charlie and I debated how on earth I would get the mud off if I didn't go into the water, the grand oak door in the middle of the house opened, and a petite, dark-haired lady with a broad smile came dancing out.

"Hello, hello, welcome, welcome," she said in what sounded like a faint Italian accent. Then she stopped in her tracks when she saw me. "Oh, my goodness, what happened to you?"

Charlie thought quickly on her feet. "Mary loves mud rambling, so went mud rambling before we came here," she said.

"Oh, how wonderful," said the lady, smiling more broadly. "I do like adventurous women. I've never heard of mud rambling, but you must come on our early morning rambles; you'd love it. We end up at the top of the farmer's fields, scaling the high hills and wading through brooks, clambering over trees and bushes... Just your type of thing, I'd have thought."

"Yes, just my sort of thing," I lied.

"Great, then I will definitely organise a serious ramble for you on Sunday morning. Now - let's get you into the shower."

If I'd had any sense at all, at that point, I would have got out of the car, turned, walked away and kept walking until I got back to London. But I didn't. I agreed that mud rambles were wonderful and smiled at her, completely oblivious to just how insane the weekend ahead was about to become.

THE BIG HOUSE IN THE COUNTRY

"Hello, you're back," said the lady with a big smile and a fancy, foreign-sounding accent. "My name's Venetta. I hope the water was OK."

"It was great, thanks," I replied. "Much better than the lake would have been."

"Yes, it's very cold in there. Lovely and refreshing, but desperately cold. Much nicer to have a warm shower after a mud ramble."

"Yes, I agree completely," I said.

The shower had, indeed, been lovely. It was in an open-air shower block at the back of the house, near the small swimming pool. The showers were proper power showers, and the water had been beautifully warm. Now I was back in the main entrance hall where Charlie had waited for me. I was wet rather than dirty and wrapped in a white dressing gown that only just about went around me. I imagined these gowns were huge on most people - making them feel swaddled, warm and safe. It barely fit me, meaning there was great danger of overexposure. With every step I took, I held the front of the gown together lest it gaped open. I didn't want our friendly host to see any of my unwaxed lady bits. I didn't want to cause alarm in this serene building in this beautiful part of the country.

"Right then...who's who?" she said, pulling out her notes and taking two sheets of paper out.

"I'm Mary; this is Charlie," I replied, putting out my hand to shake hers, but she just bowed, smiling at me and moving her hands into a prayer position.

"There's no need to shake hands," she said. "We tend to greet each other more simply."

"OK, I'll try to remember that," I said.

"You know that shaking hands is about lack of trust, don't you?" she said.

I gave her a confused look and said I didn't really know anything about that. "Yes, the handshake was developed to prove to people that you weren't carrying a weapon. If they took your right hand, that would show them you were unarmed."

"Oh," I said. "I didn't know that."

"Here, we don't need proof that you come in peace; we don't need proof of your character...we trust you and believe that you will do no wrong."

I had a sudden flashback to the peacocks and the hens in the farmyard, flapping their way out of the car's path, the angry farmer charging down the hill, and the way we'd driven off without closing the gate.

"Take a seat," she said, and I looked for a chair. There

weren't any that I could see. When I looked back at her, she was sitting on the floor in the lotus position. Good God.

Charlie and I clambered down onto the floor, Charlie executing the manoeuvre with much more dignity than I managed. I sat with my legs out in front of me. There was no point even pretending I could do the limb origami thing.

Next, there was an awkward silence while she breathed deeply and noisily. Charlie and I glanced at one another, not knowing whether to join in, ignore her or fetch her a tissue.

"Let us rise," she said.

Christ, I was exhausted already. I clambered to my feet. On the table in front of her were rice cakes, low-calorie crisps and wine... not unlike those I'd brought. She indicted them and looked back at me.

"Yum," I said, raising my eyebrows and smiling. "That's cheered me up!"

"Not really 'Yum' though, is it?" said Venetta, dropping her head to one side and looking at me in what you could describe as a maternal fashion or a patronising fashion, depending on your point of view. I decided to go for patronising.

"While you were in the shower, Charlie brought your bags in from the car," she said. "There was a suitcase which Charlie said belonged to you, and Jonty has taken to your room, along with Charlie's holdall, and there was also a carrier bag.

"I'm afraid that I couldn't help but notice that it was

full of food and drink. I don't want to be a spoilsport, but you will get the most out of this low-calorie retreat if you eat low calories. If you don't, I'm afraid you won't feel the benefit in your body, mind or spirit. Do you understand?"

I nodded like a naughty schoolgirl.

"I think it would be best if I took this bag. I will give everything back to you when you leave. If you really want them, you will find them in this cupboard. But I urge you to resist taking them. I think it would do you a lot of good if you tried to stick to the programme and just live a much simpler life while you're here. I think you will feel the benefits if you do."

Charlie and I stood there like naughty schoolgirls while she took the bag over to a cupboard and pushed it inside. "I will leave them here. They are yours to take away with you, but I think you will find that you no longer want them by the end of the course. This is the advanced yoga weekend with raw, vegan, no-sugar, and no-salt food. Under the guidance of the Guru Aaraadhy Motee Ladakee, you will find that you can cleanse and clear and direct attention to your inner self so you can focus on yogic practices. I'm afraid that will be much harder to do if you eat crisps and drink wine every night."

"Of course," I said. I looked over at Charlie. There was so much wrong with what Venetta had just said that it was hard to know where to start. She had taken our snacks - that was one bloody awful thing. Thank God I had a few more in my suitcase. The other terrible thing was that we appeared to have been booked onto the advanced course with a guru.

"Peace be with you," she said as we stood open-mouthed. "Now, let me show you around the house - please treat it like your home. I think you will enjoy your couple of days here very much. I know you will enjoy meeting the guru...we call him Guru Motee for short. His full name is very difficult to remember. Here... look at the house..."

The place was amazing, as we knew it would be from our first glance of it from the outside. We walked around behind her, listening to her sing-song voice describe the place, and I'm sure both of us were thinking the same thing - why didn't we tell her that we weren't booked on the advanced course with a guru? We were booked onto the most basic course in the brochure. But we stayed silent and just watched as we were led around. I was embarrassed about turning up covered in mud, and embarrassed about the snacks, I didn't have the strength to admit that, in addition to all that, it now turned out we were on completely the wrong course.

Venetta took us from the wide hallway with its beautifully polished wooden floors and gorgeous antique-style table to the rooms at the back of the house. She told us that she loved antiques and regularly went to London and Europe on antique-finding missions. It showed... the house boasted class and sophistication. Everything looked so expensive. She must have been making a lot of money from her yoga retreats and investing it in the house.

She took us first of all into the conservatory where the mindfulness and meditation classes were to be held. It had a lovely, warm, cosy feeling... soft rugs piled up at the side, comfy armchairs, and piles of mats and blankets in the far corner. Next to the conservatory was what looked much more like an exercise classroom. The wooden floors, the mirrors, the bar. Everything you expect of an exercise room in a gym.

"This is where the yoga takes place," she said. We walked through that to another small room at the back where one-to-one yoga classes took place. The room had mirrors all around.

"Blimey, this is all quite intensive," I said, trying to ignore the sight of myself beaming back at me from all angles in all the mirrors.

"Well, intensity is what you expect at this level, isn't it?" she said. I glanced at Charlie as I felt myself shrink a little.

We walked out of the private tuition room and back through the main yoga room, out into the body of the house, where Venetta showed us the dining room, a small but rather richly appointed place that looked more formal than previously seen.

She opened the door and showed us the outside area where I'd had my shower so that Charlie could see the swimming pool and hot tub area. There were lots of deckchairs to relax on and an outdoor table for when the weather permitted outdoor eating.

"We tend to eat outside in the summer whenever we can," she said. "But if it gets too cold or it rains, we just head for the dining room."

We walked back through the front of her home, and she showed us a sitting room with a library room trailing off it. It was a lovely house. It was a shame we had to do exercise...it would be a great place to come and chill out, read books, laze around, and eat lovely big roast dinners.

"Feel free to use any of the rooms," she said. "I'd like you to treat this place like your home... borrow any of the books you want to read, and let me know if there's anything I can do to help."

"Thank you," I said. I was tempted to say: "You could help by giving me back my snacks," but that felt a little unfair given how friendly and welcoming she was being, and given that - to be fair to her - we were on a detox yoga retreat, and it did explicitly say in the brochure that we were not to bring any food or drink into the house, and to eat only what was provide..

Venetta wandered up the stairs, pointing out all the rooms on the first floor. We were based in the loft on the top floor, there were just two bedrooms up there. Charlie and I were sharing one of them. It was a lovely big room, very plain, with wooden floors and white bed sheets, white chest of drawers and white towels. There was a kind of wet room - a large shower at the side of the room, equipped - of course - with white soap, white shampoo and white conditioner. I don't know what it was with all the white – perhaps it was about being serene, healthy, and pure. It was perfectly nice, though, if a little plain.

"I hope you'll be happy here," she said. "We have a full complement of people for the course today. The others are all based on the second floor; you are the only ones up here, so you should get lots of peace and quiet if you want to meditate or work on your yoga poses."

"Yes, I imagine we'll be doing a lot of that," I said as Venetta backed away to the door, wishing us a peaceful hour.

"Please report for the introductions at 4 pm," she said as she left.

"Of course," I said, bowing stupidly and sitting down on my bed. "I hope you have a peaceful hour, too," I added.

"You're such a dick sometimes," said Charlie, and I nodded. It was hard to disagree with her.

MEETING THE GANG

"Welcome to Vishraam," said Venetta, opening her arms as if to indicate how welcome we all were before wafting them together again, gently caressing the air between them as she did so. Venetta moved her hands into the prayer position and bowed her head. I noticed that the others in the room were doing similarly, so I kicked Charlie in the shin and we both put our hands into the prayer position and dropped our heads in a way that we hadn't done since we were sitting cross-legged in assembly, aged seven.

"As you will all know, as elite practitioners of yoga, 'Vishraam' means 'relaxation' in Hindu. We all hope you will find this weekend to be the most relaxing and energising few days you have ever spent. We are experts at ensuring the environments we create are full of kindness and joy. Please enjoy everything we have to offer. Treat the house as your own and welcome the hunger you feel on our low-calorie vegan diets. Enjoy how your body responds and lift yourself to the challenge of performing yoga here. It is only by overcoming that we reach a higher place."

There were nods and murmurs from around the room, and I realised that Charlie and I were the only people who'd had no idea what the Hindu for 'relaxation' was. I also realised that this was the second time that Venetta had referred to us as 'elite' and 'experts' which seemed both unusual and concerning. The only yoga I'd ever done in my life had left me face first in the pot plants at the garden centre; calling me an 'expert' in yoga would be like calling Kylie Minogue an expert in street fighting. No, simply not true. The opposite of 'expert', in fact.

"We're supposed to be on the bloody beginners' course," whispered Charlie.

"I know," I said to Charlie. "We *are* on the beginners' course. I don't think she realises. She's eaten too many hemp seeds and doesn't know what she's doing."

"I think we're on the wrong course. She couldn't have got it wrong twice. And look at these people - they don't look like beginners to me."

There were eight of us on the course in total. I looked around the room at them...all looking so sincere. It troubled me how thin they all were; if you stuck them all together, they would weigh about as much as I did. Blimey, yoga people are thin. Have you seen them? All wiry and serious looking. The guys on the course looked as fit and lean as athletes, but I couldn't imagine they were much fun at parties. Or anywhere. I don't imagine they could have had a day's fun in their lives. I really hoped they'd prove me wrong.

Venetta invited us to sit around in a circle while we

welcomed one another with serenity and kindness. I glanced at Charlie as Venetta said, 'serenity and kindness;' we both tried not to laugh. I didn't think what they were saying was mad or anything. Nothing wrong with serenity, and who on earth could object to a bit of kindness? I suppose I was just a bit embarrassed; I'd never heard anyone talk in such an unselfconscious way before, and I couldn't help but giggle.

I was trying hard to focus because I desperately wanted to change my life and be fitter, stronger and slimmer. I wanted to be like these people, especially the two incredibly beautiful women on the far side of the room who I found myself staring at, but it was difficult to adjust to all the sincerity. The two women must have been around the same age as me (about 30), but in all other ways, they were completely different - beautiful, elegant, relaxed, composed and slim.

"This is our safe circle," said Venetta.

Everyone was sitting with their bony legs crossed in the lotus position. They were all holding their arms out, palms up, with their hands resting gently on their knees. It was hard enough for me to get myself down onto the floor without me attempting to contort my legs into a fiendish tied-up position. We all sat there in silence.

Just when I was starting to think some of the guys in the group had fallen asleep, Venetta started chanting, and the others all joined in - deep sounds resonated through the room...sounds which made no sense. I sort of joined in, but I felt such an idiot chanting and oooing and ahhing. The loudest noise came from a very handsome man with dark hair; my God, he was good-looking, like a young Elvis Presley.

Finally, it all stopped, and Venetta told us to relax. I immediately lay back and got myself as comfortable as possible, but when I looked up, the others had remained in the lotus position and were looking at Venetta, who was looking quizzically at me.

I scrambled to sit up as quickly as my size would allow. "There's no need to sit up," she said warmly. "Just make yourself comfortable while we introduce ourselves."

There were six people in the group in addition to Charlie and me... a mixture of ages and both sexes were there...the one thing which united them, the one thing they had in common was that they were super slim and super fit looking unlike me.

I looked over to smile at the lovely dark-haired man and found myself staring at the two beautiful women on the far side of the room again...really, they were the most elegant-looking people I have ever seen. They sat there, smiling beatifically in their coordinating leisurewear. They looked simple and comfortable, but their clothing probably cost more than the average family car.

A lady who was introduced as Philippa was the slightly more attractive of the two of them. She was dressed in pale grey leggings and a matching jumper. Her clothes looked like they were made of cashmere or some other luxurious fibre. They were complemented by a soft lilac shawl thrown across her shoulders.

Her friend wore lilac leggings and a winter white woollen tunic with a grey shawl over her shoulders. They lounged next to one another with their matching perfect hair and teeth... Philippa's dark hair fell over her shoulders in waves...she reminded me of Meghan Markle: all dazzling smile and perfect figure. Sarah wasn't quite as beautiful as Philippa but still had an air of wealth, good breeding, and the same enviable taste in knitwear. There was something very fascinating about their perfection; it seemed so complete and absolute. You just knew by looking at them that their bras and knickers matched and had been purchased from some fabulous Parisian lingerie designer. There was no way she bought them in Tesco like I did. I could see Philippa's perfect fingernails, painted in a delicate shade of mocha, which matched her toenails.

As I watched her, she lifted her dark hair into a high ponytail and tied it with a lilac band that - obviously - matched her shawl. How do people manage to do that? She looked like she was living in a magazine spread. I longed to look like her.

Sarah stretched her legs out in front of her and folded herself over them, allowing me to see that her manicure and pedicure also matched perfectly... In bright red, which looked beautiful next to the lilac leggings. Her hair was also long, but it didn't seem quite as long as Philippa's, which had cascaded over her shoulders until she tied it up. Sarah's hair was in an immaculate bun that sat high on her head like a prima ballerina.

"I want to be her," I said to Charlie as Meghan Markle introduced herself.

"I've been doing yoga all my life," she said. "It was something my mother introduced to me from an early age because she ran her own yoga studio."

"Of course she did," I mumbled to Charlie. "While we

were eating crisps in front of Neighbours, Miss Perfect was meditating in the tree position...life's so unfair."

"So unfair," said Charlie. "But don't mention crisps...you're making me hungry. Still can't believe that woman stole our snacks."

We shook our heads in mutual incomprehension at the fate that had befallen our foodstuffs.

"I spend my time helping people wherever I can," said Perfect Philippa. "I also love to go for walks along the beach, and I like to bathe in the ocean when the stars are out. I sit on the rocks reading poetry at night and practice yoga daily."

It turned out that Sarah was equally well-versed in the art of yoga. She had met the gorgeous Philippa at nursery school, and they'd been best friends ever since. They smiled girlishly at one another, and I expected butterflies to emerge from between them and for tiny cartoon deer to dance around them.

"These people are so perfect," I growled at Charlie with undisguised jealousy.

"I reckon one night Sarah will do one downward dog too many, lose her mind and strangle Philippa to death in the middle of the night using just a pair of fashionable cashmere leggings."

"Ha!" I squealed rather too loudly, prompting Venetta to turn and focus on me.

"Yes, you express yourself however you feel you need to," she said. "Yoga can be a moving experience; feel you can let your voice respond to it if needed. That goes for everyone. If you want to chant or express emotion, just do that. Don't hold feelings in. Would you like to chant?"

"Who? Me?" I said.

"Yes, I wondered whether you needed to give voice to your feelings."

"No thanks."

"OK then. Why don't you tell us all your name and a little about yourself?"

"Er...sure...there's not much to say: my name is Mary Brown and I work in a DIY and gardening centre in Cobham in Surrey."

"Try again," said Venetta. "This time don't tell us about your work. Your job is something you do to bring in money so you can live your life...tell us something about that life."

"OK, well I tend to go to pubs and restaurants and watch lots of telly with my boyfriend Ted. My favourite thing is when we go out to one of those 'eat all you can' Chinese buffets and drink loads of wine. I love that."

"OK," said Venetta, with more of a sneer than a smile. "Well, it's lovely to meet you."

The rest of the room had fallen completely silent during my speech. Now they were encouraged by Venetta to speak up, one by one, and explain who they were and what they did with their time. I noticed that all of them were careful not to say where they worked. Then the focus turned back to Venetta, and she looked at us all.

"I know you have come here for various reasons; some of you are thinking of training to be yoga teachers, and others of you want a dedicated weekend of practice. But whatever you are here for, I want you to remember the fundamental principles of yoga and the importance of treating one another well and, most of all, treating yourself well. It's important that we love each other and love ourselves. You're not here to change your body; you are here to make your health better, and that, in turn, will help to change you and make you a happier, more relaxed and able person. I want you to love your body and feel happy and whole. Only when you do that will you truly be at peace and be able to create the body, relationships and life you desire. Namaste."

"Namaste," we all said.

It was time to head back to our rooms for some alone time before a mindfulness course, a short unguided yoga session, and dinner.

Charlie and I sat on our small, firm beds and looked at one another.

"I quite fancy that dark-haired man," I told her.

"Diego?" she said.

"Yes. How did you remember that?"

"I'm good with names. He's good-looking but spent all his time staring at Philippa."

"Are you saying that Perfect Philippa is more attractive than me?" I questioned.

"No, he was probably staring at her out of sympathy."

"Probably," I agreed. "I didn't think there would be men on the course. It feels quite weird in some ways."

"Why?" asked Charlie.

"The idea of them wanting to come here and leap around in yoga gear for the weekend, eating bean shoots and sun-dried tomatoes instead of going to the football with their mates and then getting hammered."

"Yeah, I guess," said Charlie. "I don't know of any men

who'd do this. Would Ted ever come to a weekend of yoga?"

"God, no," I said with a chuckle. I couldn't think of anything funnier. "He would hate it. Imagine him going to mindfulness and then 'free expression' yoga."

Charlie laughed. "I can't believe you told her you like getting pissed with your mates and having huge Chinese buffets. She couldn't have looked more shocked if you'd told her you slept in a chocolate fondue."

"What was I supposed to say then? Make it up?"

"Yes - make it up. Say something impressive like that Philippa woman did. She said she liked to bathe in the ocean when the stars were out; you said you liked to shove your face full of Kung Po chicken and beef curry. She wins."

MINDFULNESS

Charlie jogged and I waddled back down the stairs to join the group for the mindfulness session. "At least it'll be dinner time soon," she said to me in an attempt to calm me down. I think she could see the fear etched across my face. Watching the videos of yoga from the comfort of Charlie's sofa and practising the odd move in the garden centre had been OK, but now we were here, I was worried about whether I could cope. Everyone else looked so different from me...so bloody fit and healthy. And mindfulness? What was mindfulness? These were things I never came across in my normal day-to-day life.

"Do you think you're allowed wine on the retreat?" she asked. "You know, with dinner."

"You'll have to ask?" I said. "I imagine that the starter will be a plate of raw vegetables and the main course will be salad and new potatoes and pudding will be fruit salad and some light, calorie-low mousse."

"Surely not on the first night?" said Charlie, appalled at the thought. "They'll break us in gently, won't they?"

We wandered into the exercise room to find everyone in there, going into the cupboard to fetch big air-filled balls, mats and blankets.

"This looks alright," I said to Charlie as we wandered in to join them. "We're going to play on space hoppers, then have a little sleep. I might be better at this yoga lark than I thought."

Philippa and Sarah were already sitting on their balls...both pink. All the balls in the cupboard were green, so I could only assume that they had brought their balls with them. They had matching purple mats and light pink and pale purple blankets. I knew they would drive me insane with jealousy by the end of the weekend.

I collected my green ball, a rather tatty black mat and a greyish-looking blanket from the basket by the side and lay my things down to the far right of the room. Charlie positioned herself just behind me, and the two men on the course set themselves up next to me.

I knew that one of the men was called Martin; he was a rather jolly-looking chap with a warm smile and open, welcoming face. He was a bigger build than most of the others there. Not fat by any means, but less skeletal. He looked like he'd eaten sometime in the last 20 years, which the others didn't. He was completely bald and had a sore-looking rash running up the side of his right leg. I decided that he'd lost his hair because of alopecia or something. Whatever it was afflicting him, I hoped it wasn't contagious.

"I'm looking forward to this," he said. "I don't know much about mindfulness, so it'll be good to find out about it. I mean - when I say, 'don't know much' - obviously I know about serenity through Buddhist chanting."

"Yes, obviously...we all know about that," I said.

"But mindfulness is an interesting idea, isn't it?"

"Yes," I said. "I don't know anything about it either."

"Well, don't worry - we'll struggle through together," he said, and I decided right there that I quite liked Martin.

Next to Martin was the very good-looking guy with the Elvis sneer. He said his name was Diego. I smiled at him, but he looked away and seemed uninterested in talking to anyone. He just sat on his yoga ball, eyes closed, humming gently.

"OK, let's get started," said Venetta, entering the room in grey leggings similar to Philippa's and with a shawl not too dissimilar to the one Philippa had been wearing earlier.

"Oh, you've taken your shawl off," she said to Philippa, immediately discarding hers.

Charlie kicked out at my ball to check I'd seen the exchange and nearly kicked me off it.

"She's channelling Perfect Philippa," said Charlie with a small guffaw. "How bloody weird. Who would copy someone else's style?"

I decided not to share with her my thoughts about running out to buy grey leggings like Philippa's as soon as I got home.

"Yeah, weird."

"I'd like you all to sit on your ball and relax," said Venetta. "Mindfulness is about being in the here and now with no judgements or ill feelings; it's about tuning into yourself and just existing. That is a difficult thing to do when we've all got such busy lives and so much going on, so I'm going to show you some tricks to help you do it. These simple things will help you reconnect with yourself and allow you to be present here and now. They will give you a feeling of complete relaxation, and you'll feel incredibly safe and relaxed if you get it right.

"First of all, I would like you to touch the fabric of the trousers or leggings that you're wearing. Does it feel rough or smooth? Warm or cold? Feel down the seam. How does that feel? Now, feel the skin on the back of your hand. How does that feel different? How does the skin on your knuckles feel different to the skin on your hand?"

Venetta went on like this for about 15 minutes, advising us to touch different things and describe them in our heads. It sounds like a ridiculous waste of time, but it seemed to work...I found myself completely relaxing as I focused on the simple things.

"Now, touch your hair. How does that feel? What about your face? OK, now just close your eyes and think about where you are and how relaxed you are. You're safe, warm and surrounded by friends. No harm will come to you. Just relax."

By the end of it, I felt amazing. I don't know how or why it worked, but I felt completely relaxed and happy.

"Doesn't that feel good?" said Venetta, and I nodded furiously. I was slightly light-headed, like when you've had a couple of sips of wine on an empty stomach, and you just start to feel a little bit woozy and floaty...not drunk at all, just warm and lovely.

"Lots of nods, that's great to see," she said. "Remember with mindfulness that we are trying to bring the focus back to the breath...the essence of life. Caring for ourselves and loving ourselves have to start from within. We must pull our attention inside and connect to our breathing. By doing this, we can keep calm, clear our minds, and have a real understanding of ourselves and our body and what we need from yoga to help us develop awareness and affinity. If we are not fully in the present, then we aren't practising yoga, we aren't existing, we have moved too far into our heads, not in our bodies or hearts. Mindfulness can help us escape our minds when they start limiting chattering.

"Another way of incorporating mindfulness into your everyday life is to stop and look at something and describe it in great detail. Look at all the intricate patterns and try to describe colours, fibres and the way the light dances off glass and marble. By doing that, you put yourself into the details of the here and now and stop wandering off into the future or worrying about the past. I think getting into pairs for this one would be useful."

Venetta pointed at me and the very handsome Diego, which was just about the best thing that had happened to me since the idea of this whole yoga lark started. "You two together," she said. I smiled warmly at him, and he just stared back, looking frightened.

"Once you're settled in your pairs, turn to the person next to you and describe the pattern on his or her blanket.

Really look at the blanket and describe the colours, the pattern, the texture... Try to lose yourself in it completely."

"Right," I said, turning to the handsome Diego. "Do you want to go first or shall I?"

He lifted a hand and pointed gently at me. He didn't seem to want to talk to me, or anyone else, at all. I wasn't convinced that was going to get him very far in this talking game, but I continued regardless.

"Okay, sure," I said. "I'll go first. Well, your blanket is kind of browns and greys mixed up together there are some black lines in it, and it's sort of rough. Your turn."

I didn't know whether Diego was going to break his silence or whether he'd taken some sort of monastic vow and was determined to remain quiet for the whole weekend.

"Your blanket is slightly rough to the touch, like touching a cow. Not soft like a cat. The colours are muted shades of earth brown, not quite chocolate, smokier than that, and a rather dull army green. It's a slightly faded-looking green, the sort of colour that an army uniform might go if it had been through a hot wash too frequently. The colours play with one another through a criss-cross pattern, and the whole effect is reminiscent of an old lady wrapped up in a blanket, sitting by the fire on a cold November evening."

"Oh," I said, feeling completely outdone in the speaking game by the man who never spoke. "You've done much better than me."

"It's not a competition," he said. "We're all here to learn, grow, and develop...as individuals and as a group. There's no competition."

"Right," I said. "But you'd still have won if it had been a contest."

"No contest, no winners or losers," he said. "Just peace and light."

"Peace and light," I repeated, uncomfortable with the seriousness and sincerity in his voice.

"If everyone would like to stand up, we're now going to do some unguided or free-wheeling yoga just to get you limbered up and in the right frame for tomorrow's activities. If it's OK with you, I was going to do a short film of the session so we can use it to show prospective guests what our opening session is like. If anyone doesn't want to be in the video and they have clicked the tick box on the application form, then obviously will make sure they're not pictured in the video. I looked at Charlie: "Did we click any tick boxes?"

"I don't think so," she replied. "I don't really know. We booked the wrong bloody course...tick boxes were the least of my concern."

It seemed unlikely that they would want me doing yoga in their video to encourage people to come on these yoga weekends, so I decided not to worry about it too much... I was sure that their video would be full of images of perfect Philippa and her sidekick Sarah doing majestic things in expensive knitwear.

"Okay, let's start with some sun salutations, then you can move into your own work," said Venetta. I wasn't entirely sure what 'my own work' would involve since my whole yoga experience to date had been limited to falling into the pot plants after trying to do the tree position at work.

We did the sun salutations, and I was okay, to begin with: we put our arms up in the air and then bent over to touch our toes. Philippa touched her toes; I just about managed my knees. I had very little flexibility and the small problem of a large, protruding stomach to contend with.

From toe touching, we jumped back into a plank position and dropped our stomachs on the floor (to be fair, this was easy for me because my stomach was already almost on the floor), then went up into downward dog (basically, this is shoving your bum into the air with straight legs), then we went into these lunges and back up again. It all seemed much harder than anything we had watched them do on the YouTube videos, but I still didn't think it was beyond me... I thought I could have a fair shot at doing it, but then the crucial moment came.

"Okay, let's speed up to proper time now then," said Venetta, and they all started doing it at such a pace that I was struggling even to get down to touch my toes before they jumped their legs backwards and moved through the routine, I got myself in a complete mess trying to keep up with them, missing half the poses out to reach where they'd got to. At one stage, I seemed to be doing an entirely different routine to everybody else.

"Okay, let's just leave it there for a minute. Carry on doing the sun salutation if you want to, or you can do other yoga poses if you're more comfortable with those."

While the others carried on, Venetta drifted over to me and Charlie.

"Are you both okay?" she said.

"Yes," I replied. "But I'm finding it hard because I've

never done yoga before."

"What you mean – never done yoga before?" said Venetta, looking horrified.

"That's what I mean," I said. "I have never done any yoga before. I've booked onto this course to learn, so that I could go to yoga classes at my local sports centre."

"But this is the supreme advanced class; we have Guru coming into lead yoga sessions; this is the very heights of yoga. Only the best yoga people are here," she said.

"I thought yoga wasn't competitive," I replied. And watched as she blinked wildly.

"No, it's not competitive, of course not," she said.

"They will be fine," chipped in Diego from his position in downward dog. His t-shirt had ridden up to display a magnificent six pack and I was momentarily distracted.

"Look, I thought we'd booked the beginners class; we clearly got that wrong," I said. "We won't get in the way; we will just do what we can at the back. Is that okay?"

"Or we could leave," said Charlie. "If you think we should."

"No, let's stay," I insisted.

"No, stay," said Venetta. "But do remember that some of these advanced techniques are going to be very difficult for you."

"Will try our hardest," I said.

I looked around at Charlie to find her gazing at me open mouthed. "That was our route out of here," she said. "You just missed the exit."

"Come on, let's give it a go," I said, pushing myself back into downward dog. "What's the worst that can happen?

RETURN OF THE CHICKENS

"I don't think we should be here," said Charlie, when we returned to our room. "We should have sneaked out when she told us it was an advanced class. I mean - what the hell are we doing on an advanced course? It's insane."

"Yep, it's insane, but we should just try to make the most of it," I said in what I thought was a very grown-up fashion. "Let's go and have dinner. I'm sure we'll both feel better after having a nice meal."

"Yes, OK," said Charlie, giving me the sort of dejected look that one usually associated with a little girl who's been told she has to go and visit her aunt and uncle instead of going to a party. She and I made a very basic effort to get ready. This was a casual retreat, and we'd been told there was no need to get dressed up for dinner, so we were planning just to wear leisure wear and make no more effort than brushing our hair.

It was a relief to get downstairs and discover that the others had done likewise. Well, most of the others.

Perfect, Philippa and Sarah looked magnificent, of course, in elegant maxi dresses. Philippa's was in emerald green, and she wore bright red earrings and bright red ballet shoes. Sarah's dress was knee-length and red. It was tight fitting at the top, then kicked out at the waist to form a lovely full skirt. She wore it with - you guessed - emerald green earrings and green ballet flats. They were truly amazing.

Everyone else was very casual. The men seemed to be wearing exactly the same as they had worn at dinner; the women hadn't dressed up much either - like us, they'd just brushed their hair and cleaned up a bit.

"Please, take a seat," said Venetta, indicating the table in the garden. It was a beautiful setting, under trellises with vines growing over them, like at an Italian villa, with the flames from the candles sending light dancing across the glasses on the table. With the pool lying to the side of us and the silence of the evening enveloping us, it was all completely perfect… until the food arrived.

First, it was the starter...a vegetable broth with so few vegetables that tasted like the water you cook vegetables in. It was dreadful. Horrible stuff. Charlie and I were sitting next to two women who we hadn't talked to earlier: Margaret, who said she worked in high finance (she'd obviously forgotten the first rule of yoga club: don't mention your job), and a lady called Julia who was very weak-looking and complained constantly about how ill she felt. She told us about the flu she'd just had, how she had weak lungs and a terrible immune system, and how she'd been in hospital five times so far this year as she was of a very delicate disposition. The two women were polar opposites; while Julia complained of her frailties, Margaret spoke at considerable lengths of her strengths. She had a first from Oxford and then went to Harvard, then she went into the City and has worked there ever since. High finance suited her because of her combative, confident nature.

"What are you doing on a yoga retreat then?" I asked. "Forgive me for saying this, but you don't seem the type to be here. You're kind of an alpha type."

"Absolutely, I'm an alpha type, 100%. But my husband makes me come here every six months because he says they calm me down. I like coming because I lose weight. It's like a cheap spa. Not that I need it to be cheap. I have plenty of money."

"Yes, I got that," I said, rather rudely, but she was annoying. So annoying.

More food came, and I rubbed my hands in joy, then stopped rubbing them because the main course was a side plate with salad on it. No protein, no bread, no anything. Sprouting mung beans and bean sprouts with lettuce, cucumber and leaves from the garden. It was dismal.

Desert was no better...three walnuts and a sliver of watermelon. And that was it. My stomach felt like it was eating itself I was so hungry.

Just as we were starting to feel like things were as bad as they could be, Julia shrieked. "Oh my God - birds," she squealed as a dozen or so chickens came clucking into the garden.

Venetta came out and looked at them quizzically. "How did you get out?" she said, then turning to us. "The farmer must have left his gate open. All the chickens have escaped."

Charlie and I dropped our heads and looked down at the ground.

"Shit," I said. "I bet that was us."

"It can't have been. That was hours ago," said Charlie. "Perhaps the chickens have been wandering around for hours?"

Venetta called the farm, and minutes later, the farmer charged into the garden with his hands on his hips. It was the same guy who'd been shouting at us earlier. He locked eyes with me as he surveyed us all, and I looked quickly away. He must have known it was me he'd seen - I was twice the size of everyone else.

We all helped to collect the chickens. "This afternoon, someone drove into the farmyard and disturbed the birds. Does anyone know anything about that?" he asked gruffly. "I haven't been able to calm them down since, and the gate's broken."

I carried on trying to catch chickens and ignored his question. We hadn't broken the gate; all I did was open it.

"If anyone knows anything about a blue car that came into the farmyard, please let me know," he added.

We all nodded and said that we would. Then we helped to take his chickens out to his Land Rover. As we walked back through the car park, I glanced at Charlie's blue car, covered in mud and feathers.

"Thank God, he didn't see it," I said, relieved that we'd parked it in the middle of the cars so it wasn't instantly visible.

"I know," said Charlie. "What a bloody nightmare.

We'll have to sneak out and wash the car later just in case. This is all our fault. Bloody feathers everywhere - look at them."

I smiled at Charlie, but she looked too fed up to smile back.

"What's the matter?" I asked.

"I just can't cope with this little food."

"Do not fear, Mary's here," I said. "Come with me."

I led a dispirited Charlie up the stairs and told her to sit on her bed. I lifted my suitcase onto my bed and opened the compartment I hadn't hitherto emptied.

"When I went to the garage, I bought loads of snacks," I confessed. "Some were in the bag that Venetta took, but some are here..."

I tipped out crisps, nuts, rice cakes and wine. I thought Charlie was going to cry with joy. "Oh my God, I love you," she said. "You're mad and everything - really batty at times, but this is amazing. Amazing."

Then she gave me the biggest hug imaginable, and we opened wine and crisps.

LATE NIGHT CAR WASH

The thing I always notice, when I eat next to someone else, is how different their attitude to food is from mine. Charlie was thrilled that I had snacks in my bag because she felt hungry. I was thrilled that I had snacks in my bag because I love food. Charlie ate some crisps and said, 'that's better'. I wasn't like that. Once the food was open in front of me, I became obsessed with it. If the packets were open, I knew that nothing on earth would stop me from eating it all...my lust for food was like a wave crashing onto the shore.

Charlie sat back and poured herself a glass of wine, and I continued to 'pick' at the food as we sat there. Charlie was full; I don't think I know full...it's not a concept I'm familiar with. My 'picking' in these circumstances usually results in me consuming more calories after we've eaten than I do while we're eating. I had five handfuls of crisps to Charlie's two, but that was the very least of my problems around food. Because after we'd eaten our 'little snack' I continued to 'pick' and I finished the crisps, ate another packet, had some more wine, and ate some nuts, all during the 'picking' phase of the meal.

We finished the bottle of wine and were feeling nicely merry. "Shall I open another one?" I said.

Charlie smiled. "Of course, but I think we should go down and wash the car first. What do you think?"

I knew we should. The farmer was bound to come back round before we left this place, and if he saw the way the car looked - covered in dried mud and feathers, he'd know it was us, and probably make us pay for damage or something.

"Yes," I said. "Come on - let's go and do it now, then we can return for more snacks."

It was 11 pm and the house was eerily silent. Charlie and I crept down the stairs without putting the lights on, trying not to let them creak, hoping not to slip. We tiptoed into the kitchen and found two large pans and a roll of kitchen paper. We filled the pans with hot, soapy water and tiptoed towards the front door. I had a kitchen roll stuffed under one arm and a huge, heavy pan in my hands. I desperately tried not to spill any water as we went. We got to the front door, and I put down my pan and pulled the door open, as I did the most astonishing sound peeled through the house.

"Oh Christ, it's the alarm," I said. "Bollocks, how are we going to explain this?"

We stood there, in our pyjamas, carrying huge bowls of soapy water, while a man who I'd seen around the house but who appeared to have no role came running down the stairs, carrying a baseball bat. Behind him was Venetta screeching, "Be careful, be careful." She was dressed in a frilly, flirty little negligée in baby pink that looked as if it belonged in the 1950s.

When the man got level with us, he stopped in his tracks. "Did someone try to break in?" he asked.

"No," said Charlie. "We tried to break out."

"Oh, my goodness, it's you two. What are you doing?" asked Venetta, regarding the bowls of soapy water with confusion.

"Cleaning the car," said Charlie.

"At this hour?" said Venetta. "Can it not wait until tomorrow? Or when you get home?"

"No, it can't," said Charlie, looking at me for support and help.

"I've got OCD," I said. "I can't sleep unless the car is clean. It's just one of those things."

"Oh, I see," said Venetta, though she didn't look as if she had a clue what I was on about. "OK then, well if it will help you sleep, by all means, clean the car, but you'll need better equipment than that. Jonty, can you pull the hose out for them?"

Really?" he said.

"Yes, it's OCD. We need to be supportive. You do the hose; I'll get car cleaner and brushes."

The man half sneered at me as he went outside, and it struck me that he could do with coming to one of the mindfulness courses. The way he was wielding the baseball bat wasn't very 'Zen' at all.

"Here," said Venetta, handing me car cleaner and brushes. I gave her the pan of soapy water, and Charlie and I walked outside.

"What? What on earth was that?" said Charlie when we were safely out of earshot. "OCD?"

"I was struggling," I said. "I didn't know what else to say. Now, come on, let's find this hose."

All the security lights had come on outside the house like the place was floodlit. I knew those sleeping in rooms at the front of the building must have light pouring through their windows.

"We better do this quickly," I said. "Or we're going to wake everyone up."

We found the hose and sprayed it onto the car, brushing like mad and tipping car cleaner onto the sides and the back, where the mud was worse. We scrubbed for about 20 minutes until the car was sparkling clean, and we were drenched and sweating like mad. "Come on, let's go get some snacks," I said, replacing the hose and leading the way back inside.

We put the pans back, replaced the brushes and tiptoed back up the stairs. Then I took the carrier bag of snacks she'd confiscated.

"Just in case we run out," I said to Charlie. By the time we reached the room, the security lights had gone off, and the house had fallen into complete silence.

HALF A POUND OF CUMBERLAND SAUSAGES

SMACK! Morning came like a thunderclap. The sound of the alarm clock burst into the attic room. It was so loud I had to put my hands over my ears to stop my head from exploding. It felt like the whole place was shaking. Lord above, it was horrific. I sat up, switched off the alarm, and looked around me. Crisp packets were strewn across the floor, and two empty wine bottles lay beside the bed. Yep, that was why I felt so damn awful. We'd stayed up til about 3 a.m. drinking wine and laughing about my sudden-onset OCD. The alarm had gone at 5.30 a.m. Our first yoga class of the day was at 6 a.m.

"Up you get, Charlie," I said. "It's time for yoga."

"Good morning, ladies and gentlemen, welcome to Advanced level Ashtanga," said a small, scrawny woman with short, curly blonde hair tied back into a tight ponytail. "My name is Elizabeth Hill."

There were murmurs of appreciation and delight emanating throughout the room. This was obviously a famous yoga teacher brought in to run a session for us. I hoped no one could sense the panic running through me. I glanced at Charlie; she looked as horror-stricken as I felt. At least we'd placed ourselves right at the back of the room.

Then, the madness began, as we started the class with ten sun salutations. On and on we went. I just copied everyone else and tried to keep out of sight. It was all going so fast that I was struggling to keep up.

I saw Venetta had come into the room. She was dressed all in black and wandered around, looking at everyone, clapping randomly and saying, "Very good, very good." Of course, she said nothing to Charlie and me because we weren't very good. I kept catching sight of the two of us in the mirror...there was no disguising it...we were very bad.

Venetta stopped at the side and watched Philippa and Sarah for a while. They looked beautiful of course...Philippa was wearing cream, loose-fitting shorts and a matching cream top. You could see flashes of her blue crop top underneath when she bent over. Her legs were so long and tanned it was impossible not to stare at them. Sarah wore the same but with a bright pink crop top underneath. They both had ponytails. Philippa's was tied with a pink ribbon to match Sarah's crop top, and Sarah's was tied with one in the same blue as Philippa's crop top.

"I think we should match our outfits like that," I whispered to Charlie, who instantly stuck two fingers up at me and nearly fell out of downward dog.

"Now, could we all turn to face the other way?" said Elizabeth, standing next to Charlie and me.

Aahhh...no. I was at the front of the class. I stood facing everyone in my baggy yellow tracksuit trousers and Daffy Duck t-shirt.

"Turn around," mouthed Charlie.

I spun on my heels, and we were told to repeat the sun salutations...with me at the front, and no one to copy. Nightmare. Do you know how hard it is to copy someone in a mirror? I tried to copy the people behind me by watching them in the mirror. It was awful. I was all over the place. In the end, I wasn't even attempting to do sun salutations, I just moved around a bit - stretching up occasionally, touching my toes occasionally and going down into a press-up position every so often.

"And... drop into child's pose," she said, ending my embarrassment.

Venetta had left the room while we were busy downward dogging and touching our toes. I saw her creep back in again. Rather hysterically, she was wearing white shorts and a matching white top. She looked nowhere near as elegant as Philippa and Sarah, but it was clear that she was dressing like them.

I glanced at Charlie. "Did you see that?" I asked.

"Yes," she said. "The woman's bonkers."

"OK, and come out of child's pose. We're going just roll from side to side. This will loosen up the spine and massage the internal organs before we go on."

I felt I would be good at rolling from side to side. I might play my joker on this one, I thought. We began slowly moving from side to side before we rolled. I had Charlie to one side of me and Martin on the other.

"OK, and roll more; go further over," she said.

Martin had rolled himself up the mat a little, so his bottom was in line with my head. He wore rather skimpy running shorts, and I noticed that the scabby rash on his calf went all up the back of his leg. It was most unappealing. Not that I was ideally placed to go around criticising anyone else's appearance, but it wasn't very nice. And why on earth was he wearing such tiny shorts? He looked like he'd come in fancy dress as a footballer from the 1970s.

"And, have a go at rolling," said the instructor. "Just gently, roll from one side, over you go..."

I just lay there. I was enjoying the rest. I didn't plan on rolling anywhere. But as I enjoyed the short rest, Martin decided to begin rolling; he swung over, rolling his body as instructed. As he finished, there was a slapping sound, like someone had slammed half a pound of Cumberland sausages on the ground. I looked over to see that the entire contents of his shorts had escaped through one of the legs. His substantial penis and balls lay on the shiny wooden floor.

"Goodness me," he said, rolling away. "Very sorry about that."

A GURU AND A HEADSTAND

"I feel sick," I told Charlie. "I really didn't need to see the tackle of some old, bald bloke with a serious skin infection."

"So you keep saying," she replied.

"It was disgusting. Really awful."

"Never mind, we've got the guru-led session in five minutes. That should be fun."

"If Martin's still wearing those shorts, I'm not going in," I said.

We were lying on our beds, exhausted. A long walk had followed the morning yoga session (Charlie ran half of it, which annoyed me), and a swimming session, then lunch. We'd eaten our 'summer vegetable bowl', then darted upstairs for proper food (crisps).

"We should head down," said Charlie, getting to her feet and stretching out a little. I grabbed another handful of crisps and followed her down the stairs.

"Ladies and gentlemen, this is a special time on the course... The time when your meditation will be elevated, and your yoga will be given meaning. I would like to welcome the man who has made my yoga journey much more enlightened and joyful. Guru Aaraadhy Motee Ladakee."

We all looked up at the door as it swung open, and a man walked in wearing a long orange robe. Charlie nudged me, and I knew she wanted me to joke about the madness of the whole thing, but I couldn't keep my eyes off him. He was the most magnificent-looking man I had ever seen. I suppose he must have been around 60 and had longish white hair and very tanned skin.

He was the sort of guy you knew must have been devastatingly handsome when he was younger. He had a look about him that was half John the Baptist and half surfer dude. Not a common combination, I admit, but he looked as if he spent his mornings on the beach and in the waves, his bleached, tousled hair and pearly white teeth set against azure blue seas and skies. He looked as if he'd jumped off his surfboard five minutes ago. His eyes were the brightest blue I'd ever seen, set in this very handsome square face with the most amazing gentle smile. I think I fell in love with him straight away. It wasn't a sexual, *come here, I want to shag you,* sort of love, it was more serene than that. There was something quite magnificent about him. I felt wholesome, warm and happy in his presence.

"Christ, look at the state of him," said Charlie.

"He's amazing," I said, still staring at him, transfixed by the vision before me.

"It's a pleasure to be here with you today," he said, bowing and sitting before us. He dropped so elegantly and flawlessly into the Lotus position, just a small glimpse of hairy, tanned ankle as he sat and bowed over. I could only imagine how strong and flexible he was. Gosh, he was amazing.

"Om sahanaa vavatu Sahanau bhunaktu. Saha veeryam karavaa vahai. Tejasvi naa vadhee tamastu maa vidvishaa vahai. Om Shaanti Shaantihi," he chanted.

Everyone joined in. I did, too. I didn't know any words or the sounds they were making, but I chanted anyway.

"Follow me," he said. And he bent right over in the Lotus position, so his hands were stretched right out in front of him.

I tried desperately to copy what he was doing. I was nowhere near as flexible as him, but – my God – I was going to try.

He went through a series of yoga poses stopping every so often and holding them for such an unconscionable amount of time that I didn't have any hope. I decided to make up for what I couldn't do in yoga by the volume of the chats I didn't know the words to. I was aware this was making me look stupid, and I could feel Charlie glaring at the back of my head as I wailed loudly not knowing any of the words.

He kept going for about 40 minutes, moving from position to position. I was exhausted but determined not to stop. In all the other yoga sessions I'd done so far, I had given up when I couldn't do it and taken to doing my own thing. Now I was absolutely determined to try and impress him, so I would make sure I tried my damnedest to keep up and to do it properly.

"Sirsasana," he said, and around me, people started going into headstands. Oh, Christ on a bike. Well, I'd give it a go. I didn't know what I was doing or how this all worked, but I put my head down, kicked my legs up and hoped to God I was doing it properly.

Turns out I wasn't.

I flew over the top and landed on the mat with a huge slapping sound. If Martin's tackle sounded like half a pound of sausages, this sounded like a whole pig had been dropped onto the mat from a great height. I really slammed my back onto the mat. There were gasps all around the room, and Guru looked up.

"Are you okay?" he asked.

"I think so," I said.

I was far from OK. I felt winded, and my back was stinging like crazy.

"Surya Namaskar, everyone," he said. "While I tend to this little injured bird."

I giggled to disguise the pain as he leaned over and rubbed my back. I could hardly breathe; my head was pounding, and I felt about to cry, but I didn't want to show him that. I looked up, like an injured bird might look at him and he continued to rub my back and chant gently.

The strange thing was that I felt the pain subside. I'm not just saying this because he was attractive or anything; I genuinely think he had healing hands. He rubbed down my back and it felt as if the pain lifted into his hands.

"Does that feel better?" he asked

"That feels much better. How did you do that?" I asked.

"I am also a Reiki Master, I can lift the pain from you. Hopefully, that will be much better now."

"Thank you," I said, clambering to my feet. I bowed,

said Namaste, and told him I was fine to continue. I wasn't, but I didn't want to look like a total wimp.

Despite the guru's healing hands, it hurt as soon as I moved my back and attempted to join in with sun salutations. I desperately wanted to make it look as if he'd magically made me better, so he'd like me, but - bloody hell - it wasn't better at all. It was stinging. I swallowed down the pain and just carried on doing the yoga. We went from position to position, and it was tortuously hard; sweat poured down my face as I tried to do everything I could.

It was ridiculously difficult, and I definitely should've been on a beginners' course, but the lovely thing was that I did start to recognise some of the names and some of the positions, and I'd worked out which ones I could do and which ones I couldn't. Because Venetta had said right at the beginning, in her introductory talk, that yoga practice was called that because it was always a practice, there were always things to work on, I knew that no one was expecting perfection. I decided at that moment that as soon as I got back home, I would sign up for yoga classes and try to be the best I could then I would come back on one of these retreats, and the group would be amazed at how much I'd improved.

We got to savasana and I collapsed, exhausted. My back was stinging like crazy, I had a terrible headache, and every part of me hurt, so I just lay back and listened to his manly, authoritative but calming voice as he talked about the power of yoga and felt like everything was going to be okay.

The next thing I knew, Charlie was shaking me. "Where am I?" I asked.

"You're in the yoga class. You fell asleep," she said.

"Oh Christ. Where is the Guru?" I asked.

"He's gone, he told me to tell you that you did very well today and if your back isn't better go and see him, and he will treat it some more. "

"My back's not better!" I screamed. "I need more treatment."

"What is it with the Guru?" said Charlie. "He is just an old man with long hair in a ridiculous orange dress."

I tried to sit up but my back hurt so much that I could barely do it. "God that hurts," I said.

"Can you stand up?" asked Charlie, putting a hand out to help me as I scrambled onto all fours and then eased myself onto my feet.

"Yeah I'm up," I said. "But bloody hell that hurt."

"Why the hell did you do a headstand?" said Charlie. "She told us not to do anything we haven't done before. Why didn't you just go onto your knees and watch the others? That's what I did."

"I don't know," I said, dragging my mat across the room to put it away.

"Don't worry about that, I'll do it," she said, taking the mat and putting it onto the pile with the others. No one else was in the room. They had all left.

"I know exactly why you did a headstand," she said, as we left the studio and headed for the room. "You did it to try and impress him, didn't you?"

"Might have," I said, opening the door and feeling pain run all the way through my back. "Did it work? Was he impressed?"

Charlie burst out laughing. "He certainly looked shocked. I don't know about impressed."

"Fuck, it hurts," I said.

"Well, you better go and find the man with the healing hands then hadn't you?" she said, shaking her head. "If you need me, I'll be upstairs drinking the last of the wine."

"Have we got any more damn yoga today?"

"Yes - we've got Bikram before dinner."

"Christ," I said. "Great Saturday night we have before us."

Then I saw Venetta walking down the corridor. "Venetta, where's the guru? I want him to talk to him about something."

"Ahhh....about your OCD?"

"No, the OCD seems better today. I wanted him to do some more reiki on my back," I said.

"I'm sorry, Mary, he's already left to go to a meditation commune for the evening," she said, apologetically. "Would you like me to look at it? Or maybe try an ice bath?"

"It's OK, I'll go for a lie-down, and see him when he gets back."

"OK, see you for Bikram at 6.30 pm," she said. "Do come, even if your back's sore, and just do what you can. Even if you just stretch out, it would be worth coming along."

I would go along, but only because it was another chance to see the guru.

I wandered up to the room to find Charlie lying on the bed, sipping wine out of the bottle. "Not completely getting into the philosophy of this course, are you?" I said, taking the bottle from her and having a huge gulp myself.

"Mmmm," she said. "I kind of am getting into it. I think I like yoga, it's just that it's all too hard. I don't know what they're saying, and I don't know any of the practices. Unlike you, that's made me want to stay out on the fringes a bit."

"Yes," I said. "I'm not really a stay-out on the fringes sort of person."

"Nooo, really? I hadn't noticed," said Charlie. "What with the wild, loud chanting and the mad thumping headstand."

"Yeah, that really hurt. Can you take a look at my back?"

Charlie lifted up my t-shirt and almost squealed. "Bloody hell - it's bright red. It looks really sore," she said. "Wasn't the guru there to help?"

"No, he'd gone into meditation or something. I'll catch him after the next yoga class. I might just have a cool bath or something now, to try and calm it down."

"Good idea," said Charlie. "Shout if you want anything. I have painkillers here if you need them."

"I'm OK for now," I said. "I'll shout if it feels worse."

I had the bath and stepped out. It felt much worse, but nothing would stop me from going to the next yoga class to see my lovely Guru man. I dried myself and styled my hair, doing my makeup perfectly. Neither Charlie nor I had worn a scrap of make-up since arriving, but I wanted to look my best for the guru, so I trowelled it on. I didn't care what Charlie said...I knew I looked much better with makeup. On went the foundation and powder, then more foundation and blusher. Fake eyelashes, eyeliner...the works. I looked good, even if I said so myself. I'm just not the sort of person who looks good au naturel, unlike Perfect Philippa.

I walked out into the bedroom and Charlie almost choked on the wine. "Bloody hell, where are you going?" she asked.

"Yoga," I replied. "Coming?"

"Sure," she said, following me out of the door and down the stairs to our next yoga class. "Which class is this one again? Come as a drag queen?"

HOT AND SWEATY

OK, so there were two things immediately wrong with the Bikram yoga situation. The first thing was that the Guru wasn't taking it. So, I was faced with having to do a yoga class with an absolutely agonising back, made-up to perfection, without any guru to show off to. The other disaster was that Bikram was done in a very hot room, unbeknownst to me or Charlie. I mean VERY hot. Basically, a steam room. Christ, honestly, yoga is hard enough without adding in steam, heat or anything else unpleasant. How the hell was I going to cope with this?

We walked into the room that was right at the back of the house, tucked away, and it was like walking into hell. It was astonishingly hot...absolutely boiling. We could hardly see one another through the haze and heat.

"Does it have to be this hot?" I asked Venetta.

"Yes," she said. "Bikram yoga should be done in a room which is 40 °C. You'll love it when we get started. It's great exercise and very good for your skin and your organs. It allows you to really stretch.

"OK," I said warily, taking my place and immediately feeling the sweat pouring off me. It was so warm that it was uncomfortable...like being in a tropical rainforest or something. You know that feeling when you're on holiday somewhere humid, and you're in your air-conditioned room feeling all lovely, then you walk outside, and the heat and humidity hit you like a truck? Bang. Sweat begins to form on your brow, then trickle down your back, and soon you feel soaking without having done anything. It's like the tube train in summer. You get on there and can feel the sweat running down your back, under your clothes, and your hair getting damp, and you know that by the time you get to work, you're going to look like you've been swimming.

The difference between the tube on a hot summer's day or a rainforest is that no one is making you exercise there. Why would anyone do this to themselves?

We bend and stretch into a variety of poses, most of which I am familiar with now. I am a yoga queen, but I can feel my back stinging as the sweat runs down it and collects at the top of my leggings. It feels awful to be honest.

We do lots of sun salutations and I can almost get all the way through one without looking at the instructor for help, which is a good job because I can't really see the instructor, sweat is dripping into my eyes, I wipe it away. I try to do a tree pose but keep falling over. When I land on the mat, there's a splash. We're all sweating so much that it's accumulating in puddles around us. It is - let's be honest - disgusting and unhygienic. There's also a strong smell. This is what it would smell like if you poached humans. Not nice. Even the minty extract in the steam can't disguise it. It's most unpleasant.

Because we're sweating so much, I feel absolutely parched; no matter how much water I drink, I feel myself gagging for more. I'm chugging it down my throat whenever I can but I'm still hellishly thirsty.

"And relax, lie back. Time for savasana."

Savasana is THE best thing in the world. Well, maybe not THE best, certainly not up there with chips and chilli sauce, chicken tikka masala and chicken and black bean sauce, but it's in the top ten, nestling comfortably between chip butties and pizza.

Savasana is basically lying down. It is when you relax and breathe deeply after yoga to rejuvenate the body, mind and spirit. Basically, whichever way you dramatise it, what you're doing is lying on your back and having a bit of a rest. Perfect.

We were told to rise after around five minutes of relaxation and to take it easy afterwards. Bikram yoga can be very draining...we should be kind to ourselves. Charlie and I walked out of the room, our heads spinning, completely soaked to the skin with sweat. My hair was plastered down against my skull and my clothes were drenched.

We ambled into the long corridor and back to the main house.

At the end of the corridor, I could see someone waiting. As we got closer, I realised it was Guru Motee.

"Hello," I said.

"Oh my goodness, look at you, my dear," he said. "I've come to see you. Venetta said you were looking for me."

"Oh yes," I replied. "I just wanted you to check my back was OK."

"Would you like to clean up first?" he said. "Or maybe you should try and get a good night's rest, then I could treat it tomorrow after the morning walk, if it's still sore?"

"OK," I said. "Yes - good idea. I'm glad you'll be on the walk tomorrow." I smiled at him provocatively from beneath my luscious lashes, which I batted at him for extra effect. I was glad I'd done the full face of makeup now. At least I knew my face looked good, even if the rest of me didn't.

"Bye, bye," I said, as he turned to leave, bowing gracefully.

We walked back up to the room. "I think he likes me," I said.

"Who?" said Charlie.

"The gorgeous Guru. Who else? Did you see the way he looked at me just now?"

"Yep," said Charlie with a smile.

"What's so funny?" I asked.

"You'll see."

Indeed, I did see. As soon as we were back in the room, I looked in the mirror and saw the state of my face. My heavy- duty make-up was all over the place...half my face was black from mascara and eye shadow and the other half a smeary mess of brown foundation and pink lipstick. I stared at the ridiculous sight for a while.

Charlie was sitting on her bed looking into the mirror

on her compact. Obviously, since she hadn't worn makeup, she looked fine.

"My skin looks great," she said. "Training in all that heat and steam definitely reduces your pores. I've just splashed some water onto my skin and it's glowing."

I didn't answer Charlie. I just kept staring at myself. I wasn't glowing. I looked like Alice Cooper had been caught in the rain. I looked entirely ridiculous like some sort of hideously nightmarish clown.

Charlie walked over to join me at the mirror.

"What's this?" she said, leaning in to lift something off my cheek. It was a false eyelash. One of the false eyelashes that I had been provocatively fluttering at the guru earlier.

"Look. At. Me," I said, slowly, emphasising each word. "I've been talking to the guru. Looking like this. He must think I'm insane."

"Well you are," said Charlie, rather unsupportively. "Completely insane, if you ask me."

FALLING FOR THE COUNTRYSIDE

There was a loud banging on the door at 5.30 am. "Good morning. Happy Sunday," sang a much-too-enthusiastic and upbeat Venetta.

"Urghhhh," Charlie and I moaned back.

"Downstairs in 10 minutes," she said, and we both heard her skipping off to ruin someone else's day.

"Christ, does she have to be so happy and lively," said Charlie. "I mean - every morning, she's like this. I have no idea where she gets the energy from. It's quite insane. I'm not sure I even fancy this guru-led walk, to be honest."

"Oh my God - it's the guru walk!" I squealed in alarm, leaping out of bed (that's not true - I kind of rolled, and moaned as I straightened out my poor back, but 'leaping' sounds so much better). "I've been looking forward to this."

"Yeah, only because you fancy him..."

"I don't fancy him at all, I just like the idea of getting to know him better. Is that such a problem?" I asked.

"Nope. No problem at all," said Charlie, rolling back

under the duvet, trying to squeeze in a few extra minutes of sleep.

It went without saying that I wanted to look amazing on this walk. It also went without saying that I knew it was impossible for anyone to look amazing while trudging for 10 miles in fields full of cattle. Still, I had to try. My appearance had been so dire when I'd bumped into him yesterday that I simply had to look sensational, eye-catching and wonderful.

I headed for the bathroom and began the beautification process while Charlie moaned at me from her bed.

"Switch the light off, it's too early for light," she said, while I smoothed on foundation and tried to do Kim Kardashian- style contouring and ultra-dynamic eyes. When I had finished, I went to the wardrobe, making a considerable amount of noise as I pulled out my favourite leggings and t- shirt, wincing as the hangers kept slipping off the rail and clattering as they hit the floor. The leggings were black, and the t-shirt was bright pink. I usually wore a black tracksuit top with the outfit, but the last time I did that, my neighbour Dave told me I looked like a massive liquorice allsort so I don't wear the jacket with it anymore. Instead, I tied the black jacket around my waist. I looked in the mirror and smiled. Not bad for a 15-stone woman who only had three hours of sleep...not bad at all.

"Are you ever getting up?" I asked Charlie, who grunted, threw the covers off and walked hunch-back into the bathroom. She emerged minutes later in running shorts and a t-shirt, hair tied back in a ponytail, no makeup. We looked like we were dressed for completely different events...her to run a marathon, me to audition for the role of head cheerleader.

"Shall we have a bite to eat before we go?" she suggested.

All this early morning exercise before eating anything was hard core. I found exercise difficult enough without trying to do it while starving to death. I opened my suitcase and pulled out fruit, rice cakes, biscuits and diet coke, and we started munching away. Breakfast was after the run, and would no doubt comprise half a prune and a lemon pip in any case. We needed this sustenance.

We walked down the stairs and into the entrance hall, flooded with early morning light despite the unsociable hour.

"Hello, you two, lovely to see you," said Venetta. "I have some good news for you, Mary. I know how much you like mud hiking, so I have arranged for you to go hiking in the fields with the farmers this morning, instead of the guru-led walk."

Christ no. I had to stop lying. Venetta had the impression that I was a mud hiking enthusiast with OCD. I didn't want to do hiking at the best of times, certainly not in mud or when there was a perfect opportunity to spend time with the guru.

"Go on," said Charlie. "You know how much you adore a mud ramble."

"I do," I agreed. "But my back is so sore, I can't possibly go today; I'll just do the walk with the guru if you don't mind."

"Oh, what a shame!" said Venetta. "Let me tell the

farmer then. You two head out and catch up with the others. They are waiting by the gate for everyone."

"Thanks for your support," I said to Charlie.

"I couldn't resist. It was all way too funny. You - mud hiking? With the farmer whose chickens we scared! Just brilliant."

When we reached the gate, the group was just leaving. Guru Motee was leading the charge.

"Hi, hello, Guru. Please wait a minute," I shouted, waddling along at top speed, trying to catch the runaway group.

"Hello there. I thought you gone on a mud ramble," he said with a gentle smile.

"No, I decided to come on this instead. I thought it would be nice to spend some time with you," I said, smiling in a lascivious way that made him recoil slightly.

"Ah, well, I'm glad you could join us," he said. "Have you enjoyed the course? Besides managing to hurt your back. How is that by the way?"

"My back is still a bit sore, to be honest," I said. "Completely my fault though... I've never done a headstand before, so it was probably unwise to charge straight up into one."

"What? Never done one before?" he said.

"No. To be honest, I'm completely new to yoga."

"I see; quite a brave thing to do to come on such an advanced course, then?" he said, giving me that lovely big smile again.

"Yes, less bravery and more stupidity I'm afraid," I said. "We managed to book the wrong course. I think it was my fault. When we were booking the course, I jokingly added the advanced course into our basket, and I think we forgot to take it out."

"Well, at least it's been an introduction to yoga, even if you would have chosen a less intensive one."

"Yes, it has, rather. Although everything seems to have gone wrong right from the start," I told him, just to keep the conversation going. I wanted to talk to him for as long as possible.

"Tell me about it..."

"Well..." I began to tell him all about how I had put on so much weight on the cruise, then we managed to get lost and had almost killed half a dozen peacocks, and that's how I got covered in mud and was about to dive into the lake when I was told to take a shower, then when I was taking a shower Venetta spotted all our goodies and hid them..."

When I look at the guru, he's absolutely crying with laughter.

"You are the most adorable, charming woman," he said. "You seem to give yourself such a hard time about your weight, but you're really a lovely person. Be kind to yourself. Relax and learn to go with the flow a bit more. I'm sure that weight will come off when you start to treat yourself much better."

"I don't know about that," I said. "I find it difficult. I love eating so much. I know it's not good for me, and I know I'm overweight, but I love it."

"And now Venetta has taken all your snacks, so you have to eat tiny amounts."

"No, because I had loads more in my suitcase anyway,"

I said. "And - in any case - we pinched back our bag of goodies."

He was laughing at this stage.

"So, you been cheating and going up to your room and having snacks every evening after the tiny vegan supper?"

"Yes. Is that terrible?"

"No, it's not terrible, Mary. But learning to eat less food, and to focus on eating food that is good for you, and for the environment, is an important part of the course. The reason the food is given to you in small amounts if because is good for you to be deprived, occasionally, of what you think you need."

"I feel bad now," I said.

"No - you mustn't. I'm explaining why you have been given small portions. Don't feel bad; don't ever feel bad. One of the most important things in life is to spread joy and make people happy wherever you go. I know you have bad feelings about yourself with food, and I can feel the waves of negativity around you even as you talk about it; you must try to see your relationship with food more positively.

"You are a funny, self-deprecating, warm and gentle soul. I think you will go far in this life. If you go to a beginners' yoga class and learn basic yoga, you will start to feel better about your whole body, and that will change your eating habits automatically without you having to force the change. Just start very gently. Stop beating yourself up and worrying about how much you weigh and how much you eat. Carry on being your own lovely self, and do a little bit of yoga as well; try to remember some of the mindfulness work, and if you incorporate those into your life, you will find yourself transformed. I promise you. And when we leave, I'll give you my details so if you need to get in touch with me you can, and I'll help you if you need further guidance. How does that sound?"

"It sounds wonderful I said. "Thank you. There is just one more thing I need to mention."

"Oh my goodness, what's that then?" he said.

"Well, you know I said that we went into the farmer's yard and reversed through his chickens and terrified his peacock half to death?"

"This was the occasion on which you landed face first in the mud and told Venetta you liked mud hiking?"

"That's the very time," I said.

"Well, the farmer who chased after us, and who definitely saw me, is just coming to the field over there... Can you see him?"

"Ah yes, I can see him. Why are you worried?"

"Because I think he's looking for me. He half spotted me when his chickens ran in when we were having dinner, but I managed to back away and hide. I'm quite conspicuous, given my size. He will know it was me who was standing there in his chickens, flapping my arms to move them out of the way. And he is coming right towards us."

"So he is," said the guru, calmly.

"Well he might get cross," I said.

"Remember any of the mindfulness techniques? Relax, think about your environment. Lean over and touch that wooden fence there and feel the texture of it; try to relax, and don't worry."

"How the hell is touching the fence going to help me when a mad farmer comes to kill me?" I said.

"He's not going to kill you; just be calm." Strangely, I feel safer and more protected than I ever have in my life before. Just a few words from this man had put me completely at ease.

The farmer caught up with us and glared at me. He clearly knew that I had been scaring his chickens half to death. He looked at the Guru, taking in the long orange robes and beard. "I'm sorry to interrupt you, sir, but I think this lady here was in my chicken coop, and I want to talk to her about the damage she did."

"Not now, not when we are at one with nature."

With that, he walked on, and I walked on behind him. The farmer just stood there and watched us go. I needed an orange robe and a fake beard; they would get me out of all sorts of trouble.

Guru managed to get a bit of speed up, so I couldn't get close enough to talk to him anymore, so I slowed down and ambled along at a more comfortable pace. I felt great for having spoken to him, as though some sort of magic had touched me, some sort of kindness, warmth and strength of purpose that made me feel happier and more confident. When I got back, I would do beginners' yoga, I would try to remember what they said about mindfulness, and I would start to love myself a little bit more, as he had suggested. For now though, I had a half-hour walk up a steep hill to do before I got back to be greeted by half a raisin and a quarter of a peanut or some other such delicacy. Blimey, this was hard-core.

I got about halfway up that hill before the feelings of

love and gentleness departed. Everything hurt, the sun was warm, and I felt uncomfortable and horrible. I was getting tense and angry. Not with anything in particular, a couple of minutes early, I'd been feeling happy and full of joy, but this whole bloody exercising thing hurt so much. My back was stinging, and I wanted to be back in the house. Then it happened. I guess I was dragging my feet, and I caught my trainer on a rock; I went flying. I put my hand out to stop myself, but it was no good. I landed in a heap with my ankle all twisted underneath me. I screamed in pain and heard Charlie shout: "My friend's hurt her ankle."

I heard the guru shout: "Don't worry, we'll carry her back to the house. Then he ran back and saw that I had fallen, not Perfect Philippa or Sarah, who probably weighed about eight stone each. He didn't repeat his offer to carry me, but he did help me to my feet, and he and Charlie supported me while I hobbled back in considerable pain.

Once we were there, he sat me on the grass and lit candles all around me, meditating noisily as I winced in pain.

"I think you need to go to the hospital," he said gently.

"Er, yes," said Charlie. "The candles aren't going to make her better, are they?"

I nodded pathetically. "Will you take me?" I asked the guru.

"It might be better if Charlie takes you so I can run the yoga Nidra class after breakfast, but look - take this..."

He handed me a business card. It made me laugh that gurus had business cards, but I guess they had to earn a living like the rest of us. I glanced at it and saw that he lived in Twickenham. Twickenham!! That was so near to me.

"I'll go and get her bags," said Charlie, running into the house while I lay back and smiled up at Guru Motee, luxuriating in all the attention...candles flickered, the guru chanted, and everyone sat around looking at me. I felt as if I were the body at a wake as mourners wandered around me solemnly, and a priest in an orange robe spoke words of comfort.

TAKE ME TO TWICKENHAM

Charlie helped me into the flat, and I hobbled to the sofa, collapsing onto it and resting my foot on a cushion. My phone was bleeping in my bag with messages from friends. I had written about the injury on Facebook in the car on the journey back. I'd even posted a picture of the X-ray department at the hospital. When I say 'written about the injury, ' I wrote: "Just injured myself on an advanced yoga course. The guru offered to carry me, and then lit candles around me. Namaste."

It was technically true. I didn't want to say I tripped over my own feet walking up a hill because I collapsed while trying to do a headstand the day before, so I admit I made it look as if I'd hurt myself doing yoga.

Some of the responses were unnecessarily cruel.

"Carry you?" wrote Dave the guy who lives downstairs.

"What's a guru? A forklift truck?"

"Good God woman, what on earth are you doing yoga for?" wrote Dawn

The guys I went to Fat Club with had also left comments on Facebook. They were kind and supportive.

"Well done you for going, but sorry to hear about the injury."

"You poor thing - let me know if you need anything."
"Well done for trying yoga!"

What lovely people. I must catch up with the fat course people again soon. I wondered whether they had had as many problems keeping the weight off as I'd had. I know we all lost weight during our weekly meetings, but it was so damn hard to keep the weight off afterwards. Perhaps we should set up another course?

Charlie appeared in the doorway with my bag, coat and the shoe from my injured foot. "There - that's everything from the car. Fancy a drink?" she asked.

"Sure, I'll have peppermint and dandelion tea, please."

"Really? You know the mad cow isn't watching us anymore, don't you? You don't have to drink that horse piss."

"I know that, but I fancy being as healthy as possible now... you know...to develop on everything the guru was saying."

"You're obsessed with that damn guru. And you didn't seem at all interested in being as healthy as possible when we were downing bottles of wine in the room at night," said Charlie.

"Good point, well made," I replied.

"Come on, it's 4 pm, why don't we get the wine out, have a few drinks, then get a takeaway later, or something?"

"Honestly, I don't feel like it, I want to do my life

differently from now on. I'm even thinking I might go on one of those courses again, you know, in a few months when I know a bit more about how it all works, when I've practised a bit more and when my ankles better and my back doesn't ache quite as much."

"You're going to book onto another yoga course that the guru is on; that's what you're going to do."

"I just found him very enlightening, that's all," I replied. "The things he said to me on the walk made me feel good. He made me feel like I can live my life differently."

"Well, if you're going to be all boring, I'm going to go home and unpack and sort myself out for work tomorrow."

"OK, I'll call you later," I said.

Charlie gave me a kiss on the cheek and told me to take care and not do too much heavy-duty yoga until my injured ankle was better.

"OK," I said. I had no plans to do any yoga, heavy-duty or otherwise...I just wanted to track down Guru Motee.

I pulled out his business card and the leaflet that had been handed out to us all at the beginning of the course. The leaflet had a small biography of the amazing Guru. He sounded even more incredible when I read it...he'd worshipped in India and all over South Asia, then had been in California for a while, as well as Bermuda, where he'd met Catherine Zeta-Jones and became her spiritual guide.

"Catherine has a home in Bermuda, and Guru would meet and work with her there." The leaflet said. Bloody hell, I loved Catherine Zeta-Jones. I loved her. Guru

Motee had to be in my life. Everything was pointing towards it.

The business card said that his studio was in Twickenham, and I knew from what he'd said on our walk that he lived above the yoga studios. I looked up the address, pulled out my laptop and input the details. It was near Twickenham Green; I could picture exactly where it was. Where they played cricket in the summer, near the lovely pub that I'd been to so many times with Ted. Trouble was, how on earth was I going to get there with my ankle bandaged up and aching like crazy?

I picked up the phone and rang Charlie. "Hello matey, it's me," I said. "I'm sorry I was being so dull earlier; I've had a painkiller and feel much better now."

"Glad to hear it," said Charlie. "It's all very worrying when you decline the offer of a glass of wine."

"Haha, I'm not that bad," I said. "Do you fancy catching up later and going for a drink?"

"Sure, yes – shall I come over to you since you cannot move?"

"That would be great," I said. "I thought maybe we could go out to a pub we haven't been to for a while...there's quite a nice one in Twickenham near Twickenham Green."

"Twickenham? That's bloody miles away," said Charlie. "Why don't we just down a couple of bottles of wine at yours instead?"

"Because I want to go to this pub," I said. "Please."

"Oh, go on then. Why don't I come and pick you up at seven?"

"Perfect," I said. I felt bad, of course, using my lovely

friend to go and chase a lovely man, but I knew she'd understand. I'd do the same for her without batting an eyelid.

While waiting for Charlie, I did my makeup, dressed, and wrote a letter to Guru Motee. I planned to knock on the door, and if he weren't in, I would push the letter through, saying I was sorry that I didn't get the chance to say goodbye and how much help he had been to me, and I would ask whether it would be possible for me to meet up with him sometime soon.

Charlie arrived at about 10 to 7, telling me she was gagging for a glass. "It's such a pain to go over to Twickenham though," she said. "I can only have one drink when I'm driving. Let's just stay in the pub for a little while, then come back here to yours afterwards and have a proper drink. I can leave my car at yours and walk back."

"Suits me," I said, hobbling out to the car. As we approached Twickenham Green, I urged Charlie to park the car on the side of the road near where my Guru lived. "Just here," I said. "There is no point going any closer; you can never park near the pub."

"But I can see spaces," she said. "And you can't walk. Let me drop you at the pub, then I can come back here and park if there are no spaces."

"No, I absolutely insist. Park here. I'll be fine," I said.

Charlie raised her eyebrows at me and made a funny face before parking the car. I rolled out and waddled, then hobbled to the pavement. We were parked next to number 47, and I knew the Guru lived at number 27.

"See, I'm absolutely fine," I said, hobbling beside her and counting the numbers to get to number 27.

"Oh! Look at this," I said. "I've just realised this is where my guru lives."

"Oh, I see, said Charlie. "Now I get it. That's why you wanted to come to this obscure pub in Twickenham... because you want to bump into the Guru. And - by the way - when did he become 'your' Guru?"

"Shut up. I don't want to bump into him. I don't think he'll be sitting in The Three Kings in his orange robes, will he? I brought a letter with me to push through the door, so let's go and see if he's in, and if he's not, I'll leave this letter there, and we can head to the pub."

"OK then," said Charlie. "But I do get the feeling that this has got disaster written all over it."

We walked up to the door, and I pushed lightly; it opened up to reveal the smell of incense. Someone had been in there recently.

"He must be in," I said in hushed but excited tones.

We were standing in a hallway with a door leading to stairs, presumably up to his apartment, and there was a door to the right of us which led into a beautiful yoga studio. I walked in and marvelled at the beauty of it. It was lovely, with flowers around the edge, motivational posters, and beautiful soft rugs on the side. "Isn't it beautiful? Just the sort of place I'd imagine he would have."

"Yes, it is lovely," said Charlie, looking around. "Very stylish. More Philippa and Sarah's taste than the Guru's, I'd have thought."

"It's amazing," I said.

"Aren't you going to leave your letter then so we can go to the pub?"

But I was too entranced to go rushing off.

"I really like it here. Oooo, look..."

There was another door at the back of the studio. I pushed it open. It led into a smaller but equally lovely, meditation room.

"Don't you think it's got a nice feeling?"

"Yes, it has," said Charlie. "But we shouldn't have walked in here. He'll have a fit if he sees us."

"It's OK," I said. "He's a guru...he doesn't have 'fits'. I'll leave the letter, and let's go to the pub."

I pushed the letter through the door, which led up to stairs and hobbled away. I urged him to contact me in the letter and said I needed his spiritual guidance desperately. I know it said on the leaflet that we weren't to contact the Guru after the weekend, but he'd given me his card along with special permission to contact him, so I was sure it would be OK.

We walked into the pub, and I went up to the bar to order the drinks while Charlie found us somewhere to sit; then, she joined me at the bar to carry them back, with me hobbling behind her.

"I hope he liked my letter," I said.

"I'm sure he will," said Charlie. "I don't see quite what the fascination with him is though; why are you bothering to contact him?"

"I just think he's amazing; he's got this lovely aura of gentleness and calmness," I said.

"Yeah, I guess," said Charlie. "But still – I wouldn't really want to be meeting up with him regularly, would you?"

"God, yes. I think I'm in love with him," I said jokingly, and we both giggled and downed our drinks, but part of me thought that I did have such a big crush on him that it wasn't far off love.

Charlie went up to the bar for our second round, and my phone rang with a number that wasn't familiar.

"Hello, Mary speaking," I said, full of hope.

"Hello there," said a deep, mellifluous voice that I recognised immediately as belonging to the Guru.

"Oh, my goodness, it's so lovely to hear from you. Did you get my letter?" I said.

"Yes, I did. How are you feeling now?"

"Much better, thanks," I said. "Nothing's broken; just a sprain."

"I'm very pleased, Mary. Now, I can't help you with spiritual guidance. I am working with lots of people at the moment. You need someone who can focus and spend more time on you. I suggest you practice yoga and seek fulfilment through that. I can recommend lovely yoga places in the area where you could go to. Would you like me to do that?"

"Are these places where you go?" I asked. "I'd like to do yoga where you are." I was aware that I was sounding slightly stalkerish.

"No, I won't be there, but many very good teachers will be with you on your journey."

"But I wanted to see you again," I said.

"You are very kind," he said. "I hope our paths cross again sometime. I must meditate now. But I wish you joy, love and happiness."

He said 'Namaste' and put the phone down just as Charlie came back with the drinks. I noticed she had changed her mind and had a bottle of wine rather than a glass and soft drink.

"What happened to you driving home?" I said.

"Let's just get an Uber, shall we? I don't start work till 11 tomorrow, so I can get the bus back in the morning to pick up the car."

"Good decision," I said and waited patiently while she opened the bottle and filled the glasses. "Who was that on the phone?" she asked.

"Oh, just mum and dad to check I got home safely from the retreat," I lied.

"Cheers," she said.

We finished the bottle in record speed.

"Shall we get another one?" said Charlie.

I knew it was a bad idea; we already felt half drunk, but I was also at that stage where I was too drunk to think rationally about whether it was a good idea to get another one or not, so I nodded, gave her my card, and told her to put on that. She walked up to the bar, and I saw she was already staggering. Another bottle, and she would be all over the place.

By 9:30 pm, we were on the wrong side of two bottles of wine, and neither of us could speak properly. We sat there laughing, talking nonsense and generally enjoying ourselves.

"I can't feel my hands," I said, as Charlie laughed.

"Me neither," she replied. "Do you think that means that we should head home?"

"I guess," I said, staggering to my feet. We left the pub and walked outside into drizzly weather. It wasn't cold, just rainy and miserable.

"Let's go back and have another look at that yoga place," I said. "We can sit on the lovely soft rugs while we wait for the cab to come."

"We can't," said Charlie.

"Well, you can wait in the rain if you want. I'm going inside." I pushed open the door and walked back into the gorgeous room with the lovely atmosphere. Charlie followed me. We sat on the yoga mats, pulled the rugs over us and promptly fell asleep.

HOME SWEET HOME

I woke first, blinking myself back to consciousness and looking around in confusion, trying to work out where on earth I was. For a moment, I thought I was back at Vishraam; then it came to me... blimey, we'd broken into the guru's yoga studio and fallen asleep.

"How are you feeling?"

I looked up to see the guru - MY GURU - standing there. He was wearing a short, towelling dressing gown. He looked quite delicious. I mean - old - but very attractive.

"Sorry," I said. "We fell asleep."

"Where do you live?" he asked. "Shall I get you home, or would you rather stay here?"

Oh My God. Was he inviting him to spend the night? What should I do? I loved my boyfriend Ted, and he was way older than me. But he was a guru. He was a flipping guru.

"Home would be great. Thank you," said Charlie,

sitting up and running her hands through her hair. "And - sorry - we don't normally break into people's homes like this."

"That's OK, Charlie. I'll be right back," he said, smiling at me and leaving the room.

"Did you hear that? He invited me to stay the night," I said to Charlie as soon as he'd left the room. "I think he likes me."

"I'm sure he likes you, Mary, but I think he meant that you can stay here on the mats if you like."

"Nope, that was a come-on," I replied. "I think he...Oh!"

I was stopped mid-sentence by the sight of the guru walking down the stairs, accompanied by Perfect Philippa.

"Oh hello," I said. "What are you doing here?"

"I live here," she said. "We live together. He doesn't drive, so I'll take you back."

"You live together?" I said, but Charlie interrupted. "Thanks so much," she said. "A lift home would be great."

"He's way too old for her; way too old," I said, whispering to Charlie, as we walked to Philippa's car. "What's she thinking?"

"Same thing you were thinking, by the sound of it..."

We got to the car and – of course – it was one of those which bleeps when you don't plug the seatbelt in. She sat there waiting for me to click my seatbelt. "It won't go around me. They never do," I said, feeling my face sting with embarrassment.

"Would you mind trying," she said. "We can't drive to Cobham with this thing bleeping."

I tried and failed.

"I'm sorry," I said as we drove along, the noise getting louder and louder. Eventually, we reached the area in which Charlie and I both live. Philippa dropped me off first.

"Thank you," I said, rolling out and hobbling to the kerb.

"No problem," she said. "Just one thing; please don't turn up at my house again, or phone us or put letters through the door. OK? Guru is very peace-loving, but me? Not so much. Namaste."

"Namaste," I said as I hobbled away, looking back to see Charlie's face, wide-eyed and startled, beaming through the window. Perfect Philippa and the guru. Who'd have thought?

IT WAS 2 a.m. when I got back, and I crashed immediately. I didn't wake up until midday when Ted came bashing on my door to take me to lunch.

"How was it?" he asked after he'd given me a big welcome-home hug. I gave him the potted version, and he shook his head in disbelief.

"Wherever you go, you get in trouble, Mary Brown. Did you enjoy it, though, despite all the minor hiccups? You know - the lack of food, getting your snacks nicked, scaring the chickens, angering the farmer, getting covered in mud, pretending to have OCD, almost breaking your back and ankle, and being on the wrong course. Despite all that - how was it?"

"The mindfulness was really good," I said. "I liked that because I felt relaxed, warm, and happy afterwards. I'll do that again."

"What is it? How do you do it?" he asked.

"It sounds daft, but you just have to connect with yourself in the moment, and you do that by stopping and looking intently at things, like feeling the seat you're sitting on, and trying to describe little details."

"OK," said Ted, looking totally confused by the whole thing.

"What else did you do?"

"Well, this guru came in to do yoga with us, and he was excellent. Turns out he lives in Twickenham."

"Will you meet up with him again?"

"Na, I don't think so," I said. "I might do some beginners' yoga classes because I think it will be good for me, but I'll keep away from gurus for now."

WANT to know what happens next?

OF COURSE YOU DO...

IT'S "CHRISTMAS WITH MARY BROWN"

My Book

HOORAY, it's Christmas! Mary Brown's favourite time of year, and she embraces it with the sort of thrill and excitement normally reserved for toddlers seeing jelly tots.

Our funny, gorgeous and bonkers heroine finds herself dancing from party to party, covered in tinsel, decorating the Beckhams' Christmas tree, dressing up as Father Christmas, declaring live on This Morning that she's a drug addict and enjoying two Christmas lunches in quick succession.

Then there's the Christmas Post Box of Wishes and Dreams that she installs in the gardening and DIY store where she works. She plans to make customers' wishes come true, but it doesn't go perfectly. For a start, a good proportion of the notes she receives make suggestions that are positively vulgar. And physically impossible.

But she grants the wishes that she can...fixing up a date, delivering twigs and dealing with remote control mayhem.

Along the way, Mary finds herself defending the elephant in the manger and heading off to Lapland for a Christmas trip she'll never forget.

To top it all off, there's a life-changing Christmas present from the man she loves...

'It's perfect Christmas comedy...Dawn French meets Bridget Jones. Wonderful.'

My Book

ALSO BY BERNICE BLOOM

THE ORDER OF THE MARY BROWN BOOKS & ALL THE LINKS

(Ebook readers can click 'My Book' for more details):

1. WHAT'S UP, MARY BROWN?: My Book
2. THE ADVENTURES OF MARY BROWN: My Book
3. CHRISTMAS WITH MARY BROWN: My Book
4. MARY BROWN IS LEAVING TOWN: My Book
5. MARY BROWN IN LOCKDOWN: My Book
6. MYSTERIOUS INVITATION: My Book
7. A FRIEND IN NEED: My Book
8. DOG DAYS FOR MARY BROWN: My Book
9. DON'T MENTION THE HEN WEEKEND: My Book
10. THE ST LUCIA MYSTERY (out 2024): My Book
11. MARY BROWN HAS A BABY (out 2024) My Book

Or, see them all together here:

UK

https://www.amazon.co.uk/Bernice-Bloom/e/B01MPZ5SBA?ref=sr_ntt_srch_lnk_1&qid=1666995551&sr=8-1

US

https://www.amazon.com/Bernice-Bloom/e/B01MPZ5SBA?ref=sr_ntt_srch_lnk_1&qid=1666995644&sr=1-1

Thank you xxx

Printed in Great Britain
by Amazon